Theresa Murphy was born in Portland, Dorset and is the author of numerous books. She is a member of MENSA and her writing has included diverse subjects ranging from television comedy to nautical history. She lives in Dorchester, Dorset.

COMING TO THE EDGE

DCI Mattia is struggling with a case that involves politics, big business and a psychopathic killer. He's depressed: the combination of his current investigation into the murder of a young girl singer, his rocky relationship with his girlfriend, and his infatuation with a sexy private detective are all having an effect. But as members of his team are attacked, it looks like he might be onto something. Will he succeed in clearing the murder victim's husband, whom he believes to be innocent, or will his police career end in ignominy and the loss of the woman he now knows he loves?

Books by Theresa Murphy
Published by The House of Ulverscroft:

LOVE ON TURTLE ISLAND
LET ME DIE YESTERDAY

THERESA MURPHY

COMING
TO THE EDGE

Complete and Unabridged

ULVERSCROFT
Leicester

First published in Great Britain in 2011 by
Robert Hale Limited
London

First Large Print Edition
published 2012
by arrangement with
Robert Hale Limited
London

British Library CIP Data

Murphy, Theresa, *1962 –*
  Coming to the edge.
  1. Murder- -Investigation- -England- -Fiction.
  2. Police- -England- -Fiction.
  3. Detective and mystery stories.
  4. Large type books.
  I. Title
  823.9'2–dc23

  ISBN 978–1–4448–1247–3

Published by
F. A. Thorpe (Publishing)
Anstey, Leicestershire

Set by Words & Graphics Ltd.
Anstey, Leicestershire
Printed and bound in Great Britain by
T. J. International Ltd., Padstow, Cornwall

This book is printed on acid-free paper

1

It was Saturday night at the Dockers' Den, a bawdy hostelry better known to the locals as Ike's Place. It was packed by a crowd ranging from respectable town folk daringly slumming it, groups of empty-headed, grinning youths starting out on their urban careers of midnight dissipation, and the local twilight people who dwelt on the fringes of the law. The air was stuffy with perfume and body heat, and the noise close to intolerable.

The town's most popular pub, its reputation owed as much to the high class of the entertainment provided on Fridays, Saturdays, and Sundays, as it did to its notoriety. A sudden hush fell on the assembly as Tina Spencer, the star of that evening, made her way to a small stage. Stepping over an inebriated teenage girl who lay peacefully asleep on the floor, the stunning vocalist whose rhythmic body movements were always appreciated as much as her singing voice, was greeted by a mighty chorus of cheering.

Up on the stage, clad in a tight white dress that showed off her figure to breathtaking advantage, she turned to face her audience while reaching to take the microphone from its stand. As the band played the introduction she, a skilled professional who made use of every sensual nuance, gave a shake of her head that set her long black hair swinging in a practised, erotic way. Then the room fell completely silent as she began singing *Lovers' Concerto*.

When the song had ended a protracted roar of appreciative approval kept her on stage, putting on a much appreciated cleavage display each time she bowed to her grateful audience. Only when she stepped down did the tumult subside. As the more strident noises abated and conversation became possible, landlord Ike Preston stretched an arm across the bar to give Martin Spencer's shoulder a friendly squeeze.

'You are indeed a lucky man to have a wife like Tina, Marty,' Preston observed. 'And I share in your good fortune. Christmas is still three weeks away, but popular demand means that I have Tina booked solid over the festive season.'

'You don't have to tell me how lucky I am, Ike. I never forget . . . ' Spencer began, to cut off in mid-sentence, his body noticeably tensing as a group of rowdy young guys made loud and lewd comments about the lovely singer.

Preston's hand moved from Spencer's shoulder to his upper arm. The affectionate squeeze became a restraining grip as the publican urgently hissed advice. 'Leave it, Marty.'

It took much longer than the landlord would have liked for the rush of adrenalin to abate in the angry husband. Punch-ups were far from uncommon in the Dockers' Den but a brawl connected to his punters' favourite entertainer would be really bad for business.

'I'm all right now, Ike. I realize I shouldn't let this sort of thing get to me but it still does,' Spencer admits in a shaky voice.

'Don't let it,' Preston advised pointlessly, then used a sideways tilt of his head to indicate where Tina had come out of a side room to do a quarter-turn and head towards them. 'Shall I have her usual ready on the bar?'

'Please,' Spencer answered.

He knew that Tina would be seeking a much-needed spell of solitude before leaving. One year, tops, had been their so-called friends' prognosis when he, a very ordinary looking guy, had married the glamorous singer who was twelve years his junior. But they had proved the pundits wrong. Their marriage had gone from strength to strength over five years.

3

This was his favourite moment of the evening, when the gorgeous creature that was the dream of every man present walked to be at his side. It was a fantastic ego boost. Somehow separated from the distractions around them, they always spent a special time together.

Yet now something was wrong! Hardly aware of Preston placing Tina's drink of brandy in a bulge-bellied snifter glass on the bar, Martin Spencer watched a smartly dressed elderly man step in front of Tina. The band was playing, and the man moved near to Tina, his mouth close to her ear to be heard over the music. Though watchful, Spencer wasn't worried. Tina could psychologically neuter an over enthusiastic fan with a few razor sharp words.

This time, however, it was different. Instead of remaining cool while delivering some cutting remark, she was angry. In response, the man was wagging a reproving finger in her face.

Disregarding Preston's alarmed shout, Spencer pushed his way through the crowd. He ignored an angry protest as he bumped against a table and women jumped to their feet to wipe with panicky hands at dresses splattered by spilt drinks. Seeing him heading his way, the man who had been arguing with

Tina, hurried away from her, quickly leaving the pub.

Usually grateful for her husband's intervention when things turned nasty, Tina was still extremely angry. Anger that now seemed to be directed at Martin as she glared at him.

Ready to go after the troublemaker, he asked, 'What did that fellow say to you?'

Instead of the answer he had anticipated, he was shocked when Tina's rage made her raise her voice to compete with the thump-thump of music. Just then the band reached the end of a number and she was shouting loudly in the new quiet.

'Why couldn't you just keep out of it? Why make a big scene out of nothing?'

There was a screeching and scraping of chair legs over the wooden floor as people stood to surround Tina and her husband. A sea of silly faces wearing the stupid smiles of people who don't know what to expect, but were ready to happily join in once they knew what it was.

In a low, calm tone, he said. 'I simply came to help you, Tina.'

'Help me? Help me?' she yelled, seemingly mindless of the fact that the band was silent. 'All you were doing was helping yourself, giving way to your insane jealousy.'

Her behaviour was totally out of character.

Bewildered, Spencer opened the door through which she had come just minutes earlier. Gently but firmly manoeuvring her into the gap, he give her a light push, saying. 'Get your coat, Tina. We are leaving.'

He was relieved when she returned, shrugging into her coat. Wanting to help her, he reached to take her hand but the coldness of her fingers proved it was a wasted gesture. He hurried her through the baying mob towards the exit. There was a comedian up on stage who made a joke that Spencer didn't catch, but assumed was some ribald comment about the reason they were leaving early. The rabble roared with laughter.

In the car-park Spencer felt humiliated beyond belief. Unlocking the front passenger door he got the now passive Tina seated. When he had walked round and was in the driver's seat she was sitting slumped, unspeaking, closed eyes leaking tears. As he drove out of the car-park and joined the main road he heard her begin to sob.

Unable to bear the sounds of her distress, he blindly stretched out his left hand. Thankfully grasping his hand, raising it to kiss the back of it, she first sobbed and then apologized.

'I am so sorry that I treated you badly, Marty. I was terribly upset.'

'By what that man said to you.'

Her assenting nod should have been wasted in the dark interior of the car but by the dull illumination of the dashboard he caught it from the corner of his eye. This didn't add up. Necessarily thick-skinned where her work was concerned, she normally shrugged off all of the suggestive and often downright obscene remarks aimed at her.

He commented on this. 'It's not like you to be rattled by some idiot, Tina. There must have been something different on this occasion.'

'There was. It was most distressing.'

'Can you tell me about it?'

'No, not now, please. Perhaps when we get home.'

Not pressing her, Spencer made it as fast as possible through heavy late-night traffic to reach the quiet avenue in which their bungalow stood. Nothing would for either of them ever compare with the security and warmth and comfort of their home. Yet Spencer found that blissful experience was absent as he unlocked the door. Under the streetlighting her cheeks glistened with tears. She wiped them away with her fingers. A childlike gesture.

He guided her into the lounge. Helping her out of her coat, stressed at witnessing her anguish, he eased her into an armchair. Having fetched a box of tissues for her, he sat on his heels beside the chair and placed a comforting arm around her shoulders. He waited until her sobbing had eased before speaking.

'Don't worry if you find telling me too difficult. It isn't important.'

'But it is important,' she insisted.

This alarmed him. Though he knew little about her past, it had never worried him. Until now. The soft beams angled from the wall lights sharpened her colour and gave her face a fragile transparency that revealed a vulnerability that Spencer had never before seen. He was looking at a Tina whom he didn't know and the effect on him was frightening.

'I'll get us a drink,' he said, needing to think.

He had finished pouring the drinks and was about to walk back to her when the telephone rang. Picking up the receiver he listened for some time, and then said, 'I'll be there right away.'

Standing still for a moment, his eyes closed, he gave silent thanks for the phone call that presented him with the opportunity to escape from a situation he had never previously encountered, and had no idea how

8

to handle. Then his conscience clicked in and his cowardice shocked him. He had been prepared to abandon the wife he dearly loved.

'What is it?' Tina enquired. The uncertain smile on her lips, the excessive brightness in her eyes, were signs of fear.

'A job out at Ackland Road. A house with a complete power failure, all fuses blown. Why did I advertise a twenty-four-hour service in Yellow Pages?'

'Because we needed the money, and we still do,' Tina reminded him, the diversion returning her close to normal.

'You are right,' he contritely admitted. 'I've failed you in that respect.'

'Nonsense.' She put aside her own problem to argue. 'Your hard work got us our lovely home. These are tough times for everyone.'

'I should go, but how can I leave you in this state? Ackland Road is quite a way out in the suburbs, so even if I can finish the job quickly I'll be gone for some time.'

'I'll be fine. You must go, Marty.'

'If you are sure, I'll go and get changed. You be certain to lock up behind me.'

'I will,' she assured him as he went off into bedroom.

When he came back to her, wearing his working clothes and lugging his weighty toolbox, she had stopped crying. She was standing facing him, smiling with just the corners of her mouth. He knew that she was keeping a grip on herself to stop him worrying.

Seeing him to the door, she said fervently. 'I love you, and I always will.'

'Tell me that again when I get back,' he replied in a weak attempt at the suggestive banter that usually passed between them.

'I will, and I will tell you what upset me tonight.'

'Like I said, it isn't important,' he said truthfully, now certain of that.

'It is extremely important to us,' she declared earnestly as he went out of the door.

Outside, he stood on the step long enough to hear both locks click as the door closed. Satisfied, but still filled with regret at having to leave her, he hurried off to his car.

★ ★ ★

Awakened by the polite but insistent purring of a telephone, Mattia was aware of someone stirring beside him. Befuddled by being awoken from a too short sleep, what logic he could muster said it was Candace. The phone was at her side of the bed. He heard a click, then the precise tones of her doppelganger answering: *'This is Candace Dvorak. I am not at home right now. Please leave your name and number after the beep and I will get back to you.'*

Scrambling for the receiver, the flesh and blood Candace beat the beep and uttered a sleep-slurred, 'Hello.'

Mattia focused blearily on the square green digits of a dormant alarm clock. It was 3.45 a.m. Perhaps the burglar alarm at Candace's restaurant had been triggered. She switched on her red-shaded bedside lamp. The dull orange glow was easy for him to bear. He spent a moment or two looking round her flat, trying to become fully sentient by matching the none-too-familiar wallpaper and furniture with his memory. It helped. The fragmented pieces of his mind were floating back together.

Yesterday had been Saturday; the day Candace's brother had got married. Mattia was not a heavy drinker but yesterday had been an exception. Weddings always affected him adversely.

That wedding had further weakened their already ailing relationship. Candace had of late become a part of his burgeoning disillusionment with life but that was his fault and not hers. Maybe it was the approach of middle age, and something had already died inside him.

Passing him the telephone over his shoulder from behind, Candace gave way to a childish urge to embrace him, saying huskily, 'It's Melvin Petters for you, Gio.'

Taking the phone, he caught the scent of her. It was a fragrance that had once held him in chains. But no more. Irritated by her cloying behaviour, he shrugged himself free.

'Why are you ringing me on this number, Melvin?' he asked irritably.

His relationship with Candace had more or less become general knowledge at the station but he didn't like being contacted at her address.

'I tried your home number first, sir.'

Calming down, Mattia said. 'Have you forgotten that it's my weekend off?'

'No, I haven't, but the killer probably didn't know.'

Petters, though a well-above average detective sergeant, suffered from extreme self-consciousness that caused him to stammer partway through just about every sentence. That problem affected him even on the telephone. The fact that he had just spoken clearly, together with what he had said brought, Mattia instantly wide-awake.

'What's happened, Melvin?'

'A woman has been found dead at an address in Orchard Avenue.'

12

'Suspicious circumstances?'

'Most definitely.'

'Who is the informant?'

'The deceased's husband, sir. He's a self-employed electrician who was called out on an emergency late last night. When he returned home he found his wife dead.'

'Nasty,' Mattia commented, allowing himself time to think. 'Where are you now, Melvin?

'At Crescent Street, sir. I got the call at home and came straight in. A uniformed constable and Sergeant Beckett are at the scene, and I expect the pathologist is probably there by now. I've also called forensics out.'

'Good work, Melvin.'

'Do you want me to go straight out there, sir?

Mattia paused before answering. For all his high intellect, Melvin Petters was as yet too open to the influence of others to take command of a serious crime scene. Making a quick decision, he said. 'I'll come with you. Pick me up, Melvin. The fact that you know this telephone number more than suggests that you are aware of the location.'

'I am, sir.'

'I'll be ready and waiting.'

'Very good, sir.'

Mattia passed the telephone back over his shoulder. It was taken from him, proving that Candace was at least partially awake. Of late she had been prone to displays of possessiveness that made him feel threatened. She sought commitment, something that he was resolute to avoid. It would be over for Candace and him before long. Maybe it had ended the first time she had tried to own him.

Getting out of bed he stretched, cat like, releasing something into his system that filled up bone and tissues, making them glow warmly. He felt better instantly. Though enthusiasm was not on his agenda, he was ready for whatever a day that had started badly, and too soon, might throw at him.

When he returned from the bathroom and was dressing, the rhythmic sound of Candace's breathing suggested that she was sleeping. Ashamed of his spinelessness, he stealthily exited the bedroom so as not to wake her.

He took the lift down to the ground floor and stepped out into what was a dark, damp and dismal December morning. Nevertheless, he felt a fulfilling sense of freedom.

★　★　★

Chief Constable Freya Miller opening the door and stepping into the dim and ancient entrance to Crescent Street Police Station startled Melvin Petters. His surprise added to the semi-panic he always suffered in the company of others. It was similar to radio interference, their thoughts becoming more dominant in his mind than his own. Getting married and having a baby daughter had not eased his problem. Though knowing exactly what he wanted to say, he always finished up interspersing sentences with 'You know', 'I mean', and 'basically'. Mattia unkindly referred to it as his footballer's interview syndrome.

Taking a few deep breaths, he greeted the chief constable. 'Good morning, ma'am. It is unusual to see you here on a Sunday morning, particularly this early.'

She stared at him for a full minute before speaking, coolly taking an inventory. Her accent was educated and authoritative. 'Good morning, Sergeant. You wouldn't be seeing me now were it not for the fact that I was driving back from a conference in London when I learned of the Orchard Avenue incident over the radio.'

She leaned with one shoulder against a doorjamb, not in the manner of a poseur but in the natural way of a woman who was in touch with every inch of her body. Her good looks had made the strange blend of aloofness and approachability she had developed confusing for her officers. Yet Mattia had warned him that she was a high-flyer and therefore dangerous. He had warned that dangerous people are determined people who will stop at nothing at all to achieve their aims, and those practised in the black art of politics are the most dangerous of all.

Though Petters was unaffected by her attractiveness, in the three months since her appointment he had not been comfortable about having a woman in charge. He was used to male chief constables. Admittedly most of them were despoilers of their officers' achievements, but they were bearable once you let their faults slide past you. It wouldn't be that way with Freya Miller who possessed a high intellect and a sense of moral values, things the majority of her predecessors had lacked.

'Is DCI Mattia attending, Sergeant?'

Petters detected the aversion in her tone when she spoke the detective chief inspector's name. Very few in the county force, Mattia's peers as well as his superiors, tolerated him. His laid-back style had permanently settled into the lines of his darkly handsome face. Like the scar tissue of a boxer, it was his trademark. His American accent didn't help. When he was four years old his family — an

16

English mother and Italian father — had emigrated to the United States, settling in a tough area of New York. He had served in the New York Police Department before returning to England for a reason he had never disclosed.

'I'm collecting him on my way there, ma'am,' Petters replied.

She was having reservations about Mattia. That was understandable but unnecessary. Although he had scant regard for British police protocol, often resorting to what Petters judged to be NYPD methods when questioning a suspect, Mattia got results. The chief constables he'd served under had put up with his tough guy way of operating for the sake of a good crime clear-up rate. For how long Freya Miller would tolerate it was anyone's guess. If it came to a battle between Mattia and her, Petters realized it would be a war of attrition. There could only be one winner, and his money was on Mattia.

'I mustn't keep you from your duty, Sergeant,' she said, turning to the door.

They walked together out into the early hours' darkness of a winter morning, side by side but widely separated by a difference in rank. Petters held the door of her car open for her. Sitting behind the wheel, she put out a hand to prevent him closing the door.

'Impress on DCI Mattia that I must be kept informed throughout, Sergeant.'

'I will, ma'am,' he promised as he closed the car door.

It was a promise he didn't have a hope of fulfilling. Mattia was likely to ignore what the chief constable wanted even if she were to inform him personally.

* * *

As Sergeant Petters stopped the car outside of the only bungalow in the road with lights in its windows, Mattia, with an effort of willpower that took more out of him each time he reached a crime scene, clambered mentally up out of the depths of despair as he'd always had to in recent months. His work had once been impersonal but he had lately been affected by the grief, misery, and the tragedy of the cases constantly crossing his desk. He was also feeling guilty about his offhand attitude toward Candace before leaving her that morning.

He followed his sergeant up the steps and along the path through the front garden and greeted the uniformed constable standing outside of the door with a 'Good morning'. He took a deep breath and held it before entering the bungalow. At the end of a short passageway stood the uniformed figure of Sergeant Alf Beckett. Mattia asked, 'What was the method of entry, Sergeant Beckett?'

'Either invitation, or a mistake on the part of the deceased, sir. There is no sign of a forced entry.'

Going ahead of Petters, he pushed the door open to enter the room indicated by Beckett. His professional manner took over as he saw the fully clothed body of a woman lying on the floor. An elderly man who had been bending over the body straightened up to look challengingly at Mattia.

'DCI Mattia, and this is DS Petters.' Mattia made his introductions.

'Canadian or American?' he questioned Mattia's accent.

'American,' Mattia replied. 'I was expecting to see Michael Probert.'

'I am Marcus Bellingham. Mike is indisposed,' the old man explained grumpily. 'Consequently, I've been called out of retirement. This wasn't the way I intended to spend my Sunday mornings when I took my pension.'

'It's sure as hell crap compared to pruning the roses,' Mattia commented laconically before taking a look down at the body of a young woman with long, black hair. One of her eyes was blackened and swollen; blood from her nose had dried on a grotesquely swollen upper lip.

He asked, 'Was she beaten to death?'

Tilting his head back, the pathologist looked up at the ceiling as if reading from an invisible autocue. 'My initial opinion is that she was knocked to the ground, and then stamped on with great force. Her ribcage has been shattered, which leads me to suspect that my later examination will reveal that most of her vital organs have been crushed.'

At that moment a member of the forensic team came out of a room along the passageway carrying a plastic bag. Assuming that the bag contained the husband's clothing, Mattia took the opportunity to escape from Bellingham. He enquired if Spencer was now free to be interviewed, and the man with the bag nodded.

'You liaise with the forensic team, Melvin,' Mattia ordered before turning to the pathologist. 'No doubt I'll see you later today, Doctor.'

'Nothing personal, but I hope that won't be so. I'd dearly love to enjoy a roast dinner before spending the afternoon with the Sunday newspapers.'

'I don't think there is much possibility of that,' Mattia remarked, saying over his shoulder to Petters, 'Join me when you have finished here.'

Walking to the lounge, he had to steel himself to open the door and face the man whose wife lay battered to death in the nearby room. Clad in casual clothes that had plainly been hastily donned, Martin Spencer sat on a settee. On hearing Mattia enter he raised his head, his face distorted by sorrow.

'I am Detective Chief Inspector Mattia, Mr Spencer,' he introduced himself. 'I regret the necessity to intrude on your grief. I would like to clarify a few points. A full interview can be arranged later.'

'I have no objection, Detective Inspector. I will do everything possible to assist in finding who did this terrible thing.'

'I understand you had an emergency call-out last night,' Mattia said, as Petters entered the room, taking out his notebook as he arrived.

'That's right. A complete power failure at a house in Ackland Road.'

'What time was this?'

'Shortly after midnight.'

'Did it take you long to restore power?'

'There was no loss of power.'

'I don't understand.'

'There was no problem at the house, and the occupiers denied calling me out.'

'Did you believe them?'

'Yes. It was an elderly couple who were obviously as bewildered as I was.'

'So it was a hoax call. What time did you arrive at Ackland Road?'

'Twelve forty-five. I made a note of that when I pulled up outside the house. That is my usual practice, as I charge by the hour.'

With a nod of acceptance, Mattia said, 'You were at the house just a matter of minutes, I take it?'

'Just long enough to establish that I wasn't needed, and to apologize.'

'What time did you arrive back home?' Petters enquired in a confident voice that surprised Mattia.

'I would say a quarter past three, approximately.'

Suspicious, Mattia asked, 'Ackland road is only on the perimeter of town, Mr Spencer, so what took you so long?'

Spencer was either unable, or didn't want to answer. Then he spoke in a mumbling monotone that made it necessary for Petters to step closer to hear what was being said.

'There was some trouble last night between Tina and me. No, that's not strictly true. A third person was involved.'

'Please enlarge on that,' Mattia requested.

'Tina is a singer. She appears on most

22

weekends at the Dockers' Den.'

'We know the place,' Petters positively.

'Tina is . . . ' Spencer began before choking on a massive sob that shook his whole body. 'I'm sorry. Tina *was* a lovely woman. That made her a target for male attention when on stage. We learned to cope with that, but it was something different last night.'

'In what way?' Mattia prompted Spencer to continue.

'Tina was just about to join me at the bar when a man accosted her.'

'Was he known to you?' Petters questioned.

'He was a complete stranger. He frightened Tina terribly. She was so distressed that she wasn't able to tell me what it was about. She said that she desperately needed to tell me, but just could not. Then I got the telephone call.'

'And left without learning what the problem was?'

'That's right,' Spencer answered.

'How did this incident result in it taking you so long to return here from Ackland Road?' Mattia asked forcefully.

The silence that followed more than suggested that Spencer declined to answer that question. Mattia and Petters exchanged meaningful glances.

'It is difficult, but I can explain that.'

Spencer suddenly started to speak. The jerking of his body made his speech staccato. 'I have been working long hours over the past weeks. I am dog-tired most of the time. On the way back this morning I pulled into a lay-by intending to spend a few minutes trying to solve what was troubling Tina so badly, but I must have fallen asleep. When I woke up I was freezing cold. I drove home straight away.'

'How did you gain entry to your home?' Petters asked.

'With my key. No, two keys. I had security locks fitted some six months ago.'

'Does anyone else have duplicates on these two keys?'

'Only Tina.'

Mattia gently asked. 'Where did she keep her set?'

'They are in her handbag,' Petters volunteered.

'Your wife didn't identify the man who confronted her last night?'

'No. She was going to talk to me about it when I got back from Ackland Road.'

'We'll leave it at that for now, Mr Spencer, but we will want to speak to you again soon,' Mattia said.

Nodding to indicate that he understood, Spencer then spoke with his hands covering his face. 'What is the situation with . . . er . . . Tina now?'

'We'll find out,' Mattia replied, gesturing with his head towards the door as instructions for his sergeant.

2

Leaving the room, Petters was gone for only a short time. Mattia walked over to the door as he re-entered, and the sergeant whispered to him, 'Forensics have completed their work and are about to leave. The pathologist has already gone, and the deceased woman is about to be taken away.'

'Thank you, Melvin,' Mattia said, walking over to stand near to the grieving widower. 'Everything is finished here now, Mr Spencer.'

'Tina?'

'They are taking her to a chapel of rest,' Mattia replied with a white lie.

'Thank you,' Spencer said gratefully.

'Either Detective Sergeant Petters or myself will be back later. I am sorry, but a formal identification of the body is required before a post mortem can be held, Mr Spencer.'

'I won't be here,' Spencer said. 'I just can't stay in the home we shared. I will be staying at my mother's house, which is not far from here.'

'That's fine. Please give DS Petters your mother's address,' Mattia instructed.

A few minutes later Petters joined him in the passage, closing the lounge door behind him. They both had to squeeze back against the wall to permit the body of Tina Spencer to be carried past them on a stretcher.

'What's your thinking on Spencer falling asleep in a lay-by, sir?'

'The problem with his wife was obviously traumatic. Spencer didn't need to stop and ponder on it; he could have just driven home and dealt with it,' Mattia answered. 'Now, we know that we can rely on Sergeant Beckett to look after things here, so we will plan our day.'

'Which is, sir?'

Mattia paused. He needed to get his relationship with Candace back on track. 'You drop me off at the Criterion Restaurant, Melvin, then go home and have breakfast. After that, drive out to Ackland Road and make certain that Spencer's story of a hoax call and his visit during the night holds up.'

'Very good, sir.'

'While I'm at the restaurant I'll give Inspector Roberts a ring and have him organize house-to-house enquiries in this area to find out if anyone heard or saw anything unusual during last night. When you collect me from the restaurant we will pay a visit to the Dockers' Den. We need to know the identity of the man who was harassing Tina Spencer last night.' Then he added, 'I've noticed that your problem with articulation has been much less noticeable this morning, Melvin.'

'I hadn't realized that,' Petters frowned. 'It could be shock from seeing the body of that young and beautiful woman, sir.'

'I thought that you would be impervious to that by now, Melvin,' Mattia commented, pleased to use the act of getting in the passenger seat of the car to cover his duplicity. He had been struggling since he'd seen the body to force the bruised and bloodied face of Tina Spencer from his mind.

★ ★ ★

Candace Dvorak walked slowly through Sunday-quiet streets. It was early and the suburb slept with all the ugliness of its bare bones on show. Windows reflecting a grey sky that was slimy with leftover night stared blank-eyed at her. As she walked past endless rows of look-alike houses, homes in which other people dealt with their own loves and hates, their memories and sorrows, their frustrations and fears, her mind ran a replay of the early hours of that morning. Eyes closed, she had been aware of Gio leaving her bed, getting dressed and walking out of the bedroom. The sound of running water in the bathroom had eased her anxiety. She had expected him to come back with an explanation and to say goodbye before leaving. But he hadn't. The sound of the outside door of her flat closing behind him had a daunting finality to it.

It would have been different a short while ago. That had been an exquisite time in which they had been able to communicate without uttering a word. She had never questioned him on why he had left the States or about his private life over there. He had never mentioned either her marriage or her ex-husband. The past of neither of them had mattered because their present had been so good, and their future together held so much promise. Now they couldn't even look directly at each other, managing only quick, sliding attempts at eye contact that glanced off.

They were drifting apart, but not in the acrimonious way that her and Geoffrey had. Then and since, she had often wondered when the loving had stopped and the hating had begun. That was a foolish exercise. If she discovered the turning point it wasn't something to be celebrated each year. An annual raising of glasses to the end of coupledom would be absurd.

It wasn't like that with Gio. The loving remained and there were no lies between them. The fact that in recent times he had become increasingly dispirited where his work was concerned provided a simple reason for the change in him. Her dread was that Mattia might soon become no more to her than a hyphen between an unhappy past and an uncertain future.

Maybe her memory of Geoffrey influenced her. They had married young when both were equally ambitious. Taking out a frighteningly large bank loan, they had purchased an ailing restaurant. Working hard to turn the loss-making business around, they had lost interest in each other. Wearied by work and unable to accept financial responsibilities, Geoffrey had become restless.

On a Wednesday morning nine years ago, Candace had awoken to discover her husband's half of the bed cold and vacant. A note on his pillow read: *Candace. I am going away. I will not be in touch, please don't try to find me. There is much I want to do, places I want to see. At least from a distance we can be friends. Geoffrey.*

Left with a struggling business and huge debts, it had taken her five hard years to clear everything she owed to become the proprietor of what she had built into an immensely popular, thriving restaurant. She had never heard from Geoffrey again. Whether he was dead or alive she didn't know, and didn't care. That was a callous sentiment that she still couldn't believe herself capable of. She had obtained a divorce when the legally required period of time had elapsed.

Now, as she reached her restaurant and went in, she realized that Gio's leaving her apartment that morning had been an action replay of Geoffrey's abandoning her all those years ago. The hard drive of the mind captures life unevenly, but it burns the bad times in deeply.

'I'm surprised to see you, Candace,' Lewis Milford, her restaurant manager, greeted her, pulling a face in his effeminate way. 'What happened to the big plans for the weekend that you and that hunk of yours had?'

'They had to be cancelled, Lewis. Gio was called out early this morning.'

It was the lull between breakfasts and lunches, and there were only a few customers present.

'Duty called,' Lewis assumed in his camp manner. 'Sit you down, dear, and I will bring you a coffee.'

Sitting, Candace relaxed a little. Being in her restaurant helped. Though never considering herself to be materialistic, she had to

31

confess that a great sense of security came from owning a flourishing business. Success is a powerful hypnotic.

There were a few people passing outside on the street. The sight of them helped to ease her melancholia. She had of late been troubled by the way Sunday eerily changed the world into a cavernous void in which conversations and other sounds echoed hollowly. It occurred to her that this was undoubtedly something she had unconsciously picked up from Mattia.

She smiled her thanks at Lewis when he brought her coffee, then his eyes widened as he looked over her shoulder. He gave a low whistle of appreciation. 'What a man! Your hero is here; so true love is running smoothly once more, Candace.' He did his mincing walk in the direction of the kitchen, calling back, 'One more coffee coming up.'

Candace turned to face Mattia. It had been a mistake to spend hours rehearsing what she was going to say. She was sure she'd be left floundering around when nothing went according to her imaginary script. He walked across to bend and quickly kiss her before sinking tiredly into the chair across the table from her. Though he was as smartly turned-out and as handsome as ever, his black wavy hair combed neatly, she was struck by how strained he looked.

'A bad morning?' she asked and, when he answered with a nod, she added a second question. 'Murder?'

'Yes. A young woman beaten to death.'

'How awful. I didn't expect to see you until much later today, Gio.'

'I regret the way that I left your place this morning, and wanted to say sorry. Melvin Petters dropped me off. He has some enquiries to make. Then he'll come here to collect me. We have a full day ahead of us then, but with a bit of luck we'll be able to make our night out tonight, Candace.'

This was unexpected, and Candace asked prayerfully. 'Do you really think so?'

'I know that you were looking forward to it, and so was I. As its Sunday we can't make much progress with the investigation. So I'll make a positive start in the morning.'

Candace felt suddenly and deliriously happy. His enthusiasm for their night out showed that this was the Giovanni Mattia that she knew and loved. She let relief seep through her body. These past weeks there had been dread in her veins. It had been toxic and deadening.

As Lewis approached, she said. 'I'm sorry that I dragged you to the wedding yesterday, Gio.'

33

'Don't be silly, Candace. It was your brother's big day.'

'But I forced you to go,' she insisted, as Lewis put a cup of coffee in front of Mattia.

He delayed answering until an eavesdropping Lewis had remarked. 'I always cry at weddings, me.'

Returning to their conversation as her manager left, Mattia explained. 'I didn't have to go, but I wanted to be with you.'

Warmed by his words, Candace tried to snare the charm of the moment, knowing full well that within minutes of Mattia's leaving the restaurant it would become a blur, a dreamy half-memory.

★ ★ ★

It was uniformed Constable Amanda Snelling who called for Mattia at the restaurant. She explained. 'I don't have the full story, sir, but DS Petters discovered that there was nobody at home at an Ackland Road address. He has learned that the occupiers of the house are visiting relatives on the other side of town and is on his way there.'

Understanding what was happening, Mattia remarked, 'DS Petters won't be happy to miss out on things by following up a routine matter. You know that a woman has been murdered.'

'Yes, Sergeant Beckett informed me. Where are we heading, sir?'

While at the restaurant Mattia had telephoned to arrange house-to-house enquiries in Orchard Avenue, and had also contacted Marcus Bellingham, to learn that the wily old pathologist had postponed the post mortem on the murdered woman until the next morning. The Sunday newspapers had triumphed.

'The Dockers' Den pub down at the docks. The victim was a singer there last night.'

It was close to noon and the traffic was heavy. The girl at Mattia's side drove fast with the supreme confidence of someone who has never doubted their reflexes. Her skill at the wheel was reassuring in a disaster era of modern drivers who had learnt only how to pass a driving test that was unrelated to real driving. Mattia was unworried as she weaved the car through other vehicles, expertly using the gearbox, rarely touching the brakes. He had found her to be bright and instantly likeable when she had arrived at Crescent Street straight from training college eighteen months ago. She always appeared to have just got back from somewhere really nice. There was something alive about everything that she did, all that she said. She was wise with intuitive knowledge.

A pretty girl, her auburn hair was expensively messed up in the modern untidy style. Full of charm and original wit, she was a self-educated genius with free-range knowledge that was far superior to that of the taught-by-rote college graduates who had been recruited into the police in recent years. Mandy, still in her youth, was destined for eventual high rank. It grieved Mattia to know that she would only achieve her full potential at the cost of her innocence.

'Your bad luck to have a duty Sunday turn into a real-life murder weekend, Mandy,' Mattia remarked as she expertly swung the car out round a bus and safely regained her own side of the road without causing the slightest fright to the driver of an oncoming car.

'Good luck, I'd say, sir,' Mandy replied. 'I like the action; it makes me feel really alive.'

Mattia glanced sideways at the girl. She was young and eager? Good God, what an awful age! Had he ever been that young? That enthusiastic? That ambitious? He pitied her, aware that a time would come when she would wish that everything could revert to what it once had been, clean and fresh and eternal.

He spoke reflectively. 'I must have been keen at some time. As the years have gone by

I've discovered that new thoughts, novel emotions and fresh reactions become more and more rare. That's a serious handicap in a fast-changing world, Mandy.'

'I know you better than that, sir.'

'I've known me a lot longer than you have, Mandy, and I'm still not sure about myself. But I do know that I'm over the hill.'

Her light-brown eyes were friendly as she glanced sideways at him. Making amends with Candace had made him feel better and Mandy's company had really lightened his mood.

'That's nonsense, sir. I've been in awe of you from the first day I arrived at Crescent Street. I hope I don't sound like a silly little girl, but you're a man I could follow with a wordless faith, sir.'

'You would be wise to stick with the established religions, Mandy,' Mattia advised drily, shaken to discover he was vain enough to feel flattered.

They were heading down the town's skid row now. Unwashed druggies, drop-outs, and winos lounged, sat, and lay on the pavements. Mattia found it difficult to adjust to the speed at which standards were slipping, and to witnessing the crumbling of a culture. He had to admit that the morbid Marcus Bellingham had it exactly right.

'We sure live in dark and angry times. How

do you keep yourself separate from the people we have to deal with, Mandy?' he asked.

She took a time to absorb this, as if it was a code she had to decipher. Then she said pensively. 'Our reaction to it is the problem. We are all victims of our collective and individual history. I've been punched, kicked, and spat at while on duty, sir. At times such as that I remember the words of Roman Emperor Marcus Aurelius. He advised. 'If you are distressed by anything external, the pain is not due to the thing itself, but to your estimate of it; and this you have the power to revoke at any moment'.'

'Does that help?'

'Perhaps, solely by getting things into the correct perspective. I appreciate that it's not much of a deal, sir, but that's about all we can expect.'

'You are a widely read person, a self-educated academic, Mandy. Would you consider joining my team?'

Though her driving didn't falter, the way that she dug marks into her lower lip with her teeth revealed that his question had deeply affected her. Shaking her head slowly and contemplatively, she said softly, 'CID has always been my dream, sir.'

'Then make it a reality starting tomorrow morning, Mandy?'

Glancing at him from the corners of her eyes, she asked. 'Are you being serious, sir?'

'I wouldn't joke with you on something like this,' he assured her. He added. 'In police circles you are an intellectual Amazon among mental pygmies.'

'Thank you, sir,' she said with a sigh. 'But what about DS Petters?'

'You'll be working with him, not replacing him,' Mattia explained.

'I see,' she said. 'But won't you need the Chief Constable's approval, sir?'

'She probably thinks so, but I don't,' Mattia answered as arrival at their destination brought the conversation to a close.

Mattia was aware of an insidious Sunday morning creepiness about the empty dock area. For him there was something particularly surreal about deserted places that were usually thronged with people. A normally crowded café, its windows vacant and a 'Closed' sign on the door, painted a grey overlay on to an already gloomy scene.

Mattia pointed out the Dockers' Den public house which had a Christmas tree outside it, with only a few of its fairy lights working.

'Christmas is coming,' Mandy ventured.

'It must be close,' Mattia agreed. 'I noticed the supermarkets had Easter eggs on display yesterday.'

'You are a cynic, sir,' Mandy laughed as they walked together to the pub. A soft westerly breeze was herding a fog bank across the still sea towards them.

'Do I come in with you, sir?' Mandy enquired, her voice made too loud by the stillness all round them.

'Of course. I will need your assistance. There will probably be notes to be taken. This will be your last duty in uniform, *Detective* Constable Snelling.'

★ ★ ★

Things hadn't gone well for Melvin Petters. It had been 8.30 a.m. when he had arrived at 27 Ackland Road to find there was no one at home. From a female neighbour he learned that the occupiers of the house were Mr and Mrs Reyland, an elderly couple who had left fifteen minutes previously on a visit to their son's home on the occasion of their grandson's birthday. She had given him the address.

On a thirty-minute drive to where the Reylands' son lived, he was perturbed by the thought that the Spencer murder could cause him to miss his own daughter's first birthday on Tuesday. He consoled himself on the return drive to Crescent Street that Mattia had always been fair with him and would ensure that he didn't miss his very important family event.

He found the elderly Mr and Mrs Reyland with their son, daughter-in-law, and birthday boy grandson, and had verified Martin Spencer's account of the previous night.

★   ★   ★

Growing up in the New Forest had been fun. She had ridden her pony in summer through beautiful scenery unchanged over countless centuries. In winter she had tobogganed down the snow covered gentle slope at the rear of her verderer father's cottage home. That way the years had passed at a speed that in retrospect was astonishing, perhaps even somewhat scary. When little more than an infant, Amanda Snelling had had an epiphany that, though compelling, was undefined. Throughout the years that followed she was at all times certain that she had a mission of some kind. Though still undecided as an adult, she had left home to join the police.

Moving into the town to share a flat with Gabriella, a colleague, had been a wrench; a traumatic tug on an umbilical cord that she thought had been completely cut years ago. She had at first missed the smell of new-cut

41

grass and the coolness of an evening breeze softly playing music through the trees. Though perhaps never adjusting completely to living in an overcrowded town, she had known that she must persevere. It had been worth it, for now, fittingly on a Sunday morning, she had found her purpose in life. It was to bring the wicked to justice. She had been born to become a detective. She had witnessed injustice all around her, and wanted to right the many wrongs. Though far from a religious calling, it meant a great deal to her.

Keen to get into her new role, she stepped through the door of the public house behind Mattia, following him across the floor. From behind the bar the landlord, an obese figure in his fifties, suspiciously watched their approach. It took a few moments to grasp that it was her uniform that was causing concern.

There was as yet only one customer this early on a Sunday morning, a young man reading a newspaper at a table. A woman with hennaed hair, whom Mandy took to be the landlord's wife, was stacking bottles on a high shelf behind the bar.

'What can I do for you?' the landlord enquired.

'Mr Preston?'

'Yes.'

Mattia produced his warrant card. 'Detective Chief Inspector Mattia. This is Constable Snelling.'

'How can I help, Detective Chief Inspector?'

Mattia answered with a question of his own. 'One of your entertainers last night was a singer named Tina Spencer?'

'That's right.'

'I understand she had some trouble with a man as she came down from the stage.'

'Oh yes, I remember. We get our share of troublemakers in here. If I remember rightly, Marty, that's Tina's husband, went to her aid and the whole thing just fizzled out.'

'The description I have is not of a troublemaker but a respectable elderly man.'

Shrugging, Preston remarked, 'I can't be expected to remember what every potential troublemaker looks like.'

'Why don't you ask Tina herself?' the woman enquired.

Turning to her, Mattia asked, 'Are you Mrs Preston?'

'Aimee Preston, yes.'

'Tina Spencer was murdered last night.'

A distressed Ike Preston gasped loudly and whined to his wife. 'That's bloody Christmas finished. Where are we going to find someone to replace her at such short notice?'

'Did this happen close to here?' an embarrassed Aimee Preston asked quickly, obviously aware of Mandy's and Mattia's disgust at her husband's reaction.

'She was at home, Mrs Preston.'

'This is dreadful,' the landlady whispered, genuinely upset.

Preston tried to excuse his earlier reaction by saying. 'This has been an appalling shock. So young and so talented a woman.'

'Both Martin and Tina knew that with her looks she couldn't afford to take chances,' Aimee Preston informed them. 'When Martin couldn't be here to take her home he invariably arranged a taxi to collect her.'

'Do you have CCTV in the car-park?'

'No, it isn't required,' Ike Preston replied. 'Lennie Parfitt, my head of security, is a former military policeman. Lennie has a photographic memory and if anything out of the ordinary should occur he can report it, chapter and verse.'

'Was he on duty last night?'

'Yes.'

'Where would we find him if we should need to?'

'He has a house in Langdon Street,' Aimee said. 'Just behind here. Number 83.'

Chuckling, Ike Preston warned, 'You'll find

it difficult to get away from Lennie. He intended to start up as a private eye, but his army pension was too small.'

'Thank you both for your help,' Mattia told them. 'Just one last question. Did you book Tina Spencer personally, or through an agent?'

'Through Phil Crowe, her agent, at Clarence Chambers in Drake Square.'

As they turned away from the landlord and his wife, Mandy was aware of the young man at the table turning his head to them. In doing so he revealed the right side of his face. She saw that a large blemish, which she took to be a birthmark, disfigured his cheek. She could feel his eyes on her back as she and Mattia headed to the door.

'He is the type who stands out in a crowd, but not the sort you take home to meet mum and dad, Mandy,' Mattia surprised her by remarking when they were outside.

'I wouldn't take him home to meet the pig we kept in the back garden, sir.'

'If nothing else, that mark on his right cheek would put anyone off.'

'No one can be blamed for having a birthmark, sir,' Mandy's sense of justice made her protest mildly.

'Is that what you thought it was, Mandy?'

'Isn't it?'

45

'No, it was a razor slash that should have been stitched at the time. I've seen quite a few like it. For good reason the victim doesn't want to go to a hospital, so it is left to heal without being sutured. The result is a long and wide mark made up of raised ridges of original skin each side of a length of new, pinkish skin.'

'We live and learn,' Mandy remarked with a casualness that was the opposite of her true feelings. 'Where are we going now, sir?'

'We need to have Martin Spencer identify the body of his wife.'

As the car climbed a hill on the perimeter of the city, Mattia looked out at the sea far below. In the bay there were a few small sailing craft. Their sails were stirring in a modest breeze. In the middle distance were the huddled roofs of buildings in a landscape that was soft, rounded, and shadowy with the quality of old velvet. Family groups of various numbers passed by on Sunday strolls.

The surroundings were far friendlier than skid row and the dock area they had just left, yet Mattia felt equally out of place here as he had there. Maybe there was a middle ground somewhere, an environment where he could fit in, could feel at home. If that were so then it was a nirvana that had so far eluded him on both sides of the Atlantic.

'Have you ever noticed how in a city or town dusk drops fast from the sky like a theatre curtain, whereas in the countryside it rolls in slowly from the horizon?' he idly observed.

'I've never noticed, sir. But I'll certainly give it some thought.'

'Don't,' he cautioned her, 'my kind of thinking leads to manic depression.'

Smiling, she slowed the car, turned into a large housing estate and drove through a few streets before announcing. 'There's the house, sir.'

'Right,' Mattia said flatly. 'Let's collect the new widower and get it over with.'

Calling at the house was a chilling experience that forewarned Mandy and Mattia of how unpleasant the next hour or so would be. Spencer's widowed mother, elderly and frail, had kept herself in the background, taking on the appearance of a ghost haunting the house rather than a woman living in it. A dozen roses in a vase with which the old woman must have decorated the hall table at a happier time, were limp. A scattering of black-edged petals lay around the vase. For Mattia that desolate little scene summed up the despair of the situation.

Spencer didn't speak on the drive through the town. As Mattia had anticipated, he broke down when a solemn mortuary attendant had with trained but cold sympathy pulled down a covering sheet to reveal the bruised and swollen face of his dead wife. Distress caused his nod of recognition to be repetitive.

Nevertheless, it served as the formal identification Mattia required.

Spencer's continued silence made the return journey even more uncomfortable than the drive into town had been. When they pulled up outside his mother's house, he mumbled 'Thank you' before hurriedly getting out of the car, leaving the door swinging open.

Reaching over the back of his seat to close the door, Mattia joined Mandy in watching the grieving widower stagger towards the house like a drunken man. 'Come on,' Mattia said. 'Move us out of here, Mandy.'

'What's happening here, sir?'

A man and woman stood in the doorway to meet Martin Spencer. Though older, the man bore a striking resemblance to the new widower. The woman was short, dumpy and unattractive.

Opening the car door, Mattia said. 'We need to know who this is. I won't be long, Mandy.'

Allowing Martin Spencer to pass them and enter the house, the man was about to close the door when he saw Mattia approaching.

With a friendly smile he identified himself. 'I'm Stuart Spencer, Martin's brother, and this is my wife, Estelle.'

'Detective Chief Inspector Mattia.' Mattia returned his handshake.

'You will appreciate that this is a worrying time for the family. I need to ask if it is likely that my brother will need to be represented by a solicitor?'

'At this stage there is no requirement for such representation, Mr Spencer.'

'But that could change?'

'It is possible, of course.'

Lowering his head in thought, Stuart said. 'That is what concerns me. If it comes to that, then it could turn out to be extremely expensive. I have my own business, a car sales dealership on Carlton Road. Maybe I could be described as fairly rich but not wealthy. I might not have enough finance.'

'I am not in a position to advise you now,' Mattia explained. 'But I will be happy to keep you informed throughout my investigation.'

'That is most kind of you, DCI Mattia. Here is my card.'

3

On returning to the car, Mattia explained, 'That was Martin Spencer's brother, Stuart, and the timid little woman was his wife. Drive me home, Mandy. Then go back to Crescent Street, get an update from DS Petters and if there is anything important ring me.'

'We'll be home in time for tea,' Mandy predicted chirpily, turning the ignition key.

Time for tea? Time to eat, time to go to bed, and time to get up had no importance. The time you were born and the time you would die were arranged without any input from you. There were no other times to that meant anything. This brief moment of introspection had Mattia shocked to discover how embittered he had become.

When they re-entered the town he gave the policewoman directions and she gunned the engine to push the car speedily through indecisive Sunday afternoon drivers to pull up outside of the large modern block in which Candace Dvorak had her luxurious apartment.

Ducking her head to peer incredulously up at the building, Mandy Snelling gave a gasp of amazement. 'I thought that you lived close to the common, sir. Holman Street?'

'Don't practise your detective work on me, Mandy,' Mattia chided her, tapping his nose with a forefinger as he opened the door of the car.

'I wasn't probing, sir,' she pleaded with exaggerated innocence.

'The thought didn't cross my mind,' he assured her, tongue in cheek. 'If there's nothing that requires me to come to the station, I'll see you in my office at eight o'clock tomorrow morning, Detective Constable Snelling.'

He realized that it would have been an anticlimax for her if he had walked away without confirming the promotion that meant so much to her.

'Very good, sir,' a pleased Mandy Snelling replied with a pretend salute, the expression on her face as lively as a gypsy dance.

★ ★ ★

There was only stilted conversation between Mattia and Candace as he drove them through the town centre that Sunday evening. When he had called in at the restaurant that morning the old magic they'd once known had spontaneously returned. Yet now Candace had become withdrawn. Though

51

acknowledging that the cause was his preoccupation with the Spencer murder, Mattia found it impossible to prevent the details of the crime from running through his mind. He hoped that the evening they had planned would prove to be a welcome distraction. Sunday's limited choice of entertainment decided them to give the recently opened pub/theatre a try.

They were pleasantly surprised by a dining room that had some seventy tables. Those already present couldn't be described as a theatre-going crowd. They could loosely be categorized as the town's middle class. Self-celebrated folk who spoke urgently, and their talk was of big money, big business. He guessed that the majority were giving the hybrid new enterprise a test drive, just as Candace and he were.

The exact timing of the evening had been impressed upon him when making a telephone booking back at Candace's apartment. The serving of a three-course meal would begin promptly at seven o'clock, and patrons were asked to be seated in the theatre ready for the show to begin at eight-fifteen.

Three uniformed usherettes standing waiting by the entrance to the theatre caught Mattia's appreciative eye. Lent a mystique by the subdued lighting and with no duties as yet, they stood as onlookers, minor attendant-goddesses. He reproached himself. Since his early teens some siren, invisible and sitting on a rock just outside the span of his senses, had been singing her song of seduction for him. Each time he met an attractive woman he was convinced she was that ethereal beauty who had haunted him throughout his adult life. It was this drawing his attention to the usherettes. He was determined to beat this mental aberration. Candace Dvorak was enough woman for any man. His feelings for her were of a higher order.

He switched his attention to a young, hunched-shouldered man who was playing the memorable *As Time Goes By* on the piano and singing with a talent that belied his very ordinary looks. The haunting melody from the classic film *Casablanca* had an emotional effect on the diners. A hush replaced the uneven murmur of separate conversations. Candace sat nodding in time to the pianist's tempo. Sensing that he was looking at her she turned to him, her lips struggling with a tentative smile. Then the smile took hold and moved up to include her eyes.

This promise of an enjoyable evening was boosted when a waiter brought their meal. It was truly excellent fare, and Mattia was aware that the good food and ambience of the restaurant was having a spirit-lifting effect on Candace.

'I'm really looking forward to the play. I've long been an avid fan of Alan Bennett,' she said.

'As Tennessee Williams dominated my early theatre going, I know nothing about this Bennett guy, but I'm glad that we decided to give this place a try,' Mattia responded.

'So am I, it's good to see you relaxing, Gio.'

At that moment Mattia was made speechless as he noticed Detective Superintendent Ralph Bardon sitting with his wife just a few tables away. The ambitious Bardon was destined to soon blight some county by becoming assistant chief constable there. A skilled self-promoter, he had a *curriculum vitae* superior to anything the Pope could come up with.

'There goes my hope of a cop free evening,' Mattia muttered gloomily.

Following his gaze, Candace enquired, 'A colleague, Gio?'

'Not exactly. That's Ralph Bardon, an asshole rather than a policeman.'

Seeing Mattia looking his way, Bardon's stern face that had the kind of ridiculous tan that has to be topped up all year round, lightened into an easy smile that put square, yellow teeth on show. Coming from a smugly contented spot somewhere deep inside, the wide smile lacked warmth. He seemed only half-human; an example of what an overdose of self-regard can do to a man. Mattia acknowledged the smile with a curt nod.

'Forget him, Gio,' a concerned Candace advised. 'Whoever he is we mustn't permit him to spoil our evening.'

'He won't,' Mattia recklessly promised.

Candace was later proven to having been right about the entertainment. *Habeas Corpus* was a sexually orientated enjoyable play. So good, in fact, that when they were leaving cheerful talk of Alan Bennett and the play ricocheted around them.

'I'm sure that I once knew a randy clergyman like that Canon Throbbing,' Candace joked about one of the characters in the play.

'I have arrested more than a few exactly like him,' Mattia quipped.

Musak was pulsing gently in the foyer. Not the harsh stuff of discothèques, but soft, sweet, romantic ballads and instrumentals. Candace was tightening her hold on Mattia's arm when a voice close behind them ruined the moment.

'Excuse me, Gio. Might I have a word?'

They both turned to discover that it was

Ralph Bardon who had spoken. His wife, plainly under orders, was waiting some distance away.

'What is it, Ralph?'

'I am sorry to broach police business on an evening out,' Bardon began with a bogus apology. 'This Orchard Avenue case. I understand that the husband has not yet been brought in. That makes me uneasy.'

'There's no reason why it should. You are not the senior investigating officer, I am.'

'That's true, Gio, but at the risk of causing bad feeling between you and me, I have the chief constable's ear, and I am concerned enough to request that I take over as SIO.'

'There has always has been and always will be bad feeling between you and me, Ralph. I can see that such a move could prove useful in your desperate dash for promotion.'

'That is gratuitously insulting,' Bardon protested vehemently.

'I meant it to be,' Mattia assured him.

Leaving Bardon gaping open-mouthed, Mattia ushered Candace away. Candace reached out to take his arm as she had before Bardon had intruded on their obviously fragile happiness. But the link had lost its thrill.

As he was unlocking the car door, she put up a hand to lift a lock of hair back off her shoulder; the movement was delayed, as though she was uncertain whether she should speak. Then her hand dropped to her side and she remarked forlornly, 'Why does such a lovely evening have to end like that?'

'That is the effect Bardon has, Candace,' he replied. 'Devoid of talent he has shot up through the ranks like a space rocket. You don't do that unless you have massive support from outside the force.'

When they were in the car and driving away, Mattia recognized the inadequacy of the answer he had given her. Ralph Bardon was just a part of the problem. Mattia's work, linked to his growing dissatisfaction with his job, was a major problem for both Candace and him.

Though both of them had become accustomed to long silences between them, Candace found it necessary to break this one by asking, 'Will you be staying tonight?'

'I don't believe that will help either of us, do you?'

'Probably not,' she morosely agreed.

There was sparse conversation between them after that. Mattia drove home slowly after a lacklustre leave-taking from Candace at the door to her apartment, a parting that left everything flat, colourless. Reluctant to arrive at his destination, he drove slowly. It was as if the night was the only thing he had left, and even that wasn't doing much for him.

He had first met Candace on a night when she had organized the catering at a retirement do for a Crescent Street inspector. Late in the evening he had sought sanctuary from the noisy, drunken policemen with whom he didn't feel even a hint of affinity. Wandering into a side room, he had discovered it already had one occupant. Candace had been sitting with her elbows on a table, her head resting in her hands.

Raising her head she had wearily asked, 'Have you come to arrest me for loitering with intent?'

Her long dress made of white silk chiffon had traversed time. It looked modern while at the same time seeming to belong to the 1960s, but with one shoulder bare and the other draped in the style of Ancient Greece, it couldn't be dated. Her eyes had boldly run over him in frank appraisal. Having been aware of her all through the evening, he noticed that tiredness had not even slightly diminished the brilliant glow of her personality.

Shaking his head, he had answered. 'No. I lack the authority to do so. I'm a police community support officer, not a proper policeman.'

'Thank goodness,' she had said, aware that he had been joking.

'But I could issue you with a fixed penalty notice.'

'Oh dear. I didn't think that plastic policemen had even that much power. What would my punishment be?'

'You must remain in the immediate vicinity, madam, while I temporarily vacate this room to get both of us a drink.'

'I plead guilty, as long as mine is a Bacardi,' she had laughingly agreed.

On his return with two drinks, he had pulled up a chair to sit across the table from her, saying contentedly. 'This is heaven. The great escape from that bunch of heathens out there.'

'I noticed that you were apart from the others,' she had commented, her face reddening on realizing that she had unintentionally confessed to having been aware of him during the evening. Having a short while ago been in a state of desperation to get out of this place, he had then just as desperately wanted to stay.

'I guess I am anti-social,' he had said, raising his glass to toast her. 'Here's wishing you whatever you wish for yourself. I'm Giovanni Mattia.'

'Candace Dvorak,' she had responded.

Clinking her glass against his she added. 'I don't think the wish fairy would be interested in me, but I wish you the same.'

'If that is instantly granted, we'll both find ourselves sitting on that sofa in the corner of the room.'

'I'm too tired to come up with a witty comeback.'

He had given an exaggerated sigh. 'I'm relieved. I feared rejection.'

'It's academic now, as your wish wasn't granted,' she had pointed out, adding cheekily, 'So you'll never know.'

'Don't underestimate me,' he had cautioned her with a smile. 'But I would never take advantage of a lady who is drunk.'

'I am not drunk,' she had vigorously defended herself.

'Oh, it's OK then,' he had said, pretending to get up from his chair.

She had laughed a genuine laugh. Then he had guessed that it was because they both had had a hectic working day and a demanding evening, the pair of them had quickly become lost in a vacuum of quieting emotions.

A short while later the volume of noise from the hall had lessened, she remarked, ironically, 'The festivities are at an end.'

'Thank — ' Mattia had hastily stifled an obscenity, improvising with ' . . . the Lord,' as they emptied their glasses. He then asked, 'Is that it for us?'

'In what way?'

'Is this as far as we go?'

'That depends on how far you want it to go,' she had answered with a self-deprecating little smile. 'You're a man of the world who could take your pick of the women in this city, so what would you want with me?'

'I would be flattered if that were true. But if it was, then there would be only one woman that interested me, Candace.'

Aware that he meant her, she had a way of slowly raising her limpid violet eyes to look at the person she was speaking to. There was a level of intimacy in the mannerism that had a stirring effect. 'Why should someone like you feel that way about me?'

'I do feel that way. That is why I want to know if this is to be our last goodbye?'

'I have to now supervise my staff packing everything away.'

'So it is to be a case of nice-to-have-met-you?'

'Not if you don't want it to be,' she had told him. 'Do you know the Criterion Restaurant?'

'Yes.'

'You are welcome to call in at any time.'

'What time do you open tomorrow

morning?' he had eagerly enquired, only partly in jest.

That was how it had started, but now what had been the deepest, the most exciting, the most satisfying relationship he'd ever had, seemed doomed to a fate neither of them wanted.

Arriving home now, his terraced house seemed smaller and somehow unwelcoming. Never one to need companionship, always appreciating the solitude that came with living alone, he felt none of his usual contentment as he turned the key in the lock. As he stepped inside, closing the door behind him, his home felt eerily empty, as if nobody had lived there for many long years. He had the ludicrous thought that the place had died while he'd been away.

★ ★ ★

Unable to sleep, listening to Zeeta breathing regularly and softly beside him, Melvin Petters couldn't fathom what was worrying him. It wasn't his wife or daughter. As Zeeta had lovingly pointed out to him earlier, he was a natural-born worrier. That was inarguable, but this was different. It was more a feeling of unease; of insecurity than of worry: an entirely new and frightening experience.

The only clue, so vague that he felt inclined

to ignore it, was Mandy Snelling. He liked her, but her reaction to joining the CID had been somewhat girlishly enthusiastic. He had known more than one over-zealous officer who had put the lives of colleagues at risk. However, Mandy was an intelligent girl, so there was nothing about her to keep him awake through the early part of the night.

At two o'clock in the morning, Petters was still struggling to discover what was now menacing him to a terrifying degree. Music from a thoughtless neighbour's stereo was flooding the night, a disturbance that added to the unrest that had him restlessly twisting and turning in his bed. Relief of a sort only came when his thinking became distorted. He drifted through the crazy hypnagogic state into a troubled sleep in an uneasy world.

★　★　★

Arriving later than usual at the police station on Monday morning, Mattia was thankful for having made things right with Candace along the way. Wearing a pink towelling dressing-gown, she had been standing at a worktop preparing food with her back to him. She drew in a long, deep breath, and had then spoken without turning. 'Did you sleep well, Gio?'

'Far from it.'

'Join the club,' she had said, yawning.

He had taken her hand; at once realizing that she must have just come from a bath because, close-up, her stirring aroma was fresh and soapy. Warmth and feeling had been exchanged between them for a few moments. Then this closeness had for some odd reason turned them into semi-strangers, embarrassing them both. They stood back, both wearing uncertain smiles.

To reassure her he had said. 'I have to go now, but I'll be with you tonight.'

'Maybe you'll be too late,' she had managed to joke as she kissed him. 'I might take George Clooney up on his offer.'

'I don't think so. You aren't the type to settle for second best,' he had joked as he left her.

Mandy and Petters were waiting outside his office. Having earlier decided to call on Tina Spencer's agent, he instructed Petters to investigate the Spencers' financial situation.

'Give it the full works, Sergeant. Bank accounts, joint or single, savings or current, I want full details. If they are in debt, who do they owe money too, and why?'

Noticing that an eager Mandy was waiting to learn her brief, he told her, 'I want you to attend the post-mortem with me at eleven o'clock this morning, Mandy. So, first, you can check out the results from the house-to-house inquiries. Then meet me in the car-park behind Drake Square at half ten. You can leave your car there. We'll go to the lab in my car.'

When his detective sergeant and constable had left his office, Mattia sat for a few moments of reflection. Where things personal were concerned, everything with Candace was back on an even keel. That left him with the murder of Tina Spencer to concentrate on. Then, his detective's mind in overdrive, he went out of his office.

★   ★   ★

The ground floors of the fine Victorian buildings in Drake Square had been ripped out to accommodate anachronistic seasonal gift shops and fast-food outlets. But on the north side of the square the Belmont Buildings still stood sedately intact, a breakwater against the turbulent seas of change. Included in the row was the sacrosanct Clarence Chambers, home to the elite, the city's top lawyers.

Puzzled as to how a theatrical agent had come to occupy the same building as the in-crowd, he entered a spacious reception area in which a girl sat at a low, long modern desk. Wearing a red dress and a brilliant smile, she had the exotic kind of beauty that favours Asian women.

'Good morning,' Mattia said in answer to her smile. 'I'm looking for the offices of a theatrical agent, Phillip Crowe.'

'It's on the sixth floor,' she said, her smile still in place. 'Turn right on leaving the lift, and it's the last door at the end of the landing.'

The lift stopped and he stepped out into a private world high above the asphalted, pedestrian-thronged, traffic-jammed, fume-spewing madhouse below. Mattia hated city life but wouldn't want to live anywhere else. How was that for a split personality? He rapped on the agency's door before entering a small room.

An ageing woman rose up from behind an ageing desk. She didn't look like any other type. Women working in these places never did. You don't see them climbing little steel stepladders in shoe shops, or dragging barcodes over a bleeping checkout in supermarkets.

'Yes?' she challenged Mattia, peering over silver-rimmed glasses to impale Mattia with a penetrating glance.

'I want to see Mr Crowe.'

Taking off her glasses with a dramatic gesture, she gave an indulgent little smile. 'He could possibly fit you in at some time tomorrow if you would care to make an appointment.'

'It has to be now,' Mattia told her firmly, producing his warrant card. 'I am Detective Chief Inspector Mattia.'

Taken aback, the elderly woman stood undecided. A door at the far side of the room opened a crack and one eye peered out nervously through the gap. Then the door closed. An intercom buzzed on the woman's desk. Answering it, she told Mattia that Mr Crowe would see him, and indicated the door which led into another poky room.

Mattia guessed that to get himself a prestigious address Crowe had rented, probably at an extortionate rent, what was once a janitor's storeroom. He was sitting behind his desk and played the one-upmanship ruse of keeping Mattia waiting by not looking up. He used a mouse to line up a regiment of icons on the blue parade ground of a computer screen.

Then he came round his desk with his right hand extended. Close to, or possibly past retiring age, he had a tendency towards obesity. His flesh seemed to sag from his bones. 'Good morning, Detective Chief Inspector . . . ?'

'Mattia.'

'I have heard the tragic news, so believe that I know the reason for your visit.'

'It's just a matter of procedure, Mr Crowe, to build a profile of the deceased.'

'I do understand,' Crowe said, gesturing for Mattia to be seated.

'Was Mrs Spencer a big earner?'

Giving the question profound thought, Crowe ran a forefinger up and down the edge of his jaw, then his eyes lifted to meet Mattia's again. 'She certainly had the talent and the potential to hit the top and stay there. She was unlucky in being born too soon. The fame, and I use that word advisedly, that today comes via the media's ludicrous obsession with celebrity, did not exist when Tina needed publicity. She always looked disappointed at her cheque each month.'

'That suggests that she needed money badly.'

'Maybe.' Crowe shrugged. 'I had a guy come in here last week asking about Tina on the pretence that he wanted to hire her for a gig.'

'You considered it to be a bogus enquiry?'

'I sure did. It occurred to me that he was a debt collector.'

'Did he ask for her address?'

Crowe's forehead furrowed into a frown.

'No. I never divulge personal details about anyone on my books. But he did casually slip in one enquiry. I didn't really twig it until now. He asked when Tina would next be appearing at Ike's place.'

'Did you tell him?'

'It was no secret, so I told him that Tina would be at Ike's on Saturday.'

'Can you describe him?'

'Young, in his late twenties I would say. His hair was glued so that it stood up at the front in that ridiculous ski-jump style. Most noticeable about him was a long diagonal razor scar down his right cheek.'

Linking the description with the guy he had noticed in the Dockers' Den the previous day, Mattia asked. 'Did he say anything that would help identify him, Mr Crowe?'

'Nothing springs to mind,' Crowe replied, 'but Cammy Studland may well be able to help you, as she was here at the time. She was Tina's friend. I've got Cammy regular gigs at the Mississippi Club, and she told me that she had seen this bloke there often.'

'What nights of the week would I find her at the club?'

'Every night but Monday. It's a really busy club.'

'Thank you, Mr Crowe. I'll leave you my card. Call me if anything else occurs to you.'

Shaking Mattia by the hand, Crowe promised him. 'I most certainly will, and I hope that I have been of some help to you. Though I can't claim to have been close to Tina, nevertheless this kind of tragedy close to home shakes you up.'

'It most certainly does,' Mattia sincerely concurred as he left.

★ ★ ★

After visiting two banks neither of which held accounts in the names of either Martin or Christina Spencer, Petters struck lucky at the third. He was shown into the office of branch manager Justin Lorton. Battling to remain articulate he triumphed by giving an outline of his enquiry without a single stutter.

'Mr and Mrs Spencer have three separate accounts with the bank, Detective Sergeant,' Lorton announced officiously as he studied an open file that lay on his desk in front of him. 'May I ask the reason for your enquiry?'

Petters came direct to the point. 'Mrs Spencer was murdered late on Saturday night.'

'Good heavens!' Lorton exclaimed.

'Could you please detail the accounts to me individually?'

'Of course.' Turning a page of the file, the

70

manager said. 'One is a current account pertaining to Mr Spencer's business.'

'The balance?'

'That is something that has of late caused concern,' Lorton forlornly explained. 'I have delayed any action as Mrs Spencer transferred funds from her savings account to the business account. This happens regularly and in substantial amounts, but Mr Spencer's income from his trading has recently been dwarfed by his expenditure.'

'Have these transfers run Mrs Spencer's savings account dangerously low?'

'No, the transfers she made did not affect the balance of her account. Let me explain.' Picking up the file from his desk, the manager leafed through it. 'Here we are. Eighteen months ago Mrs Spencer began depositing two thousand pounds in her savings account each month without fail. In the last six months the deposits have increased to four thousand pounds per month. This is the money that she transfers in full to the business account each month.'

'Does this money come from her work as an entertainer?'

'It doesn't. She pays that in separately.'

'I have to ask where she obtained the regular larger amounts.'

The tactful Justin Lorton somehow included

an apology in the shrug that preceded his reply. 'I am unable to tell you that. Mrs Spencer made these deposits in cash.'

'Mr Spencer's savings account?' Petters finally enquired.

'Hasn't moved either way for a considerable time, remaining at less than a hundred,' Lorton answered, closing the file in a way that signalled he regarded the interview was at an end.

★ ★ ★

Heading for his car in the Drake Square car-park, Mattia noticed a woman crouching beside a Renault Clio that was parked next to his. Coming closer, he could see that a rear tyre of her car was flat. In a response that was far from gallant, he silently but strenuously berated the stupid woman for parking next to him in a spacious car-park that was less that a quarter full. This was a situation he didn't need on a day when it was essential that everything should go smoothly.

The sun, still low in the sky, cast the woman in a blinding glare as she came upright. Raising a hand to shield his eyes, Mattia saw that she had the regular features of the stars of Hollywood's boom years. Her blonde hair was styled in a way that was vaguely familiar to him. Looking down at the punctured tyre, she breathed in deeply. Her exhalation was a sigh.

'I know absolutely nothing about cars,' she confessed, speaking as if they already had a conversation in progress. 'I had a blazing row with my bank manager yesterday afternoon and now this, first thing in the morning.'

He was determined that women, even one as attractive as this, had no place on his agenda onward from his visit to Candace that morning. Then the motorist brushed aside the soft curtain of hair that had fallen over her cheek, a movement that clicked on his memory's hard drive. She was a latter-day Veronica Lake, and he liked old movies. In the way that hearing music from the 1930s and '40s did, they connected him mystically with what was now a lost generation; people who had lived through a world war. There was a contradictory pleasant kind of sadness in the link.

He asked, 'Have you got a spare wheel and a jack? I can fix this for you.'

4

'Could you fix my bank manager first?' she enquired, fun sparkling in her dark eyes.

'I'll leave that to your husband.'

She laughed a deep, throaty laugh, putting a ringless left hand on display. 'You're a smooth operator. Now you know that I'm unattached, are you ready for the Sir Galahad bit?'

She turned her head to look down at the flat tyre, and then pointed at the car's boot. 'There's a wheel in there. But I don't know about the other thing.'

'We'd better take a look.'

She unlocked and opened the hatchback. Mattia used one end of the car's wheel brace to wind down the spare wheel carrier. He kicked the tyre. Mercifully, it was fully inflated. He lifted the car's bonnet to find the jack.

'You're in luck,' he told her, managing a half-hearted smile.

Her gaze taking in his smart suit, she protested. 'I can't let you ruin your clothing.'

'I'll only get my hands dirty, and I can wash them over there,' he said, indicating a block of public toilets at the centre of the carpark.

'You are very sweet,' he heard her say as he positioned the jack under the car.

Completing his task rapidly and efficiently, he put the wheel in the car, then closed the boot before passing her the key.

Reaching out with both hands to hold his wrists, she turned his hands palms up to survey the grime on them. The physical contact sent her voice on a roller coaster ride up and down the scale. Then she cleared her throat, and words came out in a rush. 'You've got yourself filthy. I feel terribly guilty.'

'There's no need. I volunteered.'

Releasing his wrists, she became composed once more. Then she smiled. White teeth flashed and dimples dimpled. 'I really am grateful. I'm Marcia, by the way.'

Mattia hesitated. Exchanging names would draw them out of the mystery they had shared and into reality, depriving them of a certain tone of intimacy they were enjoying. Finding their identity would cost them the strange kind of secret they had shared. Anonymity would be the ultimate in relation-ships, but that was not feasible. Reluctantly, he introduced himself. 'Giovanni, or Gio if you want to be real friendly.'

'I'm the friendly type, Gio. If this was

evening I'd offer to buy you a drink.'

'If it was evening, I would accept,' he heard himself automatically say.

'But it's not an insuperable problem.' Her lips puckered provocatively. 'We could meet somewhere later. My local perhaps. Do you know the Rose and Crown on Eastgate Street?'

An image of Candace flashed through his mind, making him inwardly cringe at his susceptibility. Marcia took a step closer, deliberately increasing the temptation that was plaguing him. Trivial though the situation appeared to be, it could force him into making a possibly life-changing mistake.

Reaching into her car for a slim, expensive cigarette case, she asked a mute question by raising an eyebrow. A non-smoker, he shook his head. Taking out a cigarette she put it between her lips and lit it with a golden cigarette lighter. She drew on it deeply while waiting expectantly for his response to her suggestion. Taking the cigarette from her mouth, she tilted her head back to blow a column of smoke heavenwards. A touch of her fragrant essence rode on the smoke, tempting him, bringing him ever nearer to the edge of the chasm that he had come to dread. On the verge of him giving an answer that would betray Candace, he saw Mandy

Snelling drive into the car-park. His relief was so profound that he wanted to run across and express his gratitude by embracing the girl. He waved a welcoming hand.

At his side, Marcia made a little moue of disappointment. 'Here comes the wife.'

'Just a girl from the office,' he explained, wondering why he felt that he needed to.

'Whatever, she's very attractive, Giovanni.'

'What happened to Gio?' he enquired.

'For some reason I no longer feel very friendly,' Marcia pouted.

Mandy got out of her car and locked the door. Watching her approach, a disappointed Marcia hopefully suggested, 'Maybe some other time?'

Knowing that she was about to leave him, and aware that he didn't want it to be for ever, Mattia philosophically agreed with her. 'It's a small world.'

'Big enough for both of us to get lost and never to find each other again,' she remarked dully as she walked away.

Mattia watched her go, bemused by an abrupt cancelling of excitement, alarmed by an acute sense of loss, and puzzled as to why she so desperately wanted them to meet again.

'Have I interrupted something, sir?' Mandy asked cheekily as she came up to him.

Mattia chuckled. 'You wait here and clean up your mind, Mandy, while I go to the toilet block to wash my hands.'

He heard Marcia's car start up as he walked to the toilets. When she tooted the horn as she drove past behind him, he disciplined himself and gave her no more than a backwards wave. Yet it was a hollow victory. It was probably inevitable that the two of them would meet again.

★　★　★

Freya Miller's annoyance moved up a notch into anger as she glanced at her office clock. Ten o'clock, half the morning already gone and still not a word from Mattia. The taciturn detective chief inspector's disregard for authority incensed the county's police authority and her assistant chief constable, but she took it personally. Ever self-sufficient, she suffered from humiliating adolescent feelings when in Mattia's presence.

A knock on her office door caused her to give a startled little jump of expectation. Then she calmed down and faced the most likely situation. It would be the obsequious Detective Superintendent Ralph Bardon, a creep ready to trade his self-respect for the chance to walk the narrow and dangerous plank to high command. Nevertheless, Bardon had the establishment stamp on him, enjoying the warm security of knowing that something incredibly powerful watched over him in secret ways.

'Enter.'

'Good morning, ma'am,' Bardon said with overdone deference.

'Good morning, Superintendent Bardon. What is it you wished to speak to me about?'

She deliberately left him standing, a signal that she didn't anticipate his remaining long in her office.

'I am concerned about the Spencer case, ma'am.'

'Why so? I have appointed Detective Inspector Mattia as senior investigating officer.'

'That is mainly the problem, ma'am.'

Freya Miller didn't respond. The sudden silence was deep and somehow audibly painful. She asked sharply. 'Are you questioning my authority or my integrity, Superintendent Bardon?'

'Neither, ma'am, I could not possibly have a reason for doing so,' Bardon stammered. 'The fact is that this is a high-profile case. Monday morning has arrived and the principal suspect has not been apprehended. The media will have a field day, to the detriment of the force.'

She had to reluctantly admit to herself that he was right. Though a brilliant press officer, even Sinead Mayo had to have something to work on. 'You are not involved in the case, Superintendent Bardon, so what made you decide who the principal suspect is?'

'It would definitely seem to be the husband, ma'am,' Bardon replied, his confidence growing. 'There was no forced entry.'

'I am sure that DCI Mattia is aware of those facts.'

'With respect, ma'am, that is the point I am making: the lack of action on DCI Mattia's part.'

Breathing an inaudible sigh of relief at the timely diversion as the telephone on her desk shrilled, Freya Miller spoke sternly.

'That will be all, Superintendent Bardon.'

His discomfiture was manifested in his animated bodily movements as she turned to walk toward her desk to answer her phone.

★   ★   ★

As Mattia drove them to the mortuary, Mandy was ashamed of her childish excitement when it began to snow. Now a brilliant white carpet lay over the previously grey scenery they were passing through. She tried to sound detached as she remarked. 'This is early. We don't usually see it until after Christmas.'

'This will interest you, Mandy,' Mattia said. 'Tina Spencer's agent told me that a young guy had come into his office last week enquiring about Tina. Another entertainer, Cammy Studland, was in the office at the time. She's a singer at the Mississippi Club, and she recognized this guy as a regular there. This guy has a razor scar across his right cheek.'

'That has to be important, sir,' Mandy acknowledged.

'I agree,' Mattia said. 'We'll call on Lennie Parfitt on the way back.'

Mandy's interest was dampened by the dread of the first harrowing experience of her promotion to detective. Their destination was a square, white modern building that in the poor light of an early December afternoon had the look of a Lego construction.

When they were inside, walking down a wide corridor that had a background smell of chemicals, a sick-scared feeling came over Mandy. She murmured, 'I hope that I don't let you down, sir.'

'Don't underestimate yourself, Mandy,' Mattia kindly advised.

Finding his confidence in her reassuring,

Mandy was close behind him as he opened a door and entered into a sizeable, marbled chamber that was illuminated so intensely that she had to blink several times before her eyes adjusted to the glare. A young woman wearing protective clothing and a tight-fitting plastic cap, ushered them into a side room.

As she went in, Mandy glanced over her shoulder and saw an elderly man standing beside what was obviously a body covered by a green plastic sheet. Once inside the small room, Mattia and she were kitted out with the protective clothing, including caps.

More confident now as they went back into the main room, Mandy took a look around. There were a number of glaringly bright lights overhead, and cameras were strategically positioned. Sinks with long-handled taps were situated along one wall, together with cupboards on the surface of which surgical instruments were laid out. There was sterility in the atmosphere that was somehow tangible to a novice like Mandy.

'Good afternoon, Chief Inspector,' the pathologist Marcus Bellingham, said.

'Good afternoon,' Mattia replied. 'This is DC Snelling.'

Acknowledging Mandy with a curt nod, the pathologist reached to take a clipboard from the young woman, then moved closer to the body.

'What do you have for me?' Mattia asked.

'The dissection has confirmed my preliminary external examination. The deceased was a healthy young woman whose death was caused by extensive damage to her vital organs.'

A shiver ran through Mandy on hearing this. However, keen to learn, she paid attention as Mattia enquired whether there was any indication of sexual assault, to which the pathologist replied that there was not.

'There is this,' the pathologist said, pulling the covering sheet down a little and pointing to the dead woman's neck. 'I believe that you Americans refer to it as a hickey, but the term in this country is a love bite.'

'Could this have occurred at some time prior to the time of death?' Mattia asked.

'No,' the pathologist shook his head. 'It happened in concurrence with death.'

'That is a new one on me. I have known murders committed by psychopaths who have bitten their victims.'

'What you refer to would have been skin-breaking incidents, not love bites, Mr Mattia,' the pathologist explained. 'The skin here is unbroken.'

'Any chance of obtaining DNA from it?'

'An exceedingly slim one, but that is a possibility that I'm exploring,' Marcus Bellingham replied. 'That's the best I can do for you right now.'

'Thank you for everything. I'll be in touch,' Mattia said.

'Nothing personal, but I hope you will be contacting Mike Probert, the next time. With luck I will have crept back to my pipe and slippers.'

When they were outside, Mattia asked, 'How bad was it for you, Mandy?'

Mandy halted and stood facing him. Melting snow ran off her hair and she needed to dry her face by drawing a hand across it before she could speak. 'It wasn't as upsetting as I had envisaged. I just feel terribly sad, sir.'

'Paying a visit to Ike Preston's head of security might cheer us up.'

'What is your opinion with regard to the love bite, sir?'

'The only possibility I can come up with, Mandy, is that it's the murderer's tag, the equivalent of a graffiti artist signing his work.'

'That's really weird, sir.'

★ ★ ★

It was an impromptu but essential meeting. Freya Miller half sat on a desk in a small office in Crescent Street, while Assistant Chief Constable Reginald Wilkes was propped on a window sill; his thin body and narrow, hooked-nosed face made him look like a bird of prey perched ready to swoop. The subject they were discussing was the Tina Spencer murder, and in particular DCI Mattia's lack of communication.

'You know how highly I regard your opinion, Reg,' the chief constable said.

That was true. Reginald Wilkes, an acerbic arse-kicker in the judgement of his subordinates, was the only senior officer she had learned to completely trust since moving to the county. At the beginning she had feared that his left-wing leanings would mean he was an atheist. She had since learned otherwise.

'I don't doubt that you know my opinion, Freya, but never have I had cause to question your judgement,' Wilkes said. 'DS Bardon has spoken to me on this subject; and he has both deep concern about this case, and strong convictions as to how it should proceed were he the SIO. This is a case that we must stay on top of, Freya. I agree that Mattia has a commendable crime clear-up record, but he just doesn't conform. Possibly his most worrying trait is his womanising. The magically soft touch of a woman's skin has toppled empires, ruined kings, and destroyed religions. I don't want it to ruin the county police force, particularly with you as chief constable.'

'I am, of course, aware of DCI Mattia's peccadilloes, if that is the right term. Nevertheless, I am aware that they have never interfered with his work. I still believe that he is the correct choice as SIO.'

'Would you like me to discipline him, Freya?'

Giving this some consideration, Freya Miller said carefully, 'Perhaps a quiet word should the opportunity occur, Reg. But please avoid any confrontation at this time.'

★ ★ ★

Parfitt, a soldierly figure with close-cropped hair, greeted them enthusiastically after Mattia had made the introductions and explained the reason for their visit.

'I remember that guy who was mouthing off at Tina,' Parfitt exclaimed excitedly before making an apology. 'You will think that I've never grown up, acting like a silly kid playing cops and robbers. But I jot down everything that happens at the Dockers' Den.'

'Ike Preston told us that you were a military policeman, so I put that down to your army training, Mr Parfitt,' Mattia assured him.

86

'Now, you want to know what I have about that man,' Parfitt said, going across the room to take a notebook from a drawer in a sideboard. 'Here we are. I checked him out as he left the pub. He drove a silver Vauxhall Corsa. That's the registration number.'

Taking the proffered notebook, Mattia passed it to Mandy who walked to the far side of the room to use her mobile telephone.

Mattia said conversationally to Parfitt. 'When we were in Ike Preston's place yesterday a young guy with a razor slash scar across the right side of his face was there.'

'That's Rory Wilton. He hangs around the pub a lot, and he struck me as a suspicious character so I checked up on him. He shows all the signs of once having been in the mob.'

'The army?'

'That's right. He arrived here in the autumn working on a travelling fun fair. He stayed behind when the circus left town, so to speak.'

'What does he do for a living?'

'Nothing. He is not registered as unemployed, yet spends money like there's no tomorrow. I suspect that he's dealing drugs.'

'I'll have narcotics check him out,' Mattia said, then asked, 'Was he in the pub on Saturday night?'

'Yes. He was there.'

Mandy returned. 'The car is owned by a Maurice Trench at an address in Grentham.'

Pleased at having been provided with a positive lead to follow up, Mattia thanked Parfitt for his help. Then he and Mandy left.

Alone after dropping Mandy off at the Drake Square car-park, Mattia drove back to Crescent Street. He turned into the police station yard and parked. He sat for a while relaxing, needing to enjoy a last moment or two of freedom before forsaking the comforting solitude of his car and entering the building. Then his short sabbatical was under threat as Chief Constable Freya Miller came out of the station heading resolutely in his direction.

The sight of her excited him slightly. But there were too many problems in his present and immediate future for such a reaction to be sustained. His interest mutated into vexation.

Striding purposefully towards him, resplendent in her silver-trimmed uniform, she was up threateningly close when he unenthusiastically stepped out of the car. She stood before him, perfectly composed, breeding giving her a certain presence and a superb self-confidence.

'Good afternoon, ma'am.' He greeted her politely with a parody of a salute that resembled a peasant-like touching of a hat that he wasn't wearing.

Not returning the salutation, she said harshly, 'A fortunate meeting, Chief Inspector. I am due to give a media interview at headquarters tomorrow, and I have as yet had nothing from you on the Spencer case. I made a point of stressing to DS Petters that I wanted to be kept up to speed, and I am sure that he will have conveyed that to you.'

'He did as you told him. But there's been a lot of pressure, ma'am.'

'Not as much as I am under right now,' she complained, frowning momentarily.

He didn't doubt that she was stressed. As it was in all disciplined forces — the army or whatever — every police officer was afraid of his or her superiors. Her concern would be the county police authority. He pitied her. The hardest thing about being a success was the frenzied need to continue to be successful. The rift yawning between them had its origin in her ambition and his lack of it. She was a willing subscriber to a form of authoritarianism that he was finding increasingly difficult to endure.

Their eyes met and held for a moment. It was something of a strangely magical moment that brought uneasiness to them both. Lowering her eyes, she caught her breath and raised her head to lock on to his gaze once more. It was a look devoid of anger that seemed to ask: *Why do we insist on this pretence of ill-feeling between us?*

'I should have something for you by noon tomorrow, ma'am,' he declared casually.

'A press conference has been arranged for one o'clock tomorrow afternoon. You will be there, Chief Inspector. The newspaper people will want something substantial.'

'Feed them platitudes, ma'am. The tabloids cater for the masses, who lack the intellect to enable them to read a serious newspaper, by using large headlines and photographs as a substitute for text,' Mattia recommended.

This nonchalant suggestion served only to increase the growing tension between them. He followed it up with, 'It could endanger a lot of people to release too much information now, ma'am.'

Her eyes widened in annoyance; there was an accompanying galvanized stiffening of her shapely body. She spoke sharply. 'What should and what should not be released to the media is a decision for me, Chief Inspector. You must simply provide me with a comprehensive report by first thing tomorrow morning.'

He could read in her eyes that this was a test. He was being issued a challenge. But appeasement was weakness. His unease about the case had been increasing with each passing minute. He had to make certain that whoever had murdered Tina Spencer did not for some insane reason believe that he had cause to kill others.

'With respect, ma'am, this is my brief and I am not prepared to compromise it.'

'I'm sure there is no need to remind — ' she broke off in mid-sentence as Mandy Snelling drove into the yard.

Watching the attractive young detective get out of the car and glance their way before entering the police station, Freya Miller said, 'I understand that we have promoted PC Snelling to CID.'

Mattia nodded, the emphasis the chief constable had laid on the word *we* had revealed her annoyance at not being consulted. He countered her overt criticism. 'She has already proved herself to be a valuable member of my team, ma'am.'

'It will take longer than a few hours for that to be judged,' she said distrustfully. 'However, to return to what is at issue here. I insist on your full support.'

'You have my support, ma'am,' Mattia assured her. 'On my reckoning, doing my job properly makes my support evident.'

'Then I regret that we have to differ on

what constitutes insubordination,' she stated. 'Your up-to-date report will be on my desk by nine o'clock tomorrow morning.'

'I never work to any sort of time schedule, ma'am.'

'The fact that you don't follow any kind of routine has been a cause of exasperation not only for me but a number of other people in authority, Chief Inspector.' The shapely, cool, highly cultured, and aloof senior police-woman looked him straight in the eye. 'Regardless of any argument you may have to the contrary, I will expect your report on my desk first thing in the morning.'

Their incompatibility was fast edging into acrimony. Her unremitting censure angered Mattia. Eyes locked in a challenging glare, they stood, each waiting for the other to speak or to make a move. His self-respect demanded a decisive ending to the standoff. Though aware that his rank, possibly even his career, was at stake, he walked away.

A dismayed Freya Miller took a step forwards as if she intended to physically prevent him from leaving. Her tone became razor sharp. 'Detective Chief Inspector Mattia.'

Mattia walked on without looking back.

He entered the police station, and beck-oned to Mandy and Petters to follow him to his office. He pointed at Petters. 'You first, Melvin. Is Martin Spencer solvent?'

'Precariously so, sir,' Petters replied clearly. 'The Spencers have three accounts, his business account, and each of them has a savings account. The business is in the red, and would probably be in real trouble by now had it not been for Mrs Spencer.'

'Her earnings as a singer?'

'What she earned as an entertainer would seem to just about cover their living costs. Starting eighteen months ago, two thousand pounds was paid into Mrs Spencer's account regularly each month. Six months ago this increased to four thousand pounds each month.'

'That's a lot of money. From what source, Melvin?'

'I don't know, and neither does the bank. Mrs Spencer deposited the money herself in cash each month.'

'That's strange,' Mattia frowned.

'A couple of days after banking this money, she transferred it to her husband's account, sir.'

'In total? Every month?'

'Every penny, every month, sir.'

'This has to be significant but it complicates things,' Mattia said. 'I doubt the Revenue and Customs will know anything

about these thousands of pounds. Bring
Martin Spencer in and get a statement from
him in the morning, Melvin. We have the
identity of the man who accosted Tina
Spencer at the Dockers' Den. His name is
Maurice Trench and he lives in Grentham.
Mandy and I will be on our way there bright
and early in the morning.'

* * *

Having made an early start, Mattia and
Mandy arrived in Grentham while a winter's
dawn struggled to light a new day. Having
spent a convivial evening and night at
Candace's apartment, Mattia was enjoying a
rare occasion on which he was at peace with
himself and with the world. Yesterday's snow
was now a distant memory, and apart from
one scurrying cloud, small and light as a puff
of smoke, there was nothing ominous in the
bright-blue morning sky.

Clearmount House was an impressive
block of flats situated on a high ground above
the town. When they entered the hall Mandy
checked out the entry phone.

'Trench, No.32. It's a top-floor flat, sir.'

'Give him a buzz, Mandy.'

When a woman's voice answered Mandy
explained. 'There is nothing to be concerned

about, madam. I am Detective Constable Snelling, and Detective Chief Inspector Mattia is here with me. If possible we would just like to have a quick word with Mr Maurice Trench.'

Accepting an invitation to go up, they found a middle-aged woman waiting for them. Despite Mandy's earlier assurance that there was nothing to worry about, her apprehension took a leap in the wrong direction when she and Mattia produced their warrant cards.

'Please, do come in,' the woman managed to say timorously.

As they entered the room a man stood up from an armchair and took one step forward to greet them. He had an engagingly boyish grin that was a contradiction to his tired old face. His springy white hair was close-cut; his pale face, lean, with a straight, well-shaped nose.

'You are not with the local constabulary?' he commented, gesturing for them to be seated. More reserved, the woman took a chair on the far side of the room.

'We are in the same county force but from Sandsport,' Mattia replied. 'There are a few questions we would like to ask you, Mr Trench. You may wish that we do so in private.'

Trench apologized humbly. 'Forgive my rudeness in not introducing you. This is Thelma, my fiancée. There is nothing that I would wish to hide from her.'

Mandy and Mattia exchanged smiles with Thelma before Mattia said. 'I understand that you know a woman named Tina Spencer, Mr Trench?'

'I do, but I know her as Tina Trench.'

'Your sister,' gasped a surprised Mandy.

'I can understand you coming to that conclusion, my dear,' Trench said, with a wry smile. 'Beauty and the beast, eh! No, she is my wife.'

Holding up a hand to stop Trench, Mattia warned him, 'I have to inform you, Mr Trench that Tina Spencer was murdered in the early hours of last Sunday.'

'Oh dear God!' Trench exclaimed as, watched closely by Mattia, his face first flushed a purplish-red and then lost its entire colour, the blood draining away to leave it ashen.

'I understand that you had a confrontation with her on Saturday last in a docklands establishment named the Dockers' Den at Sandsport?'

'That is true,' Trench said quietly.

Pausing for a moment, Mattia then said. 'You said she was your wife. But she had a husband, Martin Spencer, in Sandsport.'

'I learned that only last week, Detective Chief Inspector. Can I explain? I have nothing to hide.'

'Please do.'

'It is something of a long and pathetic story, I'm afraid,' he began, his eyes looking inwards for a moment before he continued speaking. 'I suppose this tragic ending is appropriate. It begins with my insular early life. My mother was an invalid and I cared for her. I was forty-three when she died. Hoping to ease my grief, I booked a cruise around the Mediterranean. Tina Aarons, as she was then, was a singer on the liner, and we got talking. She was seeking stability, I owned my home, and was looking for a companion. A few weeks after docking in Sandsport, we were married. A marriage with such fragile foundations couldn't survive, and we drifted apart while living in the same house. There were no arguments, no animosity between us. She just left.'

'Did you make her a regular monthly allowance after she went?'

Trench shook his head. 'No. There was no contact between us until last Saturday.'

'Can I enquire what your dispute with Tina Spencer on Saturday night was about?'

'You don't think . . . ?' Trench stammered.

'I have to consider all possibilities, Mr Trench.'

'I understand.' He checked his wristwatch.

'Are we delaying you in going to your work this morning?' Mattia enquired.

'It's quite all right. I am manager of a supermarket in town, and I have an assistant manager upon whom I can rely. I met Thelma. Our friendship evolved into something special, but our desire to marry was stymied by my already having what is legally termed a wife. I had no inkling as to where Tina was, so I hired a private investigation agency. They informed me of her whereabouts last week. So I faced her on Saturday with a polite request that she agree to a divorce. Her response was far from polite.'

'Plainly because to agree would have been to expose herself as a bigamist,' Mandy remarked.

'There was also the matter of her present marriage, which the private investigator said appeared to be a happy one. It was all too much for me. I simply came home to Thelma.'

'It may sound callous, but the problem has been solved for you,' Mattia observed. 'What is the name of the detective agency, Mr Trench?'

Trench replied. 'Ridgely Investigations.

They are in your town, Detective Inspector, Conway Street. Do you have to take me in to make a statement?'

'Not unless something unforeseen should occur,' Mattia explained, bringing immense relief to the nervous Maurice Trench.

'I thank you for your help and your time, Mr Trench,' Mattia stood ready to leave, and Mandy followed suit. 'May we wish you and your fiancée all the very best for the future.'

'That is most kind,' Trench said, and Thelma smiled at them.

5

As he entered the police station with Martin Spencer, Petters was puzzled to see a man he recognized as one of the town's top lawyers waiting for them. That added a new dimension to the Tina Spencer case. Martin Spencer, teetering on the brink of insolvency, could never afford to engage so distinguished a solicitor. From Spencer's demeanour it was plain that he had never previously met Howard.

'Good morning, Officer, I am Rowland Howard, Mr Spencer's solicitor.'

'Detective Sergeant Petters,' Petters responded, his stammer resurfacing. He called to the uniformed policeman behind the desk. 'Is there an interview room vacant, Constable?'

'Number five, Sergeant.'

Before entering the room Howard requested, 'I would like fifteen minutes alone with my client, Sergeant.'

'Very well, sir,' Petters agreed, ushering the two men into the room, then shutting the door and remaining on the outside.

* * *

'There was more to Tina Spencer than we thought,' Mandy Snelling remarked as she drove them out of Grentham. 'Where do you think Maurice Trench fits in, sir?'

'Too neatly to help us,' Mattia replied.

'He seems desperate to marry Thelma, so maybe he was enraged by the way Tina treated him on Saturday night.'

'Enough to make a telephone call to get Spencer out of the house, then kill her, Mandy?'

'It's a possibility, sir.'

'There are two things against it. I just don't think Maurice Trench is capable of violence.'

'And the second thing, sir?'

'Trench was given his marching orders in the Dockers' Den, so Tina wouldn't have invited him into her home an hour or so later.'

'Do you think Spencer knew that she was married to Trench, sir?'

'No, but he was probably about to find out.'

'When he got back home after the call-out on Saturday night,' Mandy surmised.

'That seems likely, Mandy.'

'What if she did tell him, sir?'

'Then we have both a motive and the killer.'

'Yet you don't seem convinced, sir.'

'I'm not,' Mattia said absently, looking out of the car's side window as they entered the outskirts of Sandsport. He asked. 'Do you know Conway Street, Mandy?'

'I do, sir.'

'Then we'll pay Ridgely Investigations a visit.'

Glancing at the dashboard clock, Mandy enquired worriedly. 'Have you forgotten that there is a press conference at one o'clock, sir?'

'It's because I haven't forgotten that we are going to see the shamus, Mandy.'

'Shamus, sir?'

'Private detective. General George S. Patton Jnr, US Army, said in 1944 that England and the States are two countries separated by a common language.'

'If your general said that, sir, he plagiarized George Bernard Shaw, who made that observation long before 1944.'

'Did your George Bernard Shaw have anything to say about smart-ass cops who contradict their superiors?' a grinning Mattia asked.

'I am sure that he'd back me in this argument, sir.'

'OK, you win, Mandy. Pull over, that looks like Ridgely Investigations over there. Not very imposing, is it?'

Most structural conversions aren't pleasing,

102

and the Ridgely Investigations office, above an electrical store, was no exception. At the top of a flight of uncarpeted stairs, the gold-lettered sign M. RIDGELY INVESTIGATION AGENCY on the door's glass panel belonged to the Raymond Chandler/ Humphrey Bogart era. Mattia was reaching for the handle when the door was opened from the inside.

Standing in the doorway was Marcia, the woman from the carpark. The bouquet of her perfume reached him instantly. Knowledge of such things had Mattia breathe in deeply the fragrance he recognized as Chanel No. 5 *Eau de Parfum* that women dab on both the proper and improper places. Her smile came too quickly. But she coolly remarked. 'You did say that it's a small world.'

'Not this small,' a suspicious Mattia countered. Assuming that she was a departing client, he stood back, politely gesturing for her to pass.

'I'm not going anywhere,' she told him. Pointing to the sign on the door, she announced. 'I'm Marcia Ridgely.' Catching sight of Mandy, she giggled. 'The girl from the office.'

'Detective Constable Amanda Snelling,' Mattia informed her as he endeavoured to get over the shock at learning the blonde's occupation.

'Do come in.'

He hadn't introduced himself, and she hadn't enquired. Which meant she already knew who he was. Their meeting in the car-park must have been contrived. Marcia Ridgely had purposely deflated her car tyre. Why?

A modern computer on a wheeled stand stood close to a desk which had neatly arranged accessories on its top. A green metal filing cabinet completed the office furniture, except for a swivel-chair behind the desk, and two straight-backed, armless chairs which Marcia placed in front of the desk for Mattia and Mandy.

Seated in the swivel-chair, Marcia Ridgely automatically reached for a notepad and pen. Pausing for a moment, she tossed the notebook on to the desktop, self-effacingly explaining. 'Force of habit.'

'DC Snelling will take any notes necessary,' Mattia said. 'We were speaking to a Mr Maurice Trench at Grentham this morning, who said that he is a client of yours.'

'That's right. May I ask where professional sensitivity comes into this, Chief Inspector Mattia?'

'It doesn't,' Mattia informed her bluntly, noting that she was aware of both his name and his rank. His gaze sought and found hers.

Hating himself, Mattia couldn't resist holding the eye contact. He was conscious of her with all his senses. She was yet another Lorelei! With a supreme effort of self-control he averted his gaze.

He could sense the tension that was building in the private detective as she said. 'That worries me considerably. It is like this, you see; I am a one-man or, rather, a one-woman-band. I can't charge someone a fee and then grass them up to the bizzies, if you'll excuse the phraseology.'

Mandy Snelling uttered a sharp reminder. 'This is a murder inquiry, Ms Ridgely.'

'I recognize that, and I have no wish to be uncooperative.' Marcia fiddled idly with a gold ball-pen with calibrated rings that made it a calculator as well. 'This is simply a domestic matter. Mr Trench wanted to contact the woman he had married some years previously.'

'With the intention of obtaining a divorce?' Mandy half asked, half stated.

When Marcia answered with a nod, Mattia followed up on Mandy's question. 'You located the woman Trench was seeking?'

'Though my place of business is not impressive, I do have a high success rate. My father was a detective superintendent in the Met. He started this business when he retired from the police, and taught me well. Yes, I found her.'

'Mrs Tina Spencer, who had remarried without getting a divorce.'

For a brief moment the private detective lost her calm manner. Then she regained her poise before expressing her worry in words. 'This is causing me considerable discomfort. I do have a duty of confidentiality to my clients, Gio. May I still call you Gio?'

'If it will help put you at ease,' Mattia agreed. 'You are aware that Tina Spencer has been murdered.'

'What makes you believe that I know that?'

'The stunt that you pulled in the car-park yesterday morning.'

Deep in contemplation, Marcia puckered her lips. She defended herself sternly with a modicum of levity blended in. 'We are both in a very similar line of work, Gio, and I don't doubt that you have resorted to a charade or two during your career. I did offer to buy you a drink.'

'Doubtless to get information from me, not for changing a wheel that didn't require changing,' Mattia pointed out light-heartedly.

He was conscious of Mandy studying him, uncertainty making a little furrow in her brow. He guessed she feared that he was falling under Marcia's spell. Admitting that he had given Mandy good cause to think in that way, he disciplined himself to ask a meaningful question.

'From your behaviour in the car-park and your demeanour now, your interest in Tina Spencer didn't end when you completed your work for Maurice Trench, Ms Ridgely.'

'Ms Ridgely!' she smilingly scoffed. 'We are back to being formal are we, Chief Inspector? In answer to your question, I can only say that I became unintentionally involved in a secondary issue.'

'But it is no longer secondary,' Mattia suggested.

'It is nothing at the moment, but I am concerned that it might soon become something, Gio.'

'Does it have a bearing on the case that we are investigating, Marcia?'

'You'll have to trust me on this. If, as I have reason to suspect, it might have a connection with the Tina Spencer murder, no matter how tenuous, I will get in touch with you immediately.'

Though ready to trust her, Mattia detected a flaw in the arrangement she was proposing. 'It occurs to me that if you inform me as to whatever it is, you will not be able to obtain a fee from your client, whoever he or she is.'

'Please, Gio,' she begged, for a split second

losing her self-assurance. 'There is no client involved. But I am unable to say anything more right now. Please believe me.'

'I believe you,' Mattia pledged, noticing that she was now raising troubled eyes to a wall clock.

'It may seem that I am being evasive, Gio, but I do have an important client arriving any minute now.'

'We'll take up as little of your time as possible, Ms Ridgely,' DC Snelling promised. 'But I'm afraid that you will have to ask your client to be patient.'

Mattia looked around him. There was no separate waiting room. He placed his card on Marcia's desk and explained, 'In most circumstances, what DC Snelling said would hold good. But we should not stand in the way of your business. However, I would urge you not to leave it too long. When and if you have some information, please give me a call.'

'Most considerate,' Marcia said, her voice sighing away as she picked up his card. 'I will be in touch soon and do all that I can to assist you in your enquiries, Chief Inspector.'

'Thank you, Miss Ridgely,' Mattia said appreciatively adding what he suspected was useless advice, 'Whatever this problem is, try not to let it bother you too much.'

'I'll try. But I don't feel that will work for

me,' she confessed.

'I regret that, but there is no way that I can assist you until you feel that you can explain to me what your problem is.'

Accepting this with the trace of a smile, she said. 'Then I will have to find some courage and you will need to be patient, Gio.'

'That should work well for both of us,' Mattia granted. 'I am a patient man and only a fool would doubt your courage.'

'Then I will do everything I can to ease the situation by getting in touch with you as soon as I can,' she promised.

As she shook them both by the hand, she deliberately left her slim hand in his longer than necessary. There was a message in her eyes, too, but he was too mindful of Mandy's curious, probably even suspicious, gaze on him to be able to decipher it.

★   ★   ★

Mandy felt disillusioned as Mattia negotiated traffic to get them out of Conway Street. Marcia Ridgely was clearly holding something back. Her attitude more than suggested that it was something important, yet Mattia had acted as if she was just an unimportant witness on the periphery of the inquiry.

'You are very quiet,' Mattia remarked as

they headed back to the station. Then he read her mind accurately and continued, 'Marcia Ridgely is involved. I admit that she was evasive, but instinct warned me that she had reason to be careful.'

Unable to make sense of this, Mandy confessed, 'I don't understand, sir.'

'I am fairly certain that, probably accidentally, she came across some side issue when searching for Tina Spencer. Whatever it was, it frightened her.'

'She didn't strike me as someone who scared easily,' Mandy ventured.

'Though she gives that impression, I would say she has information that could put someone in peril. That means that she is herself endangered.'

Understanding dawning on her, Mandy, partly relieved, said, 'Which is why we are not taking her in for questioning?'

'Yes, the only strategy is to wait for her to come to us, as I am sure she will do sooner or later.'

'I hope it's sooner, for her sake,' Mandy remarked, as they entered the station just as Assistant Chief Constable Wilkes came down the stairs.

'Ah, Chief Inspector, it is good to see you,' Wilkes said, with no smile or any other attempt at disguising his sarcasm.

'Good afternoon, sir,' Mattia responded, prepared to let whatever was to come slide past him.

'It is a shame that you couldn't make the press conference. I expect that you have a full schedule for tomorrow?'

'Right now I am about to do some research on the National Computer, and if the results are what I anticipate, my workload for tomorrow will extend into the day after, sir.'

'That will cause some inconvenience as the local television station is planning to film a news feature on the Spencer murder at noon tomorrow. It could well be of help to your investigation were you to speak on camera. So please arrange your day so that you can be there.'

'I'll do that, sir.'

★　★　★

When Mattia had left her to talk to the assistant chief constable, Mandy hurried to find Melvin Petters. In spite of the explanation Mattia had given her, she remained uneasy over the change Marcia Ridgely had wrought in him. On finding Petters, she discovered that she lacked the courage to tell him of her anxiety. The esteem in which Petters held Mattia was a standing joke in the

111

station, so by speaking out of turn she was likely to kill off her career in CID before it was a day old. Yet she couldn't handle the worry alone, and she forced herself to tell Petters of events in the blonde private investigator's office. In fairness to Mattia, she repeated the justification he had given her afterwards.

Listening intently, giving no sign as to what his thoughts were, Melvin kept a fretting Mandy waiting for his reaction. Then at last he spoke, less hesitantly than usual. 'I can understand your concern, Mandy, but I am sure that there is no need for you to worry. From what you say this woman is extremely attractive and Gio Mattia has never concealed the fact that good-looking members of the opposite sex interest him. But he wouldn't permit that to affect his work.'

'Thank you for your advice, Melvin,' Mandy said, nibbling at her lower lip. 'I do hope that you don't consider me to be silly.'

'Not at all. The circumstances that you describe would worry me if I had known him for only a short time. It is possible to draw the wrong conclusion because it is obvious he is disliked by his superiors.'

'Why is that?'

'Simply because he is a more able detective and a better man than any of them,' Petters replied. 'He is an experienced policeman, a veteran of the New York Police Department, where he knew the kind of policing that we will never have to face, thank God.'

'You've made me feel quite humble, which is no bad thing,' Mandy confessed.

She could tell Petters wanted to say something more, but his customary reticence had returned. Then he managed to say self-consciously, 'Don't be afraid to say no to this, Mandy. You see, it's my daughter's birthday today, and we're having a bit of a tea party. What I'm trying to say is, Zeeta and I would like you to come along. I told her about you joining CID, and she would love to meet you. But I'm sure you have better things to do.'

'I'd love to come,' Mandy said enthusiastically. 'But I don't know her name, or where you live.'

'The baby's name is Sunil, and we live in Seafield Road on the Braddock Estate, number 32. It's the house on the corner of the first right turn as you enter the estate.'

'Right. Thank you, Melvin, I'll be there,' Mandy said, thrilled at the thought of socialising with a detective sergeant so soon after joining CID.

* * *

Relieved to get away from Wilkes, Mattia found Mandy and a frowning Melvin Petters waiting for him. He remarked, 'You still seem very perplexed, Melvin.'

'There is something I can't understand, sir,' Petters explained. 'Martin Spencer had a solicitor with him when I took a statement from him today.'

'Now you have troubled me, Melvin. Had he applied for legal aid?'

'I don't think Rowland Howard does legal aid, sir,' Petters replied mock-innocently.

'Rowland Howard! You are kidding.' Mattia was shocked.

'You seem to be concerned, sir,' Mandy observed nervously.

'With good reason, Mandy.' Mattia, who had made himself comfortable in a chair and was deep in thought, now sat forward. 'A top brief like Rowland Howard becoming involved in this has to be significant, but what it means escapes me. Who would want to invest heavily in representing Martin Spencer, and why? Right now, I'm about to spend an hour or more here doing some serious thinking. So both of you can leave me to it. Enjoy your little girl's birthday, Melvin.'

'I will, sir,' Petters assured him as Mandy and he walked to the office door. 'Mandy's coming to the party.'

'Good,' Mattia said with a smile, pleasing Mandy by continuing with, 'Don't stay up too late, Mandy. It is sure going to be a busy day tomorrow. By the way, we'll soon have to pay a visit to Cammy Studland at the Mississippi Club.'

'Whenever you say, sir,' Mandy agreed with a delightfully tinkling little laugh.

★   ★   ★

It was a small gathering that Mandy joined at the Petters' home. Zeeta Petters, a slender Asian girl with a sweet face and a lovely smile, greeted her warmly. Hoping that her gift wasn't too ostentatious, Mandy handed the giant cuddly toy rabbit purchased on the way to the flat, to a delightful little girl who had the same wonderfully large, dark brown eyes as her mother. The only others present were two young women neighbours, who gave her a friendly welcome when Melvin performed the introductions.

She struck an immediate rapport with Zeeta, who was smiling now as she said, 'I'm so glad that you could come today. Melvin praises you so much that I am quite jealous.'

Aware that she was joking, Mandy said, 'Melvin is totally devoted to you, Zeeta.'

During the next hour, Mandy recognized what a close bond existed between Melvin and Zeeta. It wasn't something she would have wanted for herself, at least not until some time in the far distant future. Even so she was happy for Melvin and Zeeta, her new friends.

When it came time for her to leave she felt a mixture of regret mingled with excited anticipation. She had persuaded Gabriella to accompany her on a visit to the Mississippi Club. She intended to impress Mattia by means of some freelance investigation, but couldn't free herself of a guilty feeling about press-ganging her friend into her plan.

Gabriella wasn't a clubber. From a distance she had the look of a slim, honey-haired child. In closer, the girl-child looked older and tired. Her mouth wasn't young. She always held herself tight, stiff. Her grey eyes had a wary unfriendliness, even at times when looking at Mandy.

The miracle of persuading her friend to join her on a girls' night out had been achieved by disguising it as a celebration of her promotion to CID. This deception had worked, although it had left Mandy with a feeling of guilt that she couldn't shake off.

★　★　★

After Petters and Mandy had gone, Mattia spent a rewarding hour and a half on the Police National Computer. He had learned that Rory Wilton was the alias of one Mark Willis. Willis had been released from prison five months previously after serving a sentence for GBH. Formerly a soldier, he had received an administrative discharge from the army, which in Mattia's reckoning meant that he had mental problems.

At Candace's restaurant, Mattia, aware that it was Lewis Milford's night off, wanted to tell her that he would be able to spend a complete evening with her while she was on duty in the restaurant. This was important to them both, as she had apologetically told him that she would rather not accompany him to the high sheriff event the following evening. He could understand why. It would be an oppressive, police-oriented evening that would bore her even more than it would him, and that was saying something. However, both of them understood that his attending alone would combine with his work leaving their rebonding campaign to falter, yet again. They needed to spend as much time as possible together.

As he approached the illuminated restaurant on foot, having parked his car a short distance away, he could see her inside wearing the tight-fitting black dress that was her working apparel at the restaurant. He stood admiring the beautiful, long-legged and stylish Candace move gracefully among the tables. Watching her he realized that she meant everything to him, and always would.

* * *

'Do we have to stay, Mand?' Gabriella half-whispered, plainly on edge in alien surroundings. 'I don't like this place, or the people.'

Having got them both drinks and found a table, Mandy had been relaxing when her friend had ruined everything by complaining. Mandy's purpose for being here made the atmosphere exciting. Her one worry was the presence of Rory Wilton, who leaned with one elbow on the bar. It was obvious that he had noticed her, a fact that made her fervently hope that he didn't remember seeing her in uniform on Sunday.

As a three-piece band struck up some kind of introduction, she was relieved to see Gabriella sitting quietly as a redheaded woman came out on the stage. The complexion of a redhead, skin as white and smooth as alabaster, was accentuated by the club's lighting to enhance the singer's attractiveness. She was wearing a midnight-blue dress that emphasised a figure that really needed no help. This had to be Cammy Studland.

As the singer launched into a passable but not remarkable rendition of Beyoncé's 'Single Ladies', Gabriella remained silent. Thankful for this, Mandy waited for the song to end. Then she stood up and hurried to the side of the stage before the vocalist had time to make an exit as a modest round of applause faded rapidly away.

'Miss Studland.'

Turning as she heard Mandy's call, the singer came to her, sat on her heels, smiling as she said, 'Is it an autograph, dear? I sign them at the end of the evening, and I have another performance to do.'

'I am a police officer,' Mandy explained, keeping her voice low. 'Could I have a word with you?'

'I'm not double parked, and I can't think of anything else that I could have done wrong.' Cammy Studland reacted in an amused manner.

'It doesn't concern you directly, Miss Studland, but it is important.'

With a little nod of acceptance, and a serious expression on her face, the singer suggested. 'Can this wait until ten o'clock?

My last performance will end around then, and the management here is pretty strict.'

'That's fine,' Mandy confirmed, pleased.

She returned to Gabriella and was explaining the arrangement she had made, when Mandy saw Wilton leaving the bar to head their way.

'Let me play host and increase the evening's enjoyment for you two ladies by getting you both a drink.'

Though he possessed a surprisingly engaging smile, Wilton's arrival was the last straw as far as Gabriella was concerned. 'I'm sorry, Mandy; I can't bear to spend another minute in this place.'

'Don't worry. You go home, and I'll see you there at some time after ten.'

A relieved Gabriella was reaching for her handbag when a sudden realization hit her. 'I'll be taking my car, which will leave you with no transport.'

'No problem, Gabby. I'll ring for a taxi.'

'Are you sure?' Gabriella checked, although she was already on her feet.

'I don't usually have that affect on women,' Wilton remarked in jest, having watched the exchange between her and Mandy with an amused expression on his scarred face. 'What's your poison, babe?'

Suddenly realizing she was alone with him,

120

Mandy dried up. Though she wouldn't admit it to anyone, as a country girl she often suffered an absurd loneliness in the over-crowded city. Often fear closed round her like a sodden blanket. A sick-scared feeling would come over her — hot when she woke up in the pitch black of night, ice cold in the day, as if the sun had been switched off. She had to wait for it to pass. It was useless to try to fight it.

Convinced that it would leave her in time, she got through each day by adopting a super-confident manner that instantly fooled those around her and after an unbelievably brief time even duped her. She drew in a long, sighing breath as she waited. That bogus confidence returned, and she was able to reply chirpily, 'White wine, please.'

Watching him order their drinks at the bar, Mandy couldn't believe her luck. Already feeling good about the information she expected to obtain from the singer, now she might well get more from Rory Wilton to pass on to Mattia.

Returning to place two glasses on the table, he sat and gently pushed one across to Mandy. He alarmed her by saying. 'Your face seems vaguely familiar to me. Have you been in here before?'

'Never. This is my first time.'

'Then I want this evening to be a night to remember, if that's not too much of a cliché. I'll make sure that you enjoy yourself and it won't be your last visit here. I'm Rory.'

'Mandy,' she responded with a smile.

He raised his glass. 'To us.'

Following suit, Mandy smiled again. 'To us.'

Astonished to discover that he was charming company, even though his talk was mainly a plainly fictionalized account of his own past. Nevertheless, when she glanced at her watch she found it difficult to believe that an hour had passed by.

Proving himself to be a heavy drinker, he was annoyed when she didn't keep up with him. Her belief that he hoped to get her drunk was supported by the fact that he was less friendly each time she declined a drink when he went to the bar to have his glass refilled.

Yet even this negligible change in him didn't prepare her for his aggressive manner the last time he came back with his drink. His attitude was menacing as he said. 'I saw you talking to Cammy Studland earlier. What was that about?'

'I have a sister who is trying to make it as a singer, and I was asking if she could give me some advice,' Mandy fibbed.

'Is she going to?' Wilton enquired with apparent interest, as Cammy Studland came out on stage for her last performance of the evening.

'Yes, she was very nice about it. She is going to talk to me after this song.'

'Cut the crap,' he snarled, his character changing swiftly and suddenly. 'I want to know what you are doing here.'

'Just spending what until this moment has been a pleasant evening,' Mandy countered, fighting to hide her fear.

'Come off it. The moment you walked in I recognized you as the egotistical bitch I saw in Ike's place on Sunday, parading about in your fancy uniform. Now listen to this. You and me are going to walk out of here together this very moment.'

Mandy experienced real terror for the first time in her life. It was as if an abstract chasm of time and sound and colours had opened up and she had toppled into it. Aware of his piercing, now evil, eyes boring into her, she struggled to find the courage she was aware that she would soon desperately need.

'What if I don't?' Mandy challenged with difficult to find bravado.

He smiled a crooked smile that was made even more menacing by his scar. 'The answer to that is simple. If you don't, then you will have to leave here at some time. When you do, I will be waiting outside to make you wish you had left when I said so.'

'And if I go with you now?'

'I want nothing from you other than the truth of what brought you here tonight. Don't worry; I wouldn't touch one of the filth with the proverbial barge pole.'

6

Accepting that she had no option, Mandy stood up from her chair. Trembling inside, although she guessed that it didn't show on the outside, she desperately tried to think up a plausible story to tell Wilton when they went out of the club.

Legs trembling, she walked slightly in front of Wilton, who was smiling and waving a hand to people to whom he bade a convivial farewell.

Once you step out of the door, she instructed herself, you must run. But that didn't happen. There was nowhere to run to, and if she attempted to do so her legs would refuse to co-operate. Holding her arm in a grip so tight that it was painful, he guided her to a sports car that was parked away from the other vehicles in the car-park. The heavy silence of the night was disturbed only by the crunch of their feet on gravel.

At the car she meekly got into the front passenger seat and sat still. He walked round the vehicle and got into the driving seat. Suddenly overcome by terror she seemed to split away from herself. Though separated from the frightening situation she had been lifted out of, where she was then was a scary place. Hearing the car's engine start up snapped her back into herself.

Knowing that she must escape, she grabbed the handle and pushed the door open. Her left leg was partly out of the car when Wilton delivered a blow to the side of her head. At first she felt no pain, then suddenly her right ear was agony and she half collapsed in the seat. Reaching across he slammed the passenger door closed and sent the car roaring away, wheels throwing up the gravel from the car-park.

The pain had spread from her ear into the side of her head now. She was aware that they were passing through the town centre. This unnerved her even more. The buildings on each side of the car swelled up in the night, like political speakers on the hustings, big with their self-importance. That was a strange thought. Maybe she was concussed. Then they were travelling through what she regarded as her sort of territory. Pretty cottages, the lawns were bleached as white as hotel sheets by a recent snow fall, patching black where shadows were hiding; waiting and wondering where she was being taken as frightened as a small child all alone in the night.

Yet she wasn't alone. Rory Wilton, verbose earlier, was taciturn now as he drove at speed out of town. Occasionally they would pass a car heading in the opposite direction. Though she knew it was foolish, Mandy found a measure of security in the knowledge that other human beings were sharing this terrible night with her. Then she recognized exactly where she was on seeing the Red House Motel sign glowing against a background of darkness.

Turning into the entrance, Wilton drove through narrow lanes lined on both sides by cabins. Knowing exactly where he was going he pulled up outside a cabin, and switched off the car's engine. Mandy knew that it was now or never. This time she had the door open and was out of the car before he could stop her. Soft grass felt hospitable under her feet. The sweet scent of earth that she loved rose from the ground as she ran. Filled with determination she leapt over some low scrub, and was confident that she could escape into the night.

It was then that a hard punch struck her between the shoulder blades, knocking her flat on her face. Winded, she rolled on to her side, still hoping that she could get away. But Wilton was standing looking down at her. Drawing back his foot he delivered a vicious kick to her stomach. Excruciating pain pulled her body into a foetal position. An eruption of vomit was the last thing she remembered.

★ ★ ★

'Mandy's really nice, Mel,' Zeeta remarked when their guests had left and Sunil, exhausted by her big day, was fast asleep in her cot. The little tea party was over, their guests had left, and they both should have been enjoying the exquisite pleasure of a loving couple alone in their own home. Yet Melvin's dread of something disastrous soon to happen had grown. When he didn't respond, she continued. 'I know that you like her, too.'

Feeling sad, Petters delayed his answer. The long-anticipated birthday of his daughter had passed too quickly. Why did everything wonderful in life have to be ephemeral?

His real bad feeling was still with him. The recent change in Mattia was noticeable and seemed to be affecting his work. Recognizing this transformation in the DCI, though far from being blatantly obvious, Petters feared that he had missed an important factor, something that would never have occurred had Mattia been his old vibrant self. It was both frustrating and extremely disquieting for

Petters not to be able to figure out what it was he had overlooked.

He was about to explain that he liked Mandy but her enthusiasm possibly made her a loose cannon in an organization that depended on teamwork, when the telephone rang.

★   ★   ★

A spontaneous event is always more pleasurable than even the most meticulously planned occasion. The time he had spent with Candace in her restaurant had been no exception. The evening was drawing to a close now as she came to where he sat and put an arm round his shoulders, saying quietly and happily, 'This evening has been great, Gio.'

'I have really enjoyed it,' he agreed, and then warned her, 'Neither do I intend to let it end when we leave here.'

'I've already decided that it won't,' she murmured seductively in his ear.

Ignoring the diners and her waiters and waitresses navigating the tables at speed, she bent to kiss him long and fervently. The kiss was broken; the magic of the evening was shattered, as his mobile phone rang. It was Melvin Petters.

'What is it, Melvin?'

'Gabriella McElroy has just telephoned me, sir.'

It took Mattia a moment or two to sort the name in his mind. 'Mandy Snelling's flatmate.'

'That's right, sir. She is frantically worried about Mandy, who persuaded her to go to the Mississippi Club tonight. Gabriella hated the place and went home early, leaving Mandy there, and she hasn't arrived home yet.'

'The girl is right to be worried, Melvin. Rory Wilton's real name is Mark Willis. He's got a record for violence, and he's most probably a nut job.'

'Oh bloody hell!' exclaimed Petters, who never swore. 'This may sound silly to you, sir, but over the last thirty-six hours or so, a premonition has been plaguing me. I have been dreading something happening to either Zeeta or Sunil. Now everything clicked together in my mind, and I realized it is Mandy.'

'You could be right. She is a clever and very likeable officer, but her ambition worried me. I have been meaning to have a talk with her, but now I fear that I left it too late. I mentioned to her that the woman vocalist at the Mississippi was a friend of Tina Spencer, and that the guy we knew as Rory Wilton frequents that club. He saw Mandy in the

Dockers' Den in uniform on Sunday, so he knows she's a cop.'

'Do you want me to drive out there now, sir?'

'I'm responsible for Mandy being at the club, so I'll take care of it.'

'You'll need back-up at that place, sir.'

'I'll use diplomacy, Melvin.'

'That'll be a first for you, sir.'

Smiling briefly at this, Mattia said. 'This has been a big day for you, Melvin, it being your little girl's birthday. So make sure that it ends nicely by remaining where you are.'

'If you insist, sir. But ring me if you need me.'

Mattia closed his phone slowly and thoughtfully. Though highly intelligent and efficient, Mandy was headstrong. She had perfected an appearance of self-reliance, and if there were occasional holes in it she was clever enough to patch them. But she couldn't fool Giovanni Mattia. Had she been able to, then he wouldn't be so desperately worried about her.

★   ★   ★

It was late and the Mississippi Club was only about a third full when Mattia arrived. Mandy was nowhere to be seen. He could tell

131

that the squat, powerfully built but running to fat man behind the bar had spotted him as a cop, so Mattia didn't bother with introductions.

'Are you the proprietor?' he asked.

'Merely the manager. Ace Durell is the name.'

'Is your vocalist here, Durell?'

'There's your answer.' Durell gave a little jerk of his head to indicate a redhead who was walking by.

'Excuse me, miss, I'm a police officer,' Mattia began. 'Has a young woman made herself known to you tonight?'

'Yes, she was sitting near the stage with a friend. She said she was in the police, and I agreed to speak to her later.'

'Did you?'

'No. Her friend left and then one of the regular guys joined her at the table.'

Mattia forced himself to ask. 'Was this a young guy with a scarred face?'

'It was. She left with him.'

'When was this?' Mattia enquired.

Noticing Durell send out a message by means of a discreet movement of his eyes, Mattia was aware of two heavies closing in on him. One came in from the left, leaning against the bar as he did a quarter turn to face him, while the other stayed close behind him.

'Rory Wilton,' Mattia addressed Durell. 'Where does he live?'

'No idea.' Durell shrugged, making another unobtrusive signal to his heavies. Not giving the pair an opportunity to launch an attack, Mattia swung his right arm out behind him to catch the man there a vicious backhand blow to the face. He heard the thud of the man crashing to the floor, and Cammy Studland's scream of fright as he reached to grip with both hands the right arm of the man on his left. Bending forwards as he yanked down hard on the arm he brought the man's face crashing down on the bar top. Rising above the sound of flesh being mashed against the hard wood was the cracking of nose and other facial bones breaking.

Allowing the man to slide down on to the floor, Mattia was aware of the man behind him getting slowly up on all fours. Relying on his sense of direction, Mattia back heeled him. Catching him under the chin he put the man out of action by breaking his jaw.

Using his foot to turn the man lying against the bar on to his back, he looked down at the broken face to see that he was still conscious. He asked, 'Where will I find Wilton?'

The man could make only spluttering sounds as he was in danger of choking on his own blood. Again using his foot, Mattia rolled the man on to his face. Leaving him for a while to allow the blood to drain away, he then moved him on to his back, face up. Worry over Mandy robbing him of any feeling of compassion, Mattia placed a foot on the bloodily injured man's throat, shouting a question at him for a second time. 'Where will I find Wilton?'

There was no reply until he pressed his foot harder on the throat. Then the man croaked out words that Mattia had to stoop to hear. 'Red House Motel, on the edge of the forest. Cabin 25.'

Stepping back, releasing the throat, Mattia scuffed his foot on the floor to wipe off slippery blood. An angry Ace Durell was on the phone to someone. A terrified Cammy Studland cowered against a wall. Pausing no longer, Mattia ran out to his car.

Frustrated by traffic he drove fast out of town to the edge of the forest and into the parking lot of the Red House Motel just ten minutes later.

* * *

With preparations for the high sheriff's event set to take up all of the next day, it was after midnight when weary Assistant Chief Constable Wilkes left his office. He didn't welcome seeing Detective Superintendent Ralph Bardon hurrying towards him, looking agitated.

'We have a problem, sir,' Bardon called to him, while still some ten feet distant.

Wilkes asked. 'Nothing that can't wait until morning, Superintendent?'

'I'm afraid that it requires your attention at once, sir.'

'Tell me what it is, and I'll decide,' Wilkes offered tiredly.

'It is a most grave matter. DCI Mattia has assaulted two men at the Mississippi Club, sir. Both have been taken to hospital. The condition of one of them is serious.'

'Do you know who these two men are?'

'They are both employed as bouncers at the club, sir.'

'Mattia is not a drinking man, so the men didn't receive their injuries while attempting to eject him from the club,' Wilkes reasoned.

'My understanding is that he was there making some enquiries, sir.'

'I see. That club is a disreputable establishment, Superintendent. Objection may well have been taken to DCI Mattia's questions. Do we know who started the altercation?'

'No, sir.'

Satisfied on hearing this, the assistant chief constable was already moving past Bardon when he started to give an order. 'Very well. Send someone to the hospital to ask when the injured persons can be interviewed, then take it from there.'

'Yes, sir,' a disgruntled Bardon conceded.

Walking away, Wilkes turned his head to ask, 'Where is DCI Mattia now?'

'No one knows, sir.'

The assistant chief constable went on his way without uttering another word.

★ ★ ★

Mattia parked in a dark secluded area at the motel, never doubting that the clever Mandy Snelling would not have willingly left the club with so obvious a thug. What he would face here would depend on Mark Willis's reason for taking her. If Willis had heard Mandy talking to Cammy Studland, who had been a friend of Tina Spencer's, that would put Willis in the frame for the murder. Mattia accepted that he had to be prepared for the worst situation.

There was no sign of life around the place as he moved from cabin to cabin, using his torch to check on door numbers as he went. He extinguished the light and backed into deep shadows and remained unmoving as a cabin door opened and a triangle of light split the darkness. Music suddenly filled the silence as a man reached out to drop a lighted cigarette end on the ground and step on it. Mezzo-soprano Katherine Jenkins was singing *Van Pensiero*. The beauty of the classical performance was an alien sound in the dark and dreary surroundings. The door slammed shut and the captivating song died an instant death, leaving the night to mourn.

He spotted the silhouette of a sports convertible outside a chalet; the type of car he would expect Willis to drive. Though, in the early hours of the morning all the other chalets were in total darkness, there was a narrow strip of light down the sides of the blind in the main window. Mattia rapped on the door with his knuckles.

There was no response. Waiting for less than one minute, he tried the door handle. It wasn't locked. Taking no chances, Mattia took a short, quick step backwards, lifted his right leg and sent the door crashing inwards. The small room was empty.

Disappointed not to see Mandy there, Mattia moved to a closed door in the corner of the room. Cautiously opening the door to find the room in darkness, he slid a hand along the wall in search of the light switch. Flooding what was a tiny room with light, he saw a single bed against the wall to his left.

Mandy was lying on it, fully dressed.

Mattia was moving to the bed when a bulky figure stepped out from the behind a wardrobe. Instantly ready to repel an attack, Mattia was taken by surprise when the figure reached down to pull Mandy violently up off the bed and throw her at Mattia, knocking him back against the wall. Managing to hold himself and Mandy upright, he caught a glimpse of the grinning, scarred face of Mark Willis fleeing the room.

Unable to go after Willis, Mattia laid Mandy carefully back down on the bed. Her face was unmarked. She could have been sleeping, but Mattia doubted that. With the middle finger of his right hand he searched for a pulse in her neck. His silent prayer was instantly answered when his finger located a pulse.

Taking his mobile from his pocket, he broke into a sweat as he called for an ambulance. Then he called Crescent Street to report where he had found Mandy, and the condition he had found her in. Though it was mid-winter the air was hot and humid in the chalet, and he found it difficult to breathe. It was plain that Willis had fled in the belief that he had killed the girl.

The sounds of the emergency services arriving seemed to come from afar even though they were just outside the chalet. A man and a woman wearing green overalls came in the door; the yellow patches on their backs bore the word PARAMEDIC. Mattia pointed to the bedroom.

As the paramedics moved off into the bedroom, Superintendent Bardon came in through the chalet door with two uniformed constables. Acknowledging Mattia with a curt nod, he went to the bedroom door and looked in. When he turned back he asked. 'There was no sign of this man Willis when you arrived here, Chief Inspector?'

'He was here, but he got away from me.'

Barden walked over to the far side of the room, beckoning Mattia to join him. Out of earshot of the two uniformed constables, his voice was little more than a hissing whisper when he spoke. 'I speak as a colleague now, Giovanni. The manager of the Mississippi Club lodged an official complaint less than an hour ago that two of his employees have been beaten to within an inch of their lives. We are senior officers in a disciplined force, and it is our duty to uphold the law and set an example when doing so.'

'Then let's start by doing everything we can to help DC Snelling.'

'She is being treated in there right now. It is my intention to call in for an APW to have

139

the man who assaulted her apprehended.'

'Fine,' an indifferent Mattia said, as he walked away and into the bedroom.

He stood watching the two paramedics' hurried but controlled work. Whatever they are doing is pointless, he thought dismally. He watched them try defibrillation; saw Mandy's legs kick and her body jerk as the electric power shot through her. The male paramedic crouching beside Mandy looked up at Mattia, his bland face given significance by a pair of caring eyes.

'She's stable now,' he announced.

'What's the prognosis?'

Mandy lay on a stretcher. They had put something round her head and a supporting collar round her neck. An oxygen mask made her unrecognizable as an extremely pretty, intellectually gifted young woman.

The paramedic took a long while to answer. When he did it was plain that he had sacrificed professionalism for the sake of compassion. 'The patient has bruising to the back and the abdomen, where she has been punched and kicked. I normally avoid making an early prognosis, but I'm certain that she is going to be fine.'

Not trusting himself to speak, an immensely relieved Mattia nodded in the hope that the medic would interpret it as a thank you for his

140

candour. The female paramedic, young, fair-haired and very ordinary looking, got to her feet and gave Mattia a fleeting, sympathetic smile.

He followed as they carried the stretcher out of the bedroom. The two uniformed constables and Ralph Bardon were still in the outer room. The latter seemed about to say something to Mattia, possibly to stop him from leaving. But after taking a quick look at the chief inspector's face he changed his mind. Then he appeared to have come to some sort of agreement with himself, and followed Mattia out into the night.

Standing at the rear of the ambulance as the paramedics expertly loaded the stretcher to which the still unconscious Mandy was strapped, Mattia was irritated when Bardon walked up close behind him.

'Are you thinking of going to the hospital, Gio?' the detective superintendent enquired.

'Of course. Mandy needs to have someone she knows there when she regains consciousness.'

'She will need you to be there,' Bardon granted, adding. 'Do your best to be at Crescent Street in the morning. The assistant chief constable has agreed to interviews being filmed by the local television channel in connection with the Spencer murder. Then there is the unfortunate matter at the Mississippi Club that has to be dealt with.'

Not responding, Mattia got into the back of the ambulance with the female paramedic, and her male colleague closed the door behind them.

★ ★ ★

Having telephoned Petters earlier to ask him to look up Cammy Studland's address, Mattia found the sergeant waiting for him when, after a sleepless night, he arrived at Crescent Street before eight o'clock. He had remained at the hospital for an hour until Mandy had regained consciousness. Despite reassurances from the doctors that she was in no danger, it had been an agonizing wait for him.

'What's the latest on Mandy, sir?' Petters asked as Mattia got into the car beside him.

'I am told she will be released shortly, Melvin. The poor girl took a nasty blow to the back and a hard kick to the stomach. Thankfully, no serious damage was done.'

'The same MO as the Tina Spencer murder,' Petters put into words what Mattia had been thinking all night. 'What do you expect to learn from Cammy Studland, sir?'

'It's probably a vain hope, Melvin, but she may be able to give us a clue as to what information this Willis guy wanted from Mandy.'

'Which could mean that she remains in danger,' Petters commented, before announcing, 'Here we are, sir,' as he pulled over to the kerb beside a tall, ugly building.

The vocalist's home was a bed-sit on the third floor. They had their warrant cards at the ready as she opened the door, but she waved them aside, telling Mattia. 'I recognize you from last night.'

'I regret that you had to witness that, Miss Studland.'

'I was scared for you. I have seen those bouncers give men horrible thrashings, but you are — ' she broke off, gazing at Mattia in awe.

'May we come in?' he asked; always keen to avoid misplaced hero worship.

'Please forgive my rudeness,' she said, standing to one side to usher them in.

Moving some magazines from a settee, she gestured for them to be seated. Mattia concentrated on explaining their reason for being there was DC Snelling's having been assaulted after leaving the Mississippi Club the previous night.

'I am so sorry to hear that. She is a very

attractive, nice girl. As I told you last night, I arranged to see her after ten o'clock when I had finished my final number. I assumed that it was something to do with the death of my friend, Tina Spencer.'

'Were you aware of anyone in particular being interested in her approach to you?' Petters swiftly enquired, as Cammy's unshed tears over the death of her friend threatened to put an end to the conversation.

'As always, Ace Durell, the club manager, was noticing all that was going on. He was watching the girl talking to me, and then this other chap at the far end of the bar must have signalled to him. Ace joined him and it was plain to me that they were discussing me and the girl.'

'Did this alarm you, Miss Studland?' Mattia asked.

'After spending some time at the Mississippi, Mr . . . I'm sorry, I've forgotten your name.'

'DCI Mattia.'

'Thank you, DCI Mattia. I was trying to say that very little that happens at that club now has the power to alarm me.'

'This man that Durell was speaking to . . . ?' Petters asked.

'His name is Rory Wilton, and I don't like him.'

'Has he tried to hit on you?'

'Not in any serious way, Mr Mattia, but he did on Tina one night at the Dockers' Den, and she was terrified of him. She was certain that when she went home by taxi that night, he was following in his car.'

Mattia mentally noted the fact that Willis knew where Tina Spencer lived. He could tell that Petters had also found this significant. He moved the conversation along. 'Could you run through for me once more what happened after our colleague spoke to you by the stage?'

'She went back to sit at the table with her friend. When I came out to sing again her friend wasn't there, but Wilton was sitting at the table.'

'Were Mandy — that is our colleague's name — and Wilton talking?'

'Yes, they seemed to be getting along fine. That surprised me. When I came on stage for my last number they were leaving together. She didn't even look in my direction.'

'Was anyone at the club aware that you were friendly with Tina Spencer?'

'I didn't think so. But the day on which her murder was broadcast on the radio and appeared in the local newspaper, when I arrived for work in the evening Ace surprised me by offering his commiserations.'

145

'You have been very helpful, Miss Studland. We may possibly wish to speak to you again but if that is the case, DS Petters will contact you in advance.'

'It is Tina's funeral this afternoon.'

Mattia nodded. 'We will be there. I take it that you will be attending.'

'I wouldn't miss it, even though it isn't something I am looking forward to.'

'That's understandable,' Mattia sympathised. 'Would some unsolicited advice offend you, Miss Studland?'

'Not at all.'

'It would be wise for you to find a regular venue other than the Mississippi Club.'

'I've been thinking for some time about asking my agent to find something else for me, Mr Mattia. But I can't be too picky. I need the money.' With an expression of disgust on her face, she looked around the room. 'I have a daughter aged six living with my mother because I can't have her with me in this dump.'

'Keep trying,' Mattia advised with a smile. 'Thanks again for your assistance.'

'What a world this is, Melvin,' Mattia remarked when they were in the car. 'Mandy gets punched and kicked, and Cammy Studland is struggling against invincible odds just for nothing more than a decent place to

146

live with her child. The meek have been waiting a long time.'

'I reckon they have a whole lot longer to wait,' Petters predicted. 'I am glad that the omen, or whatever it was that had me fear for Mandy's safety, wasn't as bad as I'd expected, sir.'

'I share that sentiment with you, Melvin. Before we do anything else, I'll treat you to a cup of tea at Candace's restaurant.'

'Treat! She's not likely to charge you, sir.'

'You could have let me enjoy my moment of generosity before you put me down, Melvin,' a smiling Mattia reprimanded him.

7

With everyone struggling to stay calm, thereby ensuring they remained in a state of panic, preparations for the television filming were chaotic. There was nothing unusual in this event for the studio staff, but they were all doing a headless chicken routine. Standing at the back of the studio, Chief Constable Freya Miller, Assistant Chief Constable Reginald Wilkes, and Public Relations Officer Sinéad Mayo, watched with bored impatience. Their only participation so far had been to have their voice levels monitored.

'He's done it again, Freya,' Wilkes grumbled.

'Where is DCI Mattia?' enquired Sinéad Mayo, a petite young woman whose bland prettiness concealed an admirably devious mind, which, Freya Miller admitted, was probably a contradiction in terms. Regardless, it was something she had been thankful for on many occasions when facing the public through the media.

'That's a good question,' Wilkes remarked. 'Put concisely, Sinéad, he left hurriedly earlier this morning without telling anyone where he was going, and has been out of contact ever since.'

They stepped back quickly to avoid an over-bearing television cameraman who wheeled past a large camera, dangerously close to them.

'Why are all television people so irritatingly self-important?' Wilkes asked angrily, neither expecting nor getting a reply from his two companions.

A hyperactive man wearing headphones was beckoning them to come to take their seats behind a rickety trestle-table disguised for the cameras by a blue velvet drape. A background that included the county police shield had been affixed to the wall behind the table, and a scrap of carpet placed under-neath it. No viewer would suspect that he or she was looking at a setting that had all the charm of a long-disused warehouse.

'The illusion that is television,' Wilkes mut-tered as they followed an elderly PR woman who fussily seated them behind the table.

The agitated television man gestured wildly at them. Giving up when he couldn't make them understand, he twitched at his ear-phones and smiled a meaningless smile. A few executives of the minor television station were importantly seating themselves on uncomfortable wooden chairs, their faces wearing expressions of anticipation. Mis-placed anticipation, Freya Miller cynically decided. She and Wilkes had decided that the attack on DC Snelling should not yet be released to the media.

She thought it was as well Gio Mattia hadn't turned up. This tatty studio was the epitome of the fantasy world he detested. Even though it was a live broadcast he would make some scathing remark. Yet that would be a small price to pay for his presence. He would know what to say and how to say it, even though it would offend many. Without him the broadcast would be devoid of substance.

As if reading her thoughts, Sinéad Mayo asked anxiously. 'What are we going to tell them?'

'Feed them platitudes,' Freya Miller said softly with an inward smile.

'What are you saying, Freya?' a bewildered Wilkes enquired. 'That sounded to me like a Mattiaism.'

Unable to reply without revealing that she was thinking of Giovanni Mattia in a different way to that of her two colleagues, she remained silent, annoying Wilkes.

'You will need to ask Freya that question again,' he grumpily advised Sinéad Mayo. 'It was on her authority that Mattia was retained as senior investigation officer, against the best counsel.'

Suddenly there were bright lights and cameras went into action. An announcer from local television started a voice-over giving an outline of the Tina Spencer murder. Not yet on camera, Freya Miller accepted responsibility for the difficult situation. She mimed to Sinéad Mayo to do nothing other than to introduce her.

Sinéad did as she was told when receiving a *you're on* signal from the animated man with the earphones, and then the chief constable faced the cameras.

'Good morning. I am sorry to have to inform you that Detective Chief Inspector Mattia, the senior investigation officer, has unexpectedly had to attend an emergency so is unable to be with us this morning. Consequently, I can add little to what we have already made public.'

'Is the emergency that DCI Mattia is attending this morning connected to the Spencer murder?' the television interviewer asked.

Having no idea what Mattia was doing that morning, she took a deep breath, crossed the fingers of both hands under the table, silently offered up God, forgive me, then answered, 'Yes. It forms a vital part of the investigation. However, that is all I can reveal at this time.'

To her relief, Reginald Wilkes and Sinéad

Mayo took over from her then, by making prepared statements that gave little new information but were presented in such a way that it rescued the conference from ignominy. She thanked them both warmly afterwards.

*　*　*

After visiting the restaurant for a pleasant quarter of an hour in Candace's company, Mattia and Petters stood in the pews at the back of a small church. Mattia had called on Candace to explain why he had not been in touch. She had been understanding and sympathetic. He told her about the attack on Mandy, and eased her concern by adding that, all being well, the doctors planned to discharge her from hospital shortly.

Adding to the solemnity of Tina Spencer's funeral, a thin drizzle of cold rain had begun to fall around noon. Raincoats were worn over the respectful black suits of the men and dark-coloured costumes of the women as the mourners had stood in line to enter the church.

Decoration of the church for Christmas had begun but was not yet completed. Preparations to celebrate the most important birth of all time had been postponed for a woman who had been brutally murdered. By

152

next Christmas Tina Spencer would be forgotten by all except those who had loved her. Little progress had been made in 2,000 years.

Mattia's dismal thoughts were interrupted by the Reverend Brammer appearing among a great display of flowers on the altar. Reflected light from the stained-glass windows danced little colours over his rimless glasses. He looked out thoughtfully, sorrowfully and solemnly over the congregation. There was much throat clearing, and Norman Brammer waited a touch impatiently until there was complete silence. Then he began the service in a booming voice that caused everyone to give a little jump.

Cammy Studland sat alone in an otherwise empty pew several rows in front of Mattia and his sergeant. In the front row of pews, Martin Spencer needed to be supported by his brother, Stuart. Mattia was mystified to see the lawyer Rowland Howard standing at Stuart Spencer's side. The presence of the top solicitor at the family funeral intrigued him. Stuart's wife was standing in her bashful, screwed-up stance on the far side of the lawyer. He guessed that the absence of the Spencers' mother was due to the old lady's frailty.

A tension that was almost tangible gripped

the congregation then as the vicar looked direct at Martin Spencer who, rejecting assistance from his brother, made his way unsteadily to the altar. Apparently ready to deliver a eulogy he turned to face the congregation with tears streaming down his face. Taking a paper from an inside pocket of his jacket, he unfolded it. He remained silent for some time as he bowed his head to the paper. Hands trembling, he then refolded the paper and replaced it in his pocket. Then he looked hopelessly and helplessly at the vicar.

Taking a few steps closer to the grieving widower, the sympathetic Reverend Brammer gave him an encouraging go-ahead-you'll-be-fine little pat on the arm. Shoulders back, chin held high, staring bravely but unseeingly at the congregation, Martin Spencer obviously struggled to utter words. Whatever those words would have been they were gurglingly mangled in his throat before coming out as a loud, chilling and unearthly sound that was a rattling parody of a movie Tarzan's yell.

As Stuart Spencer rushed to rescue his brother from what threatened to be a total collapse, the congregation reacted with some murmurs of sympathy while many women were sobbing.

With Martin Spencer sitting slumped after

being helped back to his seat, the Reverend Brammer thoughtfully delayed proceedings. Stuart Spencer came forward to converse briefly with the clergyman before taking up the position his brother had occupied just minutes previously.

'I am sure that we all deeply sympathize with my brother,' he began. 'He has lost a loving wife, and my mother, my wife and I have lost a family member who was most dear to us. The community has been deprived not only of a sweet-natured lady but also a talented entertainer. There is nothing more I can say about Tina, as the presence of you all here today on this sad occasion says it all.'

Head bowed, Stuart Spencer stepped down to take up his supporting stand beside his brother. After a short, respectful interval, the bearers lifted the coffin and were led by the vicar along the aisle. Following behind, able to walk only with an arm around the shoulders of his brother, Martin Spencer was unashamedly weeping. He was more imma-ture than most, more innocent, Mattia reasoned. No, that last bit wasn't true. No one was born innocent. Innocence was something that had to be strived for and few ever achieved.

Outside, the earlier rain had changed to sleet. Drivers rubbed it with gloved hands as it turned to ice on the windscreens of the cars waiting for the mourners.

'That was an experience I could have done without, sir,' Petters remarked forlornly.

'You are not on your own in that, Melvin,' Mattia confessed. 'We must have learned something from it, but it added nothing useful to our investigation.'

'You don't have any doubts that Spencer's display of grief was genuine, sir?'

'He's one hell of a good actor if it wasn't,' Mattia replied. 'Come on, Melvin. We have to see the rest of this through.'

★　★　★

With D/Supt Bardon at his side, Assistant Chief Constable Wilkes was ready and waiting when Mattia and Petters entered the Crescent Street station later that afternoon. Using a hand to convey that Petters should pass on by while he needed to speak to Mattia, Wilkes was plainly unhappy.

'There is no reason why this shouldn't be anything other than an amicable discussion, Mattia. The chief constable and I have talked this over. With a complaint having been made against you, clearly some action has to be taken. We discussed this at length, and decided that though nothing formal is required at this stage, it was decided that you should be asked to step aside temporarily as SIO.'

Employing his strategy of always giving them what they are not expecting, Mattia amiably agreed. 'If you consider that to be best, sir.'

'Thank you for seeing it our way, Chief Inspector. It is late in the day now, and with all of us expected to appear at the inauguration of the new high sheriff this evening, I suggest that you bring Superintendent Bardon up to speed on the case tomorrow morning.'

'I will do that, sir.'

'Thank you, Chief Inspector,' Ralph Bardon said with a friendly smile. There were traces of sweat on his fat upper lip. 'I hope we can have a drink together at this evening's event.'

★   ★   ★

Sickened by the sycophantic behaviour of the police officers and their wives in the ballroom of the county's foremost stately home, Mattia wandered slowly along a subtly lit landing. Able to faintly hear the Strauss waltz playing downstairs, he escaped by walking out on a balcony that formed a part of the manor's long, west-facing façade. Looking out into the night, the assault on Mandy came into his mind. Even winter daylight somehow diminishes the fears and worries that loom monstrous and misshapen when the darkness of night pours down.

Earlier in the evening he had held the manor and its pompous guests in amused contempt. That wasn't the way he felt now. Not down inside where it really counted. As the evening had progressed, so had the uneasy truce between himself and his misanthropic tendency collapsed.

In the middle distance a carol service was in progress in the grounds of the university. Distance muted the harmonious voices to a fittingly gentle level. The voice of a female soloist had a mystical quality that held Mattia entranced. Lines of multicoloured bulbs on the campus made strings of tiny bright stars sparkle against a purple sky.

Then he gave an involuntary little jump as a voice spoke softly from the shadows to his left.

'Are you another poor soul in retreat?'

The voice was a thin sound that touched Mattia's spine with a cold finger. Freya Miller came drifting like a ghost out of the darkness. She stepped out into the moonlight, her eyes a blank dark blue as she slanted a look at him.

'I startled you. I am sorry.'

'My nerves do not usually bother me, ma'am. I guess I was scared that one of those self-seeking imbeciles down there had followed me,' Mattia explained. 'I had to get away before some asshole led that gathering into several choruses of *For He's a Jolly Good Fellow*. My apologies for that crude word, ma'am.'

'An apology is unnecessary. It is proof that we are from two very different cultures. I would have said tosser.'

Though amused by her unexpected turn of phrase, Mattia didn't show it because she had kept a straight face. Then she smiled, warmly, and he smiled back.

Reminding himself of her rank, he reluctantly turned to go. 'I'll leave you to enjoy the peace out here, ma'am.'

'Must you go?' she asked plaintively. 'I would be glad of your company. I felt very alone downstairs in a crowd, but now I would find it even lonelier up here on my own. I've always preferred the behaviour of the patricians to that of the plebs but right now I'm not so sure.'

'I've never had that problem, ma'am.'

Convinced that it would be wise to get away, Mattia was stayed by the immense sadness he sensed in Freya Miller. There seemed to be something shameful, indecent, and perhaps even vulgar about being anxious to beat a hasty exit.

Seemingly confident that he wouldn't leave, she moved close to him and leaned against the marble balustrade. Mattia was conscious of the subtle aroma of her perspiration that no deodorant could subdue past eleven o'clock in the morning. Now late in the evening it was overwhelmingly potent.

She paused, tilting her head to one side as the German carol *Stille Nacht, Heilige Nacht* came drifting through the darkness to them. Closing her eyes she hummed along with the tune until it faded away as magically as it had come to them out of nowhere.

Opening her eyes, she made a dramatic what-could-be-better-than-this gesture to the understanding shadows around them. In the new quiet there were only two faint heartbeats to be heard: their heartbeats.

She murmured to herself rather than to Mattia, 'How often it happens that after the most morbid moments of despair you discover suddenly just how wonderful life can be.' Raising her voice a little she went on, 'Savour this moment. There is more than a week to go, but I do believe that this is the closest we'll get to a real Christmas.'

'Recent events prevent me from looking

forward to the holiday, ma'am.'

'I am so sorry. My only excuse for being so insensitive is the effect the night out here has had on me. I understand that DC Snelling is soon to be discharged from hospital.'

'Yes, ma'am, but I am concerned as to what psychological problems her traumatic experience may cause her. Added to that is the funeral of Tina Spencer which I attended today.'

'I do understand and sympathize, Giovanni.'

Trying not to overreact to her use of his first name, he tightly gripped the balustrade. The choir at the college commenced singing *Adeste Fidelis*, which she interpreted. '"O come all ye faithful'. I take it that you are a Roman Catholic?'

'I was in my younger days, but that was a long time ago, ma'am,' deciding at the last moment not to use her first name.

'That's a shame. Those of us in our profession who are insightful, and I have to admit we are a minority, have need of a certain measure of spirituality to sustain us.'

Mattia had no argument against that, having long regretted the partial loss of his faith. Apparent loss would be a more accurate term. He was always aware that it remained intact and infinite, buried in his inner self.

He used humour to back away from the subject. 'I always did have difficulty with the love thy neighbour bit.'

'I had gained that impression,' she acknowledged with a soft little laugh. Then she became serious to ask a question. 'I trust that you bear me no animosity where your being removed from the Spencer case is concerned.'

'I accept that you had no option, and that I am largely responsible for that, ma'am.'

The carol singing was continuing, and she paused, listening, before speaking again. Then she said, 'I feel there is something holy in the atmosphere out here this night, and I hesitate to ruin that by talking shop.'

'If you have a problem, it will spoil things even more for you if you don't speak about it, ma'am.'

'That is sound advice. But what of you? You were enjoying your quiet time before I arrived.'

'That time away from the madding crowd held no value in comparison with my enjoyment of your company, ma'am.'

'Thank you. That was a very nice thing to say. My problem is that I understand your work method, and certainly have no reservations with regard to its effectiveness. This makes me venture to ask if you would tell me, informally, your analysis of the Spencer case.'

'Due to the complexity of the case I can offer no more than what was referred to in the NYPD as a ballpark figure, ma'am.'

'A rough calculation?'

'That's it, ma'am,' Mattia confirmed. 'Looked at simply, after a confrontation in the Dockers' Den the murder victim could have had little choice but to confess to her husband that she was a bigamist. That would have been a bombshell that could have provided him a motive for murder.'

'But you have your doubts?'

'I do. There is more to it than that. When a poofter comes out of the closet it is for the express purpose of announcing. 'I am a poof'.'

Freya Miller smiled. 'I can't recommend you for a police medal for political correctness, Chief Inspector. Neither can I say that I fully grasp the point you are making. Am I right in thinking that if Tina Spencer did leap out of the closet to admit, 'I am a bigamist', she should have added, 'and also . . . '.'

'You have it, ma'am,' Mattia confirmed. 'Over a period of some eighteen months she regularly banked large sums of money. To date I have been unable to establish the source of this money.'

'Did her husband know about the money?'

'Most probably. It kept his business afloat, but he was in such turmoil over his debts that it is likely he was so relieved that he didn't take time out to think about his wife's donations.'

'He isn't the stuff Mensans are made of?'

'He is not an intellectual, but I regard him as a trusting, honest person who would have made life easier for himself had he remained as an employee rather than start his own business. It is his vulnerability that is presently my major concern.'

'With you no longer being SIO?'

'Exactly. I have witnessed too many miscarriages of justice to want to be a party to one.'

'You mistrust Ralph Bardon?'

'I would not criticize a fellow officer, ma'am.'

'That is not what I am asking you to do, Chief Inspector. I would simply value your opinion.'

'Very well, ma'am. Martin Spencer would seem to have lost the will to live since the murder. This sets him up as a patsy whom Bardon could easily railroad through the courts straight into a life sentence.'

Staring out into the darkness, seemingly no longer held in seasonal wonder by the carol singers, Freya Miller said, 'You would do me another great favour if you would kindly advise me how to avert the ghastly scenario you detailed a few moments ago.'

'I wouldn't presume to advise a chief constable, ma'am.'

'This chief constable is begging you to do so, Chief Inspector.'

'In that case, ma'am, it was Ace Durell, the club manager, who lodged a complaint against me. The proprietor of the Mississippi Club could be persuaded to drop the complaint.'

'Pray how do I do that? There are two of his employees in hospital, both severely injured. Neither do I know who the owner of the club is.'

'I don't either, ma'am. He prefers to remain anonymous, but I believe that he is based locally. Whoever he is, he can be influenced, ma'am. Obviously I must not become involved but, in all modesty, I have tutored DS Petters well in such matters.'

'I don't doubt that,' she wryly commented. 'Please continue.'

'DS Petters will know how to spread the word that a raid on the Mississippi Club is imminent. He knows not to mention any specific date for the raid. The majority of crimes in this town are planned at that club and with a threat of a police raid the

Mississippi's trade will suffer.'

'These are not tactics that I would normally condone,' Freya Miller said dubiously.

'They are tactics that work. Conscience doesn't enter into the equation in a scheme to tackle sociopaths such as the Mississippi Club people and its clientele.'

'Then the way will be clear for your return as SIO.'

'That's right, ma'am. What action is Superintendent Bardon taking to apprehend Willis?'

'I can assure you that everything is in place for an early arrest for the assault on DC Snelling. However, I must say that the superintendent does not connect Willis with the murder.'

'That is what I feared, ma'am.'

Another Christmas carol came to them through the night. Freya Miller stood in her usual rapt listening pose. The carol was *Oh little town of Bethlehem*, an all time favourite with an echo that awakened other echoes in the mind, echoes that Mattia was certain Freya couldn't bear to hear any more than he could.

'Leave it with me. I will have you reinstated as SIO as soon as possible,' she promised.

His left hand was resting on the balustrade

and, as she had spoken, she covered it caressingly with her cool, soft-skinned hand. Mattia struggled to keep himself in the police echelon where he belonged.

She said reluctantly, 'I must go down back into the fray now.'

'I wish I could ask you save the last waltz for me,' he confided.

'I think that would be a dangerous thing for me to do, Gio.'

Then he felt her hand leave his. She made no sound, neither did he turn to look, but he knew that she had gone. He had shared a few minutes of her life, breathed in the fragrance of her, and she was no longer there. Without a word of farewell she had walked away into the shadowy background from which she had emerged. But Mattia knew that their time spent together that night would return to haunt him. Already the memory of it was increasingly becoming a threat.

★   ★   ★

'I believe that you have made a wise decision,' a relieved Assistant Chief Constable Wilkes complimented Mattia the following morning.

With some leave due to him, Mattia had decided to take two days off. But it was not a holiday, as he planned a surreptitious investigation into the murder of Tina Spencer. Having received Wilkes's blessing, and called on Lennie Parfitt to learn the location of the winter quarters of the travelling funfair that had visited Sandsport in the autumn, he was heading for a showman's yard in south London.

Before leaving he called on Candace, who invited him to spend a restful evening with her in her apartment after his return on the following day. He readily accepted the invitation, welcoming the opportunity to spend time with her to erase the deep impression made on him the previous night by Freya Miller.

Uppermost in his mind as he drove north along the A3 was the conviction that Mark Willis was involved, quite probably as the perpetrator, in the murder of Tina Spencer. At present he could not come up with a motive but was sure that further investigation would solve that aspect.

He drove through the open gates of a large yard containing lorries, caravans, and fairground equipment loaded on trailers, to where a small group of men were engaged on various tasks. He was eyed with a mixture of curiosity and suspicion as he got out of his car.

'Good morning,' he greeted the group of men.

There were some unenthusiastic murmurings in response, then an elderly man who had been using a long, slender paintbrush on some baroque work on the panelling of a fairground ride, gave Mattia a cautious half-smile.

'No offence, mister, but it will save us all time if I say I can spot a copper from a mile away on a foggy dark night.'

'You are right, that cancels out time-wasting introductions, Mr . . . ?' Mattia grinned, holding out his right hand.

'Joe, Joe Stanner is the name. I don't want to be rude, but I won't shake you by the hand until I've learned what your business is here.'

'Fair enough. I'm Detective Chief Inspector Gio Mattia, but I'm not with the Met. I've come a long way to ask you about a man I believe was a former employee of yours.'

Shaking Mattia by the hand, Stanner said. 'Then you are welcome to ask away.'

'You may know the guy either as Rory Wilton or Mark Willis.'

'I know him. Took him on at the beginning of the season, and he left when we were on the back-end run.'

'At Sandsport.'

'That's right. If I knew then what I know now I would never have taken him on.'

'Did he cause you trouble?' Mattia enquired.

'Not directly, but he is trouble, bad trouble,' the showman said. 'My daughter is married to a policeman. Not my choice at the time, but I couldn't ask for a better son-in-law than Danny. He knows quite a bit about Rory Wilton, or whatever his name is. I can give him a buzz if you like, find out when he'll be free to have a word with you?'

A grateful Mattia said, 'That's good of you, Mr Stanner.'

'You may not think that when you get involved with Danny. He's a dangerous guy in many ways, not the least being the fact that he is not a team player. Neither does he have a scrap of respect for authority. I thought I should tell you this.'

'Sounds like Danny and I will get on fine, Mr Stanner.'

'You can make it Joe, now that I know you're not here to cause me bother.'

'Right, Joe,' Mattia accepted, as Stanner walked off to his wagon.

8

Replacing the telephone, Ace Durell crumpled in his chair. Phone calls from the Mississippi Club's owner always had a drastic affect on him. It was ludicrous. Ace had the appearance and gangster attitude of a latter-day Al Capone. Even the club's toughest and roughest bouncers were afraid of him.

The angry telephone voice still reverberated inside his skull as he sprang up out of his chair and left the office. There were only three customers in the large bar that early in the morning: a trio of thuggish types sitting at a table. As Ace passed them, all three turned their heads to study him in the furtive manner of those who live outside the law.

Walking to where Lance Canning, his head barman, sat at a table Ace pulled out a chair saying. 'I've just had the man on the blower.'

At all times the strict rule that the owner's name must not be used was obeyed. He was always referred to as 'the man'.

'And?' Canning enquired.

'I got a right going over about the ruckus with that cop,' Ace explained. 'I have to go out. Shouldn't be more than an hour.'

'I'll look after the shop, Ace,' Canning promised.

As he got into his car, Ace Durell's anger took over from the fright of a short while ago. There were two things that he would never permit himself: to back down, or apologize in any confrontation. But he had no option but to back down when he reached the police station at Crescent Street. Under orders to withdraw his complaint against DCI Mattia, he would do so. But he sure as hell wasn't going to say sorry.

★ ★ ★

When Mattia went in through the entrance of a London club with Detective Inspector Danny Wood he was still unable to equate the lithe and gracefully formed physique, and remarkably good-looking features of aquiline regularity of the London policeman with the rough and tumble fighter described by his father-in-law.

Mattia had immediately taken to Wood, and the feeling seemed mutual. He was invited to Wood's home for tea with his wife Ellie, and two small children. Even so, Mattia had felt guilty when his new friend had volunteered to spend his night off duty helping to find Willis.

172

'His record is a long and violent one,' Wood had said of Willis over tea, 'but it's not as interesting as the evidence that shows he is a hitman up for hire.'

'A hitman?' Mattia responded in astonishment.

'Yes, but not the sophisticated kind you see in films. We know but can't yet prove that he arranged at least two 'accidental deaths', and suspect that he killed others to order and disposed of the bodies.'

Now Danny was looking around him as they walked through the unimpressive vestibule of Valhalla. He commented, 'If this was their idea of heaven, the Norsemen lacked imagination. But I'll bet next month's salary that you'll find your man here tonight.'

They moved on further into the club which was a vast improvement on the dingy foyer. The décor exuded good taste. Music from a sizeable band trailed away as they entered. Couples stood limply holding hands in the vague, stupid way people do when a dance ends, as if they'd expected something spectacular to happen but it hadn't.

'I feel that I should apologize for bringing you to this godforsaken dump,' Wood said humbly as he ordered drinks.

'You are forgiven, Danny, even if we don't get a result.'

'I'm glad of that. It would be unbearable to have resentment from you added to everything else that weighs me down,' Wood said, obviously serious. 'You are lucky to be out in the sticks, Gio. After a quarter of a century of hard drinking to cope with being in the police here in the capital, the booze has stopped working as well as it once did.'

Able to tell that Wood was under strain from his work, Mattia said, 'I don't envy you. Where I am, the people there are aboriginals; it is their land, their climate, their territory, the soil they have grown in. People there live in one another's laps. All the hysteria of hate and love is what makes those I have to deal with what they are.'

There was a break in the conversation as Wood took a long draught of his drink before saying, 'That sounds too primitive for me. Now, we should take a covert look around for Mr Willis. You want him for GBH?'

'Assaulting a police officer, a young woman. That is important but I aim to get him for murder.'

'Then I am even more happy at being able to assist you,' Woods said with a pleased smile. 'I've been wanting to pull in that scar-faced toe rag for a very long time. Hold on — '

Wood suddenly stopped speaking. He was looking at a table around which sat two men and two women, talking and laughing loudly. Despite the dim illumination, Mattia was able to instantly recognize Mark Willis.

'What happens now?' Mattia asked.

'We can do it officially, which will involve a mountain of form-filling before we can bring him in, or we can do it my way.'

'Which is?'

'You go back to my place. Ellie will put you up for the night while I arrange to have Willis arrested. He's sure to have some gear on him,' Wood explained.

'What if he hasn't, Danny?'

Chuckling, a cold and humourless sound, Danny replied, 'He will have by the time we get him to the station.'

Aware that Wood was talking corruption made Mattia hesitant, but only for a split second. Thinking of the beating Mandy had taken wiped out any reservations he might have about gear being planted on suspects.

'And then?' he enquired.

'I'll be home in an hour or two. By then I'll have arranged for us to go together to the station first thing in the morning, where you will find him wrapped up and ready to be delivered to you.'

'I really appreciate what you are doing for me, Danny,' Mattia said. 'But I have to know there will be no comebacks. I want to nail this

Willis guy, and not have him get away on some technicality.'

'That won't happen. Trust me, Gio. That's why I want you to leave now before I ring the station.'

* * *

At home with his wife eating supper after what he considered to be his worst ever day since joining the police, Melvin Petters said complainingly, 'Superintendent Bardon is what Mattia would describe as an asshole, Zeeta.'

'Maybe Sunil is tucked up in bed asleep, but we do not want that kind of language in our home, Melvin,' Zeeta protested.

'If you had been with me for eight hours today, Zeeta, you would be calling him an asshole as well,' Petters advised her daringly.

Relenting, she reached out a slim hand to squeeze his. 'Take heart, Melvin. Now that the complaint against Gio Mattia has been dropped, you will probably be back working with him in the next day or so.'

'That isn't likely. Bardon won't give up easily. He's bringing Martin Spencer up in front of the magistrates tomorrow on a charge of murder. Gio Mattia was determined that wouldn't happen.'

'Surely Bardon must have some evidence.'

Giving a harsh little laugh, Petters said. 'Flimsy is too strong a description. In the main it is that the door of the bungalow was locked, and only Martin Spencer and his wife had the keys. So either he let himself in, or his wife opened the door to a caller, which isn't something a woman would do in the early hours of a morning.'

'You fear that the husband might be wrongly convicted of the wife's murder, Mel?'

'Anything is possible the way things are in the world today,' Petters morosely replied.

'I know that your job makes it difficult, Mel, but try to switch off when you come home,' Zeeta advised. 'The three of us here in our little home is what really matters to me.'

'And to me,' Petters averred.

'There is no need for you to tell me that,' she assured him with all the love and longing she would ever have in her eyes.

*   *   *

The drive back to Sandsport was uneventful, despite Danny Wood's dire predictions of what might occur. Together they had brought Willis out of the London police station with his hands cuffed behind him. Mattia had held the rear door of his car open while Wood had taken the handcuffs off Willis to recuff him with his hands in front of his body. Willis had sworn at them both as they had manhandled him into the back seat of the car. That foul oath was the last word he had spoken until Mattia led him into the station at Crescent Street.

'Be on the alert at all times, Gio,' Wood had advised when Mattia had slammed the rear door of his car shut. 'Even with the cuffs on he could get his arms over your head from behind and throttle you.'

'He's not likely to do that while I'm driving. It would put his life in danger as well as mine.'

'He's a psycho, so he's capable of anything.'

At Crescent Street, Willis swore obscenely once more, and then clammed up as Mattia led him into the building. He had nothing to say at the custody sergeant's desk as Mattia began the routine of booking him in for the assault on DC Amanda Snelling.

'This is just for starters,' Mattia said in an aside when Sergeant Stevens was entering data on a sheet. 'A murder charge is on the cards.'

'The Spencer case?' the sergeant guardedly asked, and when Mattia replied with an affirmative nod, he gave a low whistle. 'That won't go down too well with Mr Bardon, sir.'

'What's your point, Sergeant?'

'Martin Spencer came up before the magistrates this morning charged with that murder, sir. Thanks to his brief, the renowned Rowland Howard, he was released on bail.'

Angered by Bardon having taken advantage of the complaint against him, Mattia, trying to decide what move to make next, waited impatiently until Sergeant Stevens had secured Willis in a cell. Walking away, he saw Petters coming towards him.

'What has happened, sir?' Petters asked.

'I've brought Willis in. I'll make sure that he is charged, hopefully with attempted murder, in the morning. What's the latest on Mandy, Melvin?'

'It's good news, sir. She's leaving hospital this morning and going home for a few days' rest before returning to work.'

'That's great,' a delighted Mattia said. 'I take it that when you say she's going *home* you mean to her parents' place in the forest?'

'That's right. Superintendent Bardon released news of the attack on her yesterday. Mandy made the front page of the evening newspaper, sir.'

'He has a strange way of handling things,' Mattia mused unhappily. 'Is there anything else you are going to worry me with, Melvin?'

'No. But there's more good news that you'll want to hear right now, sir.'

'More good news is what I desperately need.'

'Then you'll like this, sir. The Mississippi Club has dropped the complaint against you.'

Drawing an inward breath in a backward sigh, Mattia silently thanked Freya Miller. Being free from an official complaint meant that he could resume as SIO of the Spencer case.

★   ★   ★

The only way he could think of to cancel out the magistrate's court remand of Martin Spencer was to work on Mark Willis.

He asked his sergeant, 'Do you know any details of the Spencer hearing this morning?'

'Nothing official, sir. I have heard that Spencer said nothing other than to give his name and address to the court, and that his solicitor dropped a broad hint that he intended to prepare and enter a plea of manslaughter.'

Taken aback by this, Mattia exclaimed, 'But that will be an admission by Spencer that he killed his wife. Martin Spencer could never afford Rowland Howard, so someone must have had a motive for engaging him.

180

Whoever it is does not have Martin Spencer's best interests at heart.'

'How do you see it, sir?'

'That whoever murdered Tina Spencer or, more likely wanted her dead, hired Howard to have Martin Spencer convicted.'

'Finding that person won't be easy, sir.'

'I accept that, Melvin, but Mark Willis is where I'll start.'

★　★　★

Gabriella held open the door of the police car and helped Mandy into the front passenger seat. Giving her a smile of thanks, Mandy wondered if her friend had been purposely sent to collect her from hospital or, as was more probable in the impersonal ambience of Crescent Street, it was just pure luck. Whichever, she was grateful.

'Are you in any pain now, Mand?' Gabriella enquired as she got into the driving seat.

'None at all. I don't think it will be long before I am back at work.'

'I'm pleased to hear that. Our flat seems terribly empty without you.' Gabriella uttered the words with feeling. Then her plain face flushed red as she realized what she had said. 'I'm sorry, that was selfish of me. After what you have been through you deserve to be resting at home with your mother taking care of you.'

'I would prefer to be going back to our place with you right now, Gabby, and returning to Crescent Street in the morning.'

Settling back in her seat as Gabriella drove out of the hospital car-park and eased into the stream of late afternoon traffic, Mandy realized that she had most probably just lied to her friend. Physically, she felt capable of going back to work right at that moment. Her problem was that she was uncertain as to whether she wanted to return to policing at all.

Knowing the way, having visited Mandy's home with her several times, Gabriella turned the car off the main road into a narrow road on which there were fewer houses on each side of them as they progressed. Then there were no houses, only trees. They were driving into the country. Mandy asked Gabriella to take another left. She did so to drive round a rutted dirt semicircle.

'Please stop here for a few minutes, Gabby,' Mandy requested, already having the passenger door partly open.

Gabriella got out of the car, too. A footpath made a series of steps leading up a grassy rise. After ascending several steps a row of untended evergreens made a screen between them and the car. Mandy panicked at being unable to see the car. That proved that though her flesh might be willing to return her job, her spirit was seriously weak. Then she regained control and they kept climbing. They paused on a grassy mound. In the bright, brittle winter sunlight they looked out at distant towns and rolling countryside that was one of nature's magical scenes.

Acutely aware that she owed Gabriella an explanation as to why they were there, Mandy told a little white lie. 'This was one of my favourite places when I was a kid. It always made me feel really good to stand here.'

'Then I am glad that we came up here. It will make you feel good again.'

Would it? Mandy couldn't answer the question she'd asked herself. Though looking out over this magnificent stretch of country-side meant a lot to her, that wasn't why she had asked Gabriella to stop. Her motive was psychological. The effect on her of being assaulted was profound. There was no doubt in her mind that to have gone direct to her parents' idyllic cottage in the forest would have made the decision for her. She would never have returned to Crescent Street.

A grey haze started to hem her in, fogging thought. Then everything seemed to snap into place and her mind was crystal clear.

Stooping, she relieved her tension by picking up a handful of pebbles and throwing them singly at a tree. The pebbles had made her fingers gritty; causing scratches that irritated a little. Slapping her hands together to clean them, she welcomed the realization that the decision about her future was still hers to make.

Mattia came into her mind, then an image of the oddly self-conscious but supporting Melvin Petters smiled at her. The horror of the attack on her faded for the first time. The change was negligible but encouraging.

She smiled fondly at her friend. 'Sorry to drag you all the way up here, Gabriella. I am ready to go home.'

★ ★ ★

Returning after being less than an hour away at lunch, Marcia Ridgely reached the top of the stairs leading up to her office and stopped when she saw that the door was partly open. She moved slowly and cautiously towards the door, and saw the marks of crushed and splintered wood where it had been jemmied. Though on edge that someone could still be inside, it never occurred to her to call for help. Using a foot to push the door open she stepped inside.

Any nervousness she had been feeling swiftly turned to anger. The office had been ransacked. Her filing-cabinet and desk drawers were open, their contents thrown on the floor. This wasn't a robbery. The intruder had been searching for something. She proved that theory by picking up and opening her petty-cash box from the floor. Two twenty pound notes and an elastic-band-secured roll of five pound notes were inside.

Disturbed by this discovery, she put her overturned chair upright and sat down. Fear was something she had never experienced, she reminded herself. All she was now was worried. It wasn't worry that whoever had broken into her office had found what they wanted, because it had never been here in the first place. What concerned her was someone was going to such lengths to get it.

She stayed seated for a further ten minutes, then forced herself up out of the chair, took off her coat and hung it up. Then she started on the task of putting everything back in its place.

★   ★   ★

Candace had a lovely home. The lounge was a surprisingly large square room with what

185

was an incongruous combination of modernism and homely comfort. Though baffled as to how she could have achieved what had to be a minor miracle, it was the one place where Mattia discovered he could relax fully. He was doing so now, sitting beside Candace on the sofa drinking coffee after a sumptuous meal. The fact that television had nothing to offer either of them that evening brought them closer.

When switching off the television set, Candace had remarked, 'There are so many soaps on, and as I work most evenings I could never keep up with any of them.'

'You do yourself a favour, Candace. I can't imagine someone with your intellect wanting to watch a soap, and certainly not keep up with the asinine storylines.'

'I don't want to do either,' she assured him, 'but there is nothing else to watch on the television except for the news broadcasts, and they only report the horrible things in life.'

'Nobody would watch them if they didn't,' Mattia remarked, and was then suddenly overcome by her presence. This evening she was radiant; she glowed. He continued without really having any idea what he was saying, or why he was saying it. 'However, we could have a serious talk tonight, if that is OK with you?'

Finishing her coffee, Candace placed the cup in the saucer and began gyrating it in slow circles with a forefinger. 'What do you want to talk about, Gio?'

'I have a question for you when I've decided how to phrase it. I've never pried into your past, and I don't want to do so now by asking what I want to know.'

The cup turned under Candace's finger for what must have been a minute before she replied, 'There is nothing we can't ask each other, so go ahead, Gio.'

'Has your one experience of marriage put you off the idea for ever?'

'That's a strange question, Gio.'

'Maybe, but your answer is very important to me,' he informed her.

'I am scared of making a complete fool of myself,' she confessed self-consciously, 'by believing that you are asking me if I have ever considered getting married again.'

'It's more than that. I am about to ask you — ' Mattia ceased speaking as his mobile phone buzzed and he reached for it.

'What do I call you now, DCI Mattia or Gio?'

Far from pleased, he identified the voice as that of Marcia Ridgely. Being very aware that though Candace couldn't hear what the caller was saying, she could hear every word that he said, he replied, 'Whichever you choose. Why are you calling me?'

'Am I ruining a special moment? Sorry, Gio, I'm not very good where romance is concerned. I'd have buggered up arrangements in Paradise.' She giggled with her usual flippancy. Then her manner changed. He could detect an underlying panic in her voice as she continued, 'I need to see you, Gio, tonight.'

'What's happened?'

'My office was broken into at lunchtime today.'

'Have you reported it to the police?'

'That's what I'm doing now.'

'This isn't the conventional way to do it.'

'I don't do convention.'

You don't need to tell me that, Mattia thought, and then asked, 'What was stolen?'

'Nothing. It's not like that. It's scary, Gio, which is why I need to see you, fast.'

'I'll come to your office tomorrow.'

Reacting badly to this, she protested, 'That won't do. I'm in danger, Gio, and it is connected to the case you are investigating.'

'Are you saying that last bit just to rope me into something you are mixed up in?'

'That is insulting, Gio, but you are forgiven because I do joke around. But where business is concerned you can rely on me one hundred per cent. Having said that, I'll start by confessing that I held back a lot when you were at my place. I knew a hell of a lot more than I told you then, and I am ready to be straight with you now.'

Able to tell that she was speaking honestly, he said, 'Calm down. I'll come to see you. Where are you?'

'I'll be at the Rose and Crown in about ten minutes.'

'It will take me a half an hour or more to get there.'

'Whatever, I'll be here when you arrive.'

'Is it important?' Candace asked flatly when he closed his phone.

He nodded, shamefaced at exaggerating or, more likely, lying. 'That was an informant. I have to go out.'

He didn't have to go, but the panic he'd detected in Marcia made him fear for her. He would have to be an entirely different person from what he was to be able to refuse her in these circumstances.

'Have you the time to . . . ?' she began as he fetched his coat.

'To what, Candace?' he asked, although he was pretty sure that she wanted him to ask the question he had been about to ask when his phone had interrupted.

That moment of what he now considered

to be weakness had passed. Though put out by Marcia's phoning him, he had to face the fact that he had her to thank for saving him from making a commitment that he had long ago promised himself that he would never make.

'Never mind,' she responded bleakly.

The sight of her patent disappointment made him ask himself if hearing from Marcia was the reason why he was now backing away from his earlier intention. It was a question that he was unable to answer. It shamed him to acknowledge that Candace was aware of this. With good reason for doing so, she would doubt that he would ever again come so close to asking the question she had earlier been anticipating so eagerly.

Their parting was a lifeless, mute hug. In the hall he paused by the door, about to come back to take her in his arms. Then he opened the door and went out quickly.

★   ★   ★

Marcia Ridgley didn't have to tell the barman at the *Rose and Crown* her preference. He poured a Martini as he saw her approaching. Was that a sign of local fame, a reason to rejoice, or an ominous signal that she was leading a bloody boring life? Who gives a monkey's, she muttered as she raised her glass to her lips. A cheery disposition was the norm for her, so she shouldn't be in such a grumpy mood. Fear must be the cause of it. Hopefully Giovanni Mattia, a rarity in a modern world where effeminate men predominated, would have a cure for what ailed her when he arrived.

She shut her eyes tight, trying to pretend that she didn't feel the dread that had started throbbing and was spreading, reaching out all through her. Among an assembly of couples and elite cliques, she was alone at the bar. But that wasn't something that had ever bothered her before. Even so, she needed more alcohol to see her through whatever time would pass before Mattia came to her rescue. She pushed her empty glass across the bar for a refill.

'This isn't like you, Marcia,' remarked Brad the barman, who she had for some time been aware had the hots for her, but didn't have the proverbial snowball in Hades' chance. 'Are you drinking to forget?'

'Medicinal purposes, Brad.' She gave him her bland smile, learned in the no-animation school of sophistication. 'The stress of life in the twenty-first century. How do you slow down after an evening in this place?'

'I've got a great psychiatrist who has an

answer for everything. I get to bed about two in the morning after taking two Seconal tablets that knock me out with shameful swiftness.'

'Geeze, I envy you, Brad.'

'Don't,' he advised her solemnly. 'There are side effects. For instance, I can't . . . '

She raised a hand, palm towards him like a traffic cop. 'Spare me the details. One of my major weaknesses is extreme sensitivity. I don't want to throw up in front of all these people.'

'Thanks for your sympathy,' he remarked clearly hurt, with a haughty toss of his head.

'Any time, Brad, any time,' she said repentantly, but only until she saw him reach for an ice cube and pop it into his mouth. A poor substitute for a cold bath.

Then she moved off to a vacant table on seeing Mattia come in through the door. The sight of him sent a tingling from the nape of her neck down to the base of her spine.

9

The *Rose and Crown* wasn't a place that Mattia would choose to visit were it not for this meeting with Marcia. Good pubs don't offer entertainment. They had clocks that were ahead of time and air that had an anaesthetic quality due to poor ventilation, where you could spend a vacation in total freedom from time and the outside world.

Eyes adjusting to the dim illumination, he spotted Marcia. She was wearing a polished bronze satin dress tightly draped around her narrow waist by a long sash that criss-crossed over her full breasts and tied into a halter around her neck. She sat at a small oak-wood table that was some distance from the bar. Her dark eyes monitored his approach. She looked cool but he knew that she had to be on red alert; otherwise she wouldn't have called him. Fixing him with a steady look, uncertainty was slightly creasing her brow. She looked away suddenly. Then she was back with him, and the creasing had become a deeply etched furrow.

As he got nearer her palpable sadness was a sign, an omen that called for caution on his part. Yet his burgeoning regret at coming here was swiftly defeated by the tremendous power of her presence.

Putting down her glass of what he guessed was Martini, she half rose from her seat, asking, 'What can I get you to drink?'

Her voice sounded mechanical. It had the self-consciousness stiffness of a telephone-answering machine. Mattia noticed that her eyes were bright and smoky at the same time, hiding the thoughts behind them.

'Nothing for me, thanks,' he responded as he took a chair across the table from her.

'That's thrown me,' she said in a quiet voice.

As she picked up her glass, her hand movements made jerky by nerves caused her fingers to slip a little, sending a tiny amount of drink splashing over the rim. Embarrassed, she dabbed at the small damp spot on the tabletop with a handkerchief. She kept her eyes down as she spoke. 'If you had a drink I could at least pretend that this is a social occasion.'

'What sort of an occasion do you want it to be, Marcia?'

'That's an impossible question. If I knew the answer I might not have asked you to meet me here. It is good of you to agree to see me, Gio.' She was subdued; totally different from the other two occasions he had met her. She was no longer a wiseacre with all the wise words, snappy with the quickies of repartee. Yet she had retained her bewildering gift for saying one thing with her mouth and another with her eyes.

'It's no problem,' he assured her recklessly. 'Am I right in thinking that we are here because of the break-in at your office?'

'Indirectly, yes.'

'But nothing was stolen?'

'No. As I tried to explain on the telephone, it wasn't that kind of a break-in. Not a robbery.'

Mattia sensed that her answer had added a new and unwelcome dimension to the murder investigation. 'I think you should explain, Marcia.'

'I need to be absolutely honest with you, Gio, because I need you as a friend. I require your help. But now that you are here, I don't know where to start.' She alarmed Mattia for a moment by reaching her hand across the table to him. But she jerked it back quickly before it touched him. It took her a moment to regain her composure.

'Let me start for you,' he suggested. 'Someone expected something important to them to be in your office but it wasn't there when they gained illegal entry.'

She shrugged, but that simple gesture implied much. Her face was expressionless, but the tendons in her neck were taut against her skin. Silent for a long moment, she then nodded as if answering a question she had silently asked herself. 'Just how much do you know about this, Gio?'

'Nothing. What I just said is my theory, and that's as far as it goes. I need you to tell me the rest.'

She double-checked. 'If I do so, will it be off the record?'

'You have my word on that,' he said, starkly aware that he was taking yet another giant step into the unknown. Moving closer still to the precipice.

Marcia lowered her voice to a confidential whisper. 'When I located Tina Spencer for Maurice Trench, he asked me to approach her on the subject of his wanting a divorce. He was willing to pay me for this extra service. It seemed like easy money, but I changed my mind the moment I met Tina.'

'She didn't want a divorce?'

'I don't think she cared either way about that because she was terrified. She told me that she was certain that someone was intending to kill her.'

'Obviously a correct assumption, Marcia.'

'I had better start by explaining that Tina

Spencer had an unusual history.'

'In addition to being a bigamist?'

'I'll say. She became a prostitute at the age of fifteen. Her home was in Basingstoke and having made something of a name for herself as a singer in amateur concerts and charity events, she had decided to seek stardom as soon as she was old enough to leave home. But her home life was so bad that she ran away to London while still a schoolgirl.

'What followed is a story that was all too familiar to me when I lived in London and had started out in business by tracking down debtors and doing some fringe detective work. In London, Tina Aarons, whose real name was Carol James, became friendly with Kath Harmon, another would-be singing star. The contrived names these hopefuls — and there was and most probably still is, countless others like them — choose for themselves are pathetic. They begin life as plain Jane Smith, take on some exotic name for a brief period of failed auditions, and then end up as toms in Paddington. Changing their names is their first mistake. Once they get their dreams and daydreams mixed with reality they became completely disoriented — real schizos.'

'I take it this sad story becomes even more tragic, and is the reason why Tina feared for her life,' Mattia predicted, his experiences in

New York making him reluctant to hear more.

'Brace yourself, Gio. Tina and her friend Kath Harmon were paid to provide the *entertainment* at some kind of sleazy siorée a wealthy guy was giving in Kensington. Something horrible occurred, I am not certain of the details, but Kath Harmon, who had just turned fifteen, never left that place alive. Tina was paid hush money, and poor Kath's body was dragged out of the Thames some months later. Her death remains an unsolved murder to this day.'

'Hold it there, Marcia. I do need a drink now,' Mattia interrupted, as he stood up and took her empty glass from the table. 'I'll get you a refill.'

'Thank you. The guy behind the bar knows my poison.'

Returning with their drinks, Mattia sat down before commenting, 'You seem to know all the details. Did Tina Spencer tell you all this?'

'Not verbally. She gave me a briefcase and asked me to take it home and study what was inside. Unaware of what I was letting myself in for, I agreed. It was packed with documents she had collected over the years. There were newspaper cuttings of Kath Harmon's body being discovered, and she had even kept the note that had been passed to her with the money she was given to keep her mouth shut about her friend's death.'

'Was there anything on the note to identify who gave her the money?'

'Not directly, but there were loads of newspaper cuttings about him in the briefcase.'

'And she was blackmailing him.'

'That's right. There was evidence of this in the briefcase, too. How did you know that?'

'She had a regular substantial income.'

'Only over the last couple of years, to my knowledge.'

'Eighteen months or so,' Mattia concurred. 'The contents of this briefcase would seem to be the motive for Tina Spencer's murder, and — '

'For the break-in at my office today,' Marcia finished his sentence for him. 'Before I could return it to her I learned that she was dead. She pulled a flanker on me, Gio, clearly hoping to divert the threat to me. It didn't work.'

'It didn't work for her, and it might not yet work for you. It was discovered that she no longer had the incriminating evidence then learned that you did.'

'That's what has me scared and why I called you. I can't remember the details, but there was something in the papers that pointed to whomever she was blackmailing having a contact here. Do you think I am in danger?'

'Possibly, but just how much danger you are in depends on several factors. He is aware that you know his identity. It would be logical for him to expect that you would carry on with the blackmail,' Mattia answered, intrigued by her mention of a local link. Mark Willis would be regarded as no more than a tool, not an associate.

'He is a VIP. He was a Member of Parliament, a backbencher, at the time of Kath Harmon's death, but he is a cabinet minister now.'

'Junior or senior?'

'Senior. I might as well tell you. It's Kendal Stafford-Smythe.'

This was really bad news. VIP was a gross understatement when used in relation to the influential Stafford-Smythe. Mark Willis could be his hit man, which meant that Marcia was in deep trouble were he not under lock and key. Mattia intended him to remain that way, but Stafford-Smythe could afford to send a dozen like him to stop Marcia from putting the bite on him.

'I am *really* in danger, aren't I, Gio?'

With a curt nod, he asked, 'Your home will be the next place where they will start looking for the briefcase. Is that where it is?'

'No. I have a friend, Cheryl House, a single mum. She is an accountant but unemployed because of having to look after her young son. Consequently she is struggling financially, and I help her out by getting her to do my books. As you know, my office is small. Cheryl rents an old cottage on a farm, and has plenty of space. So before I realized how dangerous the briefcase was, I took it to Cheryl's place with the latest batch of my financial documents.'

'Is there any way in which these people can link you with Cheryl?'

'I don't believe so. I rarely visit her, and I don't record what I pay her, otherwise she would have to declare it and most probably lose some or all of the social security benefits she receives.'

'That's good. We don't need to worry about her right now, so let's concentrate on you. What sort of home do you have, a house, flat, bungalow?'

'A flat.'

'Where?'

'Carlton House in Micheldever Street.'

'That's a highly populated area, which is in your favour,' Mattia commented. 'Do you have intercom?'

'Yes, nobody can get in without me first

having them identify themselves and then opening the communal door.'

'Don't forget that it is possible to slip in behind someone who has been admitted by another tenant.'

'I've prepared for such an eventuality by having a peep-hole in my front door, plus double locks and a strong chain.'

An impressed Mattia said. 'Then you are pretty secure, Marcia. You can telephone me at any time if you feel you are in danger.'

She managed a smile for him. 'Thank you, Gio, you are very kind.'

'I hope you feel better about things now.'

'I do, much better.'

Sensing that someone was studying him, Mattia looked anxiously around. He feared that he had been followed, and that his meeting with Marcia Ridgely was no longer a secret.

Then his worry wasn't eased but diverted by the sight of Lewis Milford, the manager of Candace's restaurant, standing at the bar. Aware that Mattia had seen him, he turned quickly away to begin a conversation with his male companion, who slipped a possessive arm around his waist. It perturbed Mattia that Milford, despite his own sexual uncertainty, was the type to view infidelity as something unprincipled if not a mortal sin.

'To use a much hackneyed phrase, you look as if you've seen a ghost,' Marcia remarked.

'I probably will before long,' Mattia predicted morbidly. 'What I've just witnessed is most likely the death of a relationship. Do you mind if we get out of here?'

'Not at all,' she agreed willingly, recognizing how badly disturbed he was.

Grateful for the fact that Milford was not positioned between them and the door, Mattia held Marcia's elbow to guide her through the crowd. Outside, the crisp air of the night held a welcome feeling of freshness rather than cold discomfort. Neither of them spoke as they walked the short distance to their cars. As they neared their vehicles, Mattia noticed a slowing down in the rhythm of her smooth way of walking. It was as if she was averse to their reaching the point where they would part.

Then her face went serious as she gazed out at the stillness and silence of the evening. With what sounded like a sigh, she said dully, 'I don't like this time of day. Do you ever have a feeling that you don't belong?'

'Maybe you were born out of time, Marcia. In the 1940s the world would have been your oyster. You would have been one of Hollywood's top stars,' Mattia suggested.

'You mean?' she asked, pulling her blonde

hair around to partly cover one eye, and giving him a sultry look.

'That's it, Veronica Lake,' Mattia said, wavering on the edge of temptation. 'I suppose you are used to people telling you that.'

'Yes. When I was young and silly I made the most of looking like her. But as the years have passed, so do the people who make that comment become older. There's not much fun in being a pensioner's pin-up.'

'Her real name was Constance Ockelman.'

Looking at Mattia in amazement, she gasped. 'How on earth do you know that?'

'I'm what I suppose should be called a posthumous fan.'

'Maybe that's the link between you and me,' she said seriously. Too seriously for Mattia's comfort. 'We are kindred spirits, maybe even twin souls.'

She stood facing him, leaning back against her car. The nearness of their bodies caused them both to feel the jarring impact of new and sudden emotions.

'Here we are, Gio, two absurd ships trying to pass in the night, both scared that we're about to sink. I'm sorry to involve you like this. It was wrong of me in our circumstances. If we were an item we'd have made incontestable rules together, and neither of us is the type to mess with definite rules.'

'We are not an item,' he told her, with far less resolve than he would have liked.

'Why are all the good things in life, the things you really yearn for, always buried under a ton of taboos?' she pondered desolately.

Then, with her self-confidence now at least partially restored, she had tuned back into her mystique, part of which was a strange impression of obscurity. She was the type you could spend a lifetime with yet never know completely. That gave her a powerful magnetism.

'Now I feel that I should apologize for speaking out of turn.'

'There is no need.' He took her car keys from her hand and unlocked the door for her.

'I am sorry if I have caused problems between you and someone you love.'

'You have more important things to worry about than my love life, Marcia.'

'That's true. Nevertheless, there is no way that I can stop caring about you.'

Raising her right hand, fore and middle fingers together, she kissed them lightly then touched the fingertips against Mattia's lips. She smiled impishly. 'That's a disconsolate woman's version of a Masonic handshake.'

He held her car door open as she slid into

the driver's seat, and they remained still, looking at each other in silence for some time, he from where he stood with one arm resting on the car's door, she from where she sat in the driving seat.

Using words to break the spell that held them both, he said, 'Goodnight, Marcia.'

She responded with a meagre, 'Goodnight, Gio.'

With that he closed the car door to prevent any further conversation. This displeased her. She started the engine, and turned to give him a long and potent look.

He stood watching the car move away, thinking of all the sensible things he should have said, but hadn't, and the silly things that he shouldn't have said, but had.

★　★　★

Wrestling with a myriad of unwanted thoughts that crowded his mind, Mattia drove slowly towards Candace's apartment after leaving Marcia. It was essential that he devise a strategy. Lewis Milford was an inveterate gossip. In the morning he would be unable to resist telling Candace that he had seen him with another woman. How could he handle any challenge from her? To claim that it was strictly police work would be to lie. There was nothing that could induce him to lie to Candace.

Would it be wise, when he reached Candace's home, to explain that the informant he had met that evening had been a woman? If he did that, then if at the restaurant in the morning Lewis did report seeing him with a woman it would not have too drastic an impact on Candace. Yet she was a bright woman who was likely to see through such a charade.

Just as he had realized how much she meant to him, their relationship could well be under serious threat. Whatever it was that had ailed him of late was now ruining everything. If he lost Candace he would have nothing. What then? Marcia could not fill the void losing Candace would create. Alluring though the blonde was, how long would it be before her anachronistic magic ebbed away and she moved from the past world of pleasant dreams into the harsh reality of the present? When that happened, as it was certain to, Marcia would prove to be just another in a long line of short-lived distractions. In comparison, Candace was an exceptional woman who seemed immortal in her feminine beauty.

Maybe it would be advisable for him to telephone Candace now to say that it was so late he considered it better to go back to his own place rather than disturb her. He could assure her that he would call at the restaurant to see her first thing in the morning. That way, as his policy for dealing with personal matters had always been, if there was a problem then he could face it head on.

That wouldn't work. If he went home now it would be to a sleepless night in which the threat to his relationship with Candace would grow out of all proportion. The tension in him would increase unbearably as, through long hours, he anticipated the crisis that morning was likely to bring. Making a firm decision, he pressed his foot on the accelerator and followed the route to her apartment.

* * *

Candace made certain that Mattia's return to her apartment would wipe his earlier departure from the memories of both of them. Closing the door behind him, she hugged him to her. Gently changing her embrace to one of his own he kissed her passionately.

When they parted, she told him breathlessly. 'These last few hours have been torture for me, Gio.'

'I know that I caused it,' he said apologetically, 'and I will make it up to you now.'

By asking me the question you were about to ask before you left? she mentally suggested, but said nothing as they moved into the lounge and she poured each of them a drink. Before sitting she went to the CD player to make a careful choice. As she came back to join him on the settee the distinctive voice of Karen Carpenter followed her, singing *Close to You*.

'I hope you like this one,' she said hopefully.

'It's fine, helping me to relax,' he assured her. '*Top of the World* would be too much to stand after the day and evening I've had.'

Placing both hands around her glass, she cupped it gently as she looked down into it as if it was a crystal ball. She was thankful that it wasn't. The last thing she wanted right then was to know the immediate future. No, that wasn't true. She had already guessed the immediate future but was sure that Mattia wouldn't confirm it for her now. Wherever he had been that evening, whoever he had been with, had changed him. There was no hope of him tendering the proposal she was sure that he had been leading up to earlier in the evening before his telephone had interrupted.

'Did what you were told this evening help, Gio?' she enquired.

'It presents the possibility of having the murder charge against Martin Spencer dropped, but adds more complications to the investigation. My way forward is to make Mark Willis talk.'

'Not by using your fists?' Candace urgently asked for assurance.

'You know me too well,' Mattia told her with a smile. 'You don't have to worry about that, Candace. It would delight Ralph Bardon to find even a hint of a bruise on the prisoner after I've left him.'

'So I have no need to worry?'

'Not in the slightest,' Mattia told her reassuringly although the thought entered his mind that she would have much to worry about if Lewis Milford snitched. Then he went on. 'I'll confine my punches to Willis's body.'

Though aware that he was fooling around, Candace could only respond with a feeble smile, not a laugh. A framed photograph on the sideboard caught her attention. It was of Mattia and herself on holiday in Newquay the previous year. She didn't like photographs. For her they were reminders of passing time, of mortality. This one had slipped through the net because she was so fond of it.

'What is your next move, Gio?'

'My first call will be the hospital to see Mandy. Then it will be Crescent Street to interview Willis.'

'You aren't ready yet to have him charged with murder?'

'No, not yet. I am constantly working on that and will soon have a result.'

'Maybe I can help you put these problems aside until the morning,' Candace shyly suggested. Her eyes were steady and direct, deep and warm as they watched and waited for a reaction from him.

'I am absolutely certain that you can,' Mattia replied as he reached for her.

★　★　★

Arriving at her office at nine o'clock in the morning, Marcia Ridgely picked up the small stack of mail from behind the door. Placing the letters on her desk, she was taking off her coat when the telephone rang.

It was unusual to receive a call this early. Lifting the receiver she uttered a curious rather than a nervous, '*Hello.*'

'At last, sleepy head,' a man's voice exclaimed in satisfaction. 'I've been trying to get in touch with you for the past half an hour. The thing is I urgently need that file you were telling me about.'

'I was telling you about? Who are you?'

'You are kidding, aren't you, Marcia? You are not doing much for my self-esteem. It's Giovanni Mattia.'

Now she was nervous. Really nervous. 'You don't sound like Gio.'

'I've got a bit of a cold in the head. That always makes me sound different, especially on the telephone. The thing is can you bring that file to me at the pub this evening? It is really important that you do . . . '

Convinced that it wasn't Gio at the other end of the line, Marcia quickly replaced the receiver. As she did so she was ashamed to notice a tremor in her hand. Recent events in her life were eroding the nerves of steel that once she was so proud of.

Receiving a telephone call so soon after reaching the office meant that she was being watched. That the caller was pretending to be Mattia made it obvious that she had also been under surveillance when Gio and she had been together at the *Rose and Crown*. Realizing this accelerated her desire to get away from her office. She desperately wanted to get away from everything, but that was an impossibility.

With an effort, she calmed herself by fighting her fears and having the real, self-sufficient Marcia Ridgely take over. A sensible strategy was needed. The situation as she had discussed it with Gio in the *Rose and Crown* had been given a new and frightening angle by whoever had just telephoned her.

It was essential that she telephone Mattia to report this latest incident. At that moment she considered it to be no exaggeration to think that her life was in danger. Picking up the telephone she dialled his mobile. She fumbled the cigarette case out of her handbag and managed to light up with a trembling hand as she waited for a response. But the regular droning sound went on and on, taunting her.

Accepting that there would be no answer, she hung up, battling against a rising panic by controlling her breathing.

★   ★   ★

With a busy day ahead, Mattia had started out carly on a drive through the forest. Arriving at the Snellings' quaint cottage, he introduced himself to the smiling lady who answered the door saying that she was Mandy's mother. She invited him in.

He was pleased to find Mandy dressed in a polo-neck sweater and sitting in an armchair beside the bed. But her face registered the ordeal she had recently endured. However, delighted to see him, she smiled an easy smile and the trouble lines were gone.

'Walking wounded, sir,' she described herself.

'It's great to see you are making progress, Mandy.'

'I feel good about everything except for being bored,' she complained.

'Make the most of it, Mandy. It won't be long before you are back in harness and wishing you had time to relax in that armchair.'

'Nevertheless, I'm ready for an update, sir.'

'You first, Mandy,' Mattia insisted. 'Melvin is so concerned about you that I think his wife has cause to be worried.'

'I hardly think so, not with her looks,' Mandy laughed, before making a prediction. 'I expect to be back at Crescent Street before the end of the week.'

Mattia noticed how her hands lay twitching slightly in her lap. He advised, 'Don't rush it, Mandy. It isn't wise to hurry this kind of thing.'

'That is what I've been telling her.' Mandy's mother lent him support as she entered the room carrying two cups of coffee on a tray.

'Thank you for the coffee, Mrs Snelling,

and your support,' Mattia said.

'You are welcome to the coffee, Mr Mattia, but I am afraid that my support doesn't carry much weight.'

'You fuss too much, Mum,' Mandy chided, and then eagerly turned to Mattia. 'It was a relief when Melvin told me that you have Willis safely locked away. Has he been charged yet, sir?'

'Not yet,' Mattia replied, then, seeing disappointment cloud her face, he hastened to explain. 'I'm keeping a careful eye on the time limit for doing so but once he is charged I won't be able to ask him questions that I'm not yet ready to put to him.'

'To tie him in with the Tina Spencer murder,' she deduced. 'Can I ask how the Spencer case is going, even though I'm not fit for duty, sir?'

'I think that is permitted,' he replied, mock seriously, and then went on to recount his meeting with Marcia Ridgely and the revelations about Tina Spencer's past and the politician she had been blackmailing.

'She had a lurid history,' Mandy commented in wide-eyed surprise. 'I wouldn't think that her husband knew anything about it, sir.'

'I doubt that he does, but it worries me that he will very soon.'

'What effect will that have?' Mandy mused. 'Is it possible that learning these terrible things about her will lessen his grief over losing her, or will his suffering be increased by learning that the woman he loved had a dark side that she'd hidden from him?'

Avoiding the cynicism he had gained over the years, Mattia gave a neutral answer. 'I avoid venturing into that area of speculation, Mandy.'

'It's a woman's thing, really,' Mandy excused him. 'But you think that her past was the motive for her murder, sir?'

'It looks that way. Tina Spencer was costing the politician a lot of money, so it follows logically that he hired hit man Mark Willis to get rid of her. The flaw in that reasoning is that Tina was not likely to have opened the door to Willis. There were only two sets of keys to the bungalow. Her keys were in her handbag, her husband had his keys with him, and there was no sign of forced entry.'

She looked out of the window for a few minutes, intently watching a robin hopping around in the garden. Then she spoke without turning to Mattia, 'I have a theory, but hesitate to put it to a senior officer, sir.'

'Well don't,' he advised. 'Put it to Gio Mattia who is ready to welcome any help available, especially from a thinker like you, Mandy.'

'Thank you, sir.' She turned to him then, her pretty face showing how pleased she was. 'It occurred to me that the murderer could have put the keys to the bungalow back into Tina's handbag.'

'But where would he get them from in the first place?'

'Willis was at the Dockers' Den last Saturday night, wasn't he?'

'He was.'

Quiet for a moment in thought, Mandy pondered. 'Tina wouldn't have her handbag with her when she was performing there on stage.'

'And her husband took her home, so he would unlock the door of the bungalow and she wouldn't know that her keys were missing,' Mattia murmured, then he raised his voice to tell her, 'You are a marvel, Mandy.'

'Not until my theory is proven,' Mandy modestly warned.

'Only Tina's fingerprints were on her handbag but he would have worn gloves. We need to know that access to Tina's handbag was possible,' Mattia said. 'I can find that out from Lennie Parfitt. I have to leave you, Mandy, but I'll do my best to come back soon.'

'I'd like that if you can, sir. But don't fret if you can't make it, as I'll have company. Melvin and Zeeta Petters have promised to visit again.'

10

A visit to Lennie Parfitt left Mattia feeling good. The would-be private eye explained that when a highly popular singer such as Tina Spencer was holding all present enchanted, anyone could have stealthily entered the small room unnoticed where the performers left their personal belongings. This made him determined to gather evidence that would result in Mark Willis facing a murder charge as well as one of assaulting a police officer.

Bracing himself for a dismal journey through the housing estate he had travelled before with Mandy, he drove off to the elderly Mrs Spencer's house. She answered his knock on the door, her faint smile suggesting that she had recognized him.

Doing his best to make it appear that he was making a social call, he smiled. 'Hello, Mrs Spencer. I would like to have a word with Martin if that is convenient.'

'I'm sorry, dear, he's not here,' she replied. 'He's not been able to get back to his own business yet, but is at such a loose end wandering around the house that he has been helping his brother out at the garage.'

'That's on the outskirts of town?' Mattia checked.

'That is right, dear, Carlton Road.'

Thanking her for her help, and needing to revise his best-laid plans for the day, he hurried back to his car and telephoned Petters. 'Where are you, Melvin?

'At home having lunch, sir.'

'Stay there. I'll be along in around twenty minutes to pick you up. We need to have a word with Martin Spencer, who is out at his brother's place of business.'

'I'll be waiting for you, sir.'

Petter was already outside his home when Mattia pulled up his car. He got into the car, asking, 'Is everything right with you, sir?'

'Why do you ask?'

'You sounded strained on the phone.'

'Thinking in booster gear, that's my problem, Melvin,' Mattia answered, taking a moment out for a swift study of a blonde pedestrian wearing a light-grey artificial fur coat and matching hat that added to her attractiveness, before going on, 'But don't get swell-headed if I tell you that the assistant chief constable recently agreed with me that you are the man to watch when promotion comes up in CID.'

'Thank you for that, sir. I am grateful,

because everything I know about policing I learned from you. Did I say that without stammering, sir?'

'I think you did, but try saying it again. Hearing it gave my ego a massive boost.'

There were three salesmen present in the car showroom, one of whom hurried forward to greet them. 'Good afternoon, gentlemen.' He indicated the line of cars with a sweep of an arm. 'What interests you?'

Mattia felt Petters nudge him and saw him move his eyes sideways to indicate a side window. Through it Martin Spencer could be seen washing a car.

'That's the man we want to see. Sorry,' Mattia apologized to the crestfallen salesman as they left the showroom, to join a glum Martin Spencer.

'Sorry to trouble you, Mr Spencer,' Mattia said. 'We hope you can answer two questions.'

'I'll be pleased to try.'

Stuart Spencer was standing coatless in the doorway of a nearby impressive house which Mattia assumed was his home, watching them with undisguised curiosity.

'When you reached your home on returning from the Dockers' Den on Saturday night was it your wife or you who unlocked the front door of the bungalow?'

Spencer hesitated as his brother approached,

saying jocularly, 'Keeping my staff from working, DCI Mattia? I can't allow this.'

'It's OK, Stuart,' Martin said, and then turned to Mattia. 'It was me who unlocked the door. Tina was too upset to do even the simplest of tasks at that time.'

'Thank you, Mr Spencer.'

'I believe you said you had two questions?'

'That is correct,' Mattia confirmed. 'When your wife was on stage on Saturday night, did you see anyone enter or leave the cloakroom where she had left her coat?'

'Including her handbag, eh, DCI Mattia?' Stuart Spencer questioned.

'Good thinking, Mr Spencer,' Mattia acknowledged.

Still in a good-humoured mood, Stuart Spencer remarked, 'I asked my brother the same question, and he replied that the pub was too busy to notice anything like that. You are seeking to rule out a third set of keys. You would seem close to having the charge against my brother dropped.'

'I would advise against raising the hopes of your brother or your family.'

'I appreciate your warning,' Stuart Spencer said, reaching out to shake Mattia by the hand. 'But even a glimmer of hope is welcome right now.'

'You are, of course, free to think as you

wish,' Mattia agreed, walking a little distance away with Stuart Spencer following him. 'How did your brother come to have a top lawyer?'

'It came as much a surprise to Martin as it did to you and me. I was relieved that my brother was to have such worthy representation, but I was puzzled enough to make enquiries. I was told that a benefactor who wished to remain anonymous had engaged Mr Howard to defend Martin.'

He has not made a very good job of it so far, Mattia thought, before asking, 'Can you think of anyone who would go to such considerable expense to help your brother?'

'Quite frankly, no.'

'You have been very helpful, Mr Spencer. I will keep you informed.'

★   ★   ★

'Hopefully,' Mattia said to Petters when they returned to Crescent Street, 'interviewing Willis will be, to quote Winston Churchill, the beginning of the end.'

'I think what Churchill said was the end of the beginning, sir.'

'I bow to your superior education, Sergeant,' Mattia responded with fake humility.

'What interview rooms are available, Peter?' Mattia asked the custody sergeant.

'Number two is all yours, sir.'

'Good. I want Mark Willis.'

This made the custody sergeant uneasy. 'That presents me with a problem, sir.'

'Why so?' Mattia asked, aware that Petters was as shocked as he was.

'Uhm . . . Mark Willis has been released without charge, sir.'

'When?'

'Nine o'clock this morning, sir.'

'The assistant chief constable sanctioned extending Willis's detention a further twelve hours. That period won't end until six o'clock this evening.'

'That is correct, sir, but I had to obey orders.'

'Whose orders?'

'Detective Superintendent Bardon, sir.'

'I'll see — ' Mattia began, then he surprised the custody sergeant and Petters by loudly speaking a name. 'Mandy!'

'What is it, sir?' Petters asked anxiously.

'Willis is on the loose and DC Snelling is unprotected. Take my car and get out to the home of Snelling's parents in the forest, Melvin. Stay with her until I have seen Assistant Chief Constable Wilkes and have a constable sent to relieve you.'

'Very good, sir,' Petters said before hurrying away.

'Thanks, Peter,' Mattia gave the custody sergeant a pat on the shoulder as he left him.

Taking the stairs to the third floor he rapped on the door of Wilkes's office.

'Enter.'

As Mattia walked in, Wilkes looked up from a document to enquire in a manner that said that he already knew the answer, 'Is there a problem, Chief Inspector?'

'I would describe it as a crisis, sir,' Mattia answered. 'Are you aware that Willis has been released without charge?'

'Of course. I am the Assistant Chief Constable. Let me explain the situation. Detective Superintendent Bardon has correctly — '

'Excuse me for interrupting, sir. With a man such as Willis on the loose, have either Mr Bardon or yourself arranged protection for DC Snelling?'

The superior manner that Wilkes had adopted on Mattia's arrival in his office instantly deserted him. He reached for the telephone on his desk. 'Good God!'

'Don't panic, sir. I have sent Sergeant Petters to her parents' home with orders that he remain there until you appoint an officer to take over from him.'

Embarrassed, Wilkes made arrangements

on the telephone that he should have attended to hours before. When he eventually finished the call, Mattia reminded him, 'You were going to explain, sir.'

Wilkes cleared his throat. 'On checking the record of detention in this case, Superintendent Bardon became aware of a number of contraventions of procedure.'

'It is unfortunate that his dedication to procedure didn't extend to ensuring the safety of an injured colleague, sir.'

Glaring at Mattia, Wilkes said angrily, 'Your attitude since entering my office is something that I would not normally tolerate. However, I accept that the onus for the oversight, a most serious oversight, concerning the safety of DC Snelling rests with me. Return to your duties, DCI Mattia.'

Coming out of Wilkes's office, Mattia heard his name called and saw a uniformed constable hurrying towards him.

'I tried to reach you in your office, sir. There is someone in reception asking for you.'

'Thank you, Constable,' Mattia said, as he wondered, what now!

*　*　*

As Mattia came down the stairs into the reception area, Marcia Ridgely stood up and walked to meet him. The concerned expression on her face worried him before she had spoken a word. What she said when she began speaking, magnified his disquiet tenfold.

'Forgive me for coming here to see you, Gio.'

'Has something happened?'

His question was made superfluous by the nervous state that she, normally completely self-possessed, was in. She nodded, and was unable to stop the movement of her head for a few seconds. 'Yes. I have been trying to get you on the phone for an hour or more.'

Puzzled, he patted his jacket pocket. His mobile was not there. Then he had the answer. It was in the glove compartment of his car, which was now no doubt parked outside a cottage in the forest.

'I'm sorry, Marcia. I left my cell phone in my car, which my sergeant is using in an emergency involving DC Snelling.'

'The girl from the office.' She smiled briefly as her usual dry humour momentarily returned. This short-lived change of mood left her even more disturbed, and her voice quavered as she went on, 'Earlier this morning I went to my office as usual. As soon as I unlocked the door I had a phone call.'

'From whom?'

'Supposedly from you.'

'Someone pretending to be me?' he queried, looking around him to see the door of a room opposite was open. 'We'll go in there and you can tell me all about it.'

When they were in the room he closed the door and ushered Marcia into a chair at a table. He took the chair opposite to her, saying. 'Tell me all about it, Marcia.'

She recounted the whole episode of the telephone call in detail. Listening intently, learning about the incident perturbed Mattia deeply.

Finishing her report, she asked anxiously, 'This is serious, isn't it?'

'Very,' Mattia agreed, knowing that he could increase the danger she was in if he pretended otherwise.

'It is all about the file I obtained from Tina Spencer,' she began hesitantly. 'I wish that I'd never seen the damn thing. As they are watching me, what if I was to get rid of it in a way that lets them know that it has gone?'

'I don't think that would work, Marcia. They would assume that you had made a copy.'

'That's not what I wanted to hear, Gio.'

'It's the truth, which is all you'll ever get from me,' he told her bluntly. 'There is a way, but it has rough edges that I need time to smooth down.'

'How much time?'

'I could probably be ready to put the idea into action by tomorrow. I have to put it to my superiors first.'

'How soon can you do that?'

'I will get to it right away.'

'Can you tell me what the plan is, Gio?'

'I must follow police procedure by having it sanctioned before I can discuss it,' Mattia explained. Then he studied her closely before commenting. 'You still look extremely agitated, Marcia.'

'For selfish reasons,' she humbly confessed. 'I have faith in both you and your plan, Gio, but I am concerned about my safety before you can put that plan into action.'

'Keep as low a profile until you hear from me, but if there is anything that worries you, give me a buzz straight away.'

'I will do exactly as you say, Gio,' she solemnly promised.

★   ★   ★

The day so far had gone reasonably well for Detective Sergeant Melvin Petters. Though thankful that Mandy had been alarmed to learn that Willis had been freed from custody, her anxiety was eased by having Petters there. She was relieved further when a uniformed constable arrived to take over from Petters, leaving a marked police car conspicuously parked outside the cottage.

Driving back into town, Petters' satisfaction that Mandy was safe was spoiled for him by his increasing concern for Mattia. The DCI's attitude had taken a turn for the worse. He was as keen and efficient as ever in his handling of the Spencer investigation, but he was going about it in an arrogant way that annoyed his superiors more than ever. Petters anticipated that Mattia's growing unorthodoxy would result in big trouble very soon. D/Supt Bardon had already set things in motion to make sure that this would occur.

He called in at Candace's on the excuse that he was desperate for a coffee and the visit intensified his feeling of foreboding. Though Candace had tried to greet him in her usual friendly manner, he knew her well enough to know that she was troubled. It was unlike the easy-going Candace to be pensive, to be so distant, and he had somehow convinced himself that the cause lay in her relationship with Mattia.

'Has Gio been under pressure today, Melvin?' she had enquired anxiously, proving his theory to be correct.

Guessing that she had been expecting Mattia to ring her, and that he hadn't, Petters had answered sensitively. 'Most probably, Candace. This murder investigation is stressing us all.'

'I expect it is,' she had said with a listless smile.

He had been grateful that an influx of lunchtime customers had precluded any further conversation between them. Her palpable sadness had been a sign, an omen that had fuelled his premonition that something bad was soon to happen. He had recently been weighed down by such a premonition. Mattia's free-thinking had become so radical of late that alarm bells were ringing in the police chain of command.

His dread was confirmed on returning to Crescent Street to find the station agog with speculation. He learned that the chief constable and assistant chief constable had been at Crescent Street throughout the afternoon, and that Mattia was now with them in Wilkes's office. This didn't bode well for Mattia, and it greatly worried Melvin Petters.

It had been obvious to him for some time that when, not if, his superiors came down on Mattia, they would come down hard. That would cause considerable upheaval at Crescent Street. Petters, who in the way of most people didn't like change, was aware that

231

things wouldn't go on as they were. Until he had become Mattia's sergeant, police work had disappointed him. It had seemed an aimless existence that he had often hated. Working with Mattia had made every day an adventure for him, and he dreaded losing the benefits of both the pleasure and wisdom he received from that working relationship.

With difficulty, he forced himself to accept an undertermined and agonizing waiting time until Mattia emerged from what he doubtless considered to be a kangaroo court.

* * *

The atmosphere in the assistant chief constable's office was frigid. For Mattia the main problem was Bardon being present together with Freya Miller and Reginald Wilkes. He had stated that there was evidence that Tina Smith had been blackmailing a Member of Parliament, and he had been told by a senior officer in the Metropolitan Police that Mark Willis was a hit man. Both Wilkes and Bardon had subtly ridiculed the hypothesis, while Freya Miller had remained quietly on the sidelines.

'I would be grateful if you would clarify the point you are making, Chief Inspector,' Wilkes now said, opening up a discussion that

Mattia believed would soon become a rancorous argument.

'With respect, sir,' Bardon quickly began, 'I fail to see how there can be a point to be made, as Martin Spencer has been charged with murder, and preparations for his trial are already under way.'

'Motive?' Mattia requested.

'I consider learning that night that his wife was married to another man is sufficient,' Bardon replied, bestowing a superior smile on the two senior officers present.

'His statement affirmed that he didn't know that.'

'If that is the truth.'

Bardon turned away. Mattia stared at him, saying, 'Then if Spencer lied we have a scenario in which she tells him that she is not only married to him but is also married to the man she was arguing with in the Dockers' Den that evening. He decides to kill her but then he gets an emergency call-out. So he tells her, 'I shouldn't be long, but wait up for me so that I can murder you when I get back.'

Though obviously angered by this, Bardon said nothing, and it was Wilkes who responded. 'I am bound to say that your satire is unwarranted, particularly when the subject is the murder of a young woman.'

'Maybe, but it is far less ironical than charging Martin Spencer with murder without a shred of evidence against him, sir.'

'The chief suspect in your opinion, DCI Mattia, is this drifter, Mark Willis?'

Admiring Wilkes's restraint that permitted him to calmly ask the question despite the rage that his riposte had provoked, Mattia was about to reply when Bardon jumped in first.

'Perhaps that is a possibility, sir,' Bardon suggested patronizingly. 'Willis could have got himself a set of keys cut for the Spencer bungalow, sir.'

Wilkes's suppressed rage exploded. 'May I remind you, Detective Superintendent Bardon, that this is a high-level police meeting, not some schoolboy forum. You will refrain from making sarcastic comments.'

'At this stage I recommend that DCI Mattia, as the Senior Investigating Officer, be given the opportunity to put forward how this contentious investigation should proceed.' The chief constable made her proposal referee-style.

'Surely the only way to proceed is to continue to prepare the case against Martin Spencer, ma'am.' Bardon gave his opinion. 'After all, Willis has been released without charge.'

'I am uneasy about that, Superintendent,' Freya Miller said with authority. 'At the very least you should have consulted with DCI Mattia before taking action.'

Noticeably cringing from this criticism, Bardon made an excuse. 'I had to act. DCI Mattia had been absent for some time, ma'am.'

'You acted wrongly, Superintendent,' Wilkes said dismissively.

'Please describe the situation as you see it, Chief Inspector,' Freya Miller invited.

'Martin Spencer isn't, and never has been, in the frame in my opinion, ma'am.'

'Please continue.'

'There is a file of evidence detailing the blackmailing of a Member of Parliament by Tina Spencer, and the incident that led to that blackmail. I am uncertain whether this file makes mention of the part played by Willis in the murder of Tina Spencer, but I am certain that it will.'

'You haven't actually seen this file?' Freya Miller enquired.

'No, ma'am, but I can obtain it.'

Keenly interested, Wilkes asked. 'How long will it take you to do so?'

'I have some inquiries to make first. I can't be sure how long that will take.'

Wilkes looked at Freya Miller, the expression on his face asking *can I handle this*.

The chief constable gave a curt nod of assent. Wilkes turned to Mattia.

'All other action in this case, including the preparation for Martin Spencer's trial, will be suspended pending your becoming in possession of this file of evidence. I must add that the circumstances are such that a time limit must be imposed. You have forty-eight hours to achieve your aim.'

'Is it possible for you to get the file within that time, Chief Inspector?' Freya Miller enquired sympathetically.

'It will have to be, ma'am,' Mattia replied, as all four of them stood to leave.

'You are putting yourself to a lot of trouble for a dead prostitute, Giovanni,' Bardon remarked.

'There are rules in the civilized jungle that apply even to hookers,' Mattia retorted.

With a ghost of a smile, Bardon gave him a pretend friendly slap on the shoulder in passing. Mattia had to make an effort not to examine the shoulder that had been touched. He shrugged off the nasty notion that something horrible had permeated the material of his jacket to stain and infect the skin of his shoulder.

★　★　★

Fearing the worst when Mattia returned from his meeting with the top brass, Petters followed him into his office. Taking a seat, it pleased him to notice that Mattia displayed no sign of being worried, until he remembered that the Chief Inspector never displayed his feelings. But when Mattia confidently began giving him an update, and then enthusiastically set out his plans for the immediate future, Petters realized that his dread had been groundless.

First relating to him what he had learned from Marcia Ridgely, Mattia went on to describe what had taken place in the meeting he'd had with the chief constable, Wilkes, and Bardon.

'You are SIO again now, so what was Bardon doing there, sir?'

'Looking after his own interests as usual, Melvin,' Mattia replied. 'But he came apart at the seams when Wilkes turned against him.'

'That surprises me, sir.'

'It did me, and I still can't understand it. Maybe I misjudged Wilkes.'

'What's the first move, sir, to get this briefcase?'

'That is important, but before that I want to find out who is Stafford-Smythe's connection on our patch. I've had a word with DI Ray Wilding about Rory Wilton, who we now know is Mark Willis. Ken was aware of him, but is certain that he hasn't been dealing since living here. That means Willis, who hasn't signed on as unemployed has, without any means of support, been residing at an expensive motel since staying here after the travelling funfair left.'

'So you conceive it possible to find Stafford-Smythe's contact here through Willis. But that will mean locating Willis.'

'Not if what I plan to do this evening works out, Melvin, and I am confident that it will.'

'Then I should be with you, sir.'

'Relax,' Mattia said. 'This won't require two of us. You go back to spend the evening with Zeeta. I'll see you back here in the morning, and bring you up to speed then.'

★ ★ ★

'Do you still have a man named Wilton staying in cabin 25?' Mattia asked the young man behind the reception desk at the Red House Motel.

'I'll go get the proprietor,' he replied sulkily.

The woman he came back with gave Mattia a look that was a blend of annoyance and hostility. She dropped the hostility but retained the annoyance when he produced his warrant card.

Opening a ledger and running a finger down the page, she replied, 'No, he left a short while ago. He had stayed here for some time.'

'How did he pay the rent, in cash?'

'Always regularly by cheque.'

Mattia's antenna buzzed. He enquired, 'His personal account?'

'Not his account, no.'

'What name was on the cheque?'

Screwing her forehead into a deeply ridged frown, the woman shook her head. 'I am very sorry, but I just can't remember.'

'It is very important, Mrs . . . ?'

'Mumford, Elizabeth Mumford.' she answered. Then her frown was wiped out by a recollection. 'Just a minute. You are in luck. We haven't been to the bank since Mr Wilton left. If you wouldn't mind waiting I'll go and get the cheque.'

'Thank you,' said Mattia, gratefully, eagerly anticipating seeing the cheque.

'Do you remember this Wilton guy?' he asked the boy, on the desk.

'I didn't have much to do with him, thank goodness. He wasn't a very pleasant person.'

'I'm with you there,' Mattia agreed. 'Did you notice if he had any visitors while he was here?'

'I never saw any.'

A smiling Mrs Mumford returned then, presenting the cheque she had in her hand to Mattia. 'How is that for service, Officer?'

'That's what makes you the best motel in a ten-mile radius.' Mattia, though desperate to take a look at the cheque, politely joined in her banter.

Amused, she informed him. 'This is the *only* motel in a twenty-mile radius.'

'Even better,' Mattia congratulated her wryly.

Then he took a look at the name on the cheque. It was 'A.C.E. Durell.' It had to be the manager of the Mississippi Club! That didn't fit right in Mattia's mind. Ace Durell wasn't buddy material for a cabinet minister. Even so, Durell presented a starting point that Mattia was thankful for.

He said. 'I will need to keep this cheque, at least until tomorrow, Mrs Mumford. I will, of course, give you a receipt for it.'

'That's fine. It's only seven hundred and fifty pounds so we'll survive until you return it.'

He completed the receipt for the cheque, hiding his impatience as he expressed his thanks again and politely took his leave of Elizabeth Mumford. On the drive through the town he wondered what the reaction would be when he walked into the Mississippi Club.

It was sure to be dramatic.

As he had anticipated, there was barely concealed panic when he entered the club. Ace Durell was standing at the far end of the bar when Mattia entered. He came rushing up, roughly pushing a couple of bar staff out of his way. His eyes narrowed slightly, then widened again as he studied Mattia carefully in the yellow light.

'I want no trouble,' he hissed.

'You won't get any unless you start it,' Mattia advised. 'Could we go into your office?'

'I prefer to stay here.'

'Suit yourself.' Mattia checked that the top of the bar was dry before taking the cheque from his pocket and laying it on the bar facing Durell. 'Is that your cheque?'

'You don't need to be a detective chief inspector to work that out for yourself,' Durell observed disdainfully.

'But being a detective chief inspector means that I can ask you to say if the cheque paid the rent at the Red House Motel for a man using the alias of Rory Wilton?'

Looking to the left and right as if seeking help in answering Mattia's question, Durell remained silent but gave a nod of assent.

'Why were you paying his rent?'

'That's a private matter.'

'The fact that Wilton is known to the Metropolitan Police makes it a matter that I can insist you explain, Durell.'

'I did it as a favour for a friend,' Durell reluctantly mumbled.

'Just the one cheque?'

Giving the question a lot of thought before answering, Durell said. 'No, there were more.'

'Well, that is all for now,' Mattia surprised Durell by saying. Then astonished him by stretching an arm across the bar to shake him by the hand. 'Thank you for your co-operation, Mr Durell.'

11

Suspicious, Durell hesitantly took Mattia's hand. Working on the principle that no matter how tough most guys are they are soft in the belly, Mattia tightened his grip. He then yanked hard to crush Durell's stomach painfully against the bar. Breath was knocked from his body in a rasping gush; the club manager struggled to continue breathing as Mattia made a pretend continuance of the handshake while tightening his grip and twisting the arm.

Leaning across the bar, his head close to Durell's, he asked. 'Who is the friend you did the favour for?'

'I think we had better go into my office,' Durell rasped, using his spare hand to lift a flap in the bar.

Releasing Durell's hand, Mattia stepped through the gap in the bar and followed him into the office. Closing the door behind them, Durell seated himself behind his desk. Mattia used the intimidating psychological technique of sitting on the edge of the desk looking down on his subject. Raising his head to return Mattia's gaze, Durell shivered involuntarily.

'What you are asking of me will cost me my job, possibly even my life,' he complained.

'Just doing *my* job, as the old cliché goes,' Mattia explained blandly. 'Just tell me who told you to pay Wilton's rent, and why.'

'I don't know why.'

'But you do know who.'

Durell shook his head. 'The man never wants his name mentioned. I have to respect that.'

'I take it that *the man* is the guy who owns this place,' Mattia ventured. 'Right now you have to respect the law and tell me his name.'

'You realize the trouble I will be in if I do?'

Mattia stood up to move closer to him round the desk. 'It looks as if I'm going to have to make you realize the trouble you will be in if you don't.'

'The two men you smashed up are still in hospital. You won't get away with that sort of thing a second time,' Durell summoned up the courage to warn Mattia.

Reaching out to take a lapel of his jacket in each hand and pull him violently to his feet, Mattia brusquely ordered, 'His name, asshole!'

'Dominic Wellman,' Durell stammered.

Releasing him so that he half fell into his chair, having to cling to the desk to prevent himself from crashing to the floor, Mattia walked out of the office. Following him out, Durell watched him until he went out through the main door of the club.

The name given him by Durell meant nothing to Mattia. He checked his watch as he got into his car and saw that it was 9.30. There could be no rest for him that night until he had answers to some vital questions. These answers could be found only at Crescent Street; he started his car and drove fast to the police station.

On arrival he was surprised to find the assistant chief constable still in the building, and he remarked, 'You are working late, sir.'

'There are a few problems perturbing me, Chief Inspector.'

'Anything that I can assist you with, sir?'

Wilkes glanced up to find Mattia's stare and hold it. He said, 'Not at this time, but it seems that I will want to speak to you shortly.'

'Am I due or, more correctly, overdue for a reprimand, sir?'

'With an attitude like yours that is quite likely,' Wilkes wryly responded. 'But that does not concern me right now. The fact is that I have come to share your opinion that Martin Spencer is not a murderer.'

'I am relieved to hear that, sir. My reason

for coming here this evening is to gather some information that will prove that fact. There is still a lot of my forty-eight hours remaining.'

'When that time is up, or before it is if you are ready, the chief constable and I will want to go through everything with you.'

'I assume that DS Bardon will not be present.'

'You assume correctly,' Wilkes replied with a forcefulness that astounded Mattia.

'Very good, sir. Goodnight, sir.'

'Goodnight, Chief Inspector.'

Wilkes walked away leaving Mattia still pondering on the assistant chief constable's mind change about Martin Spencer. Mentally probing every possibility to explain Wilkes's different outlook, he drew a blank each time. Giving up, he made his way to run a check on Dominic Wellman.

Having determined that he had no criminal record, he learned that Wellman was the chairman of the board of directors of a large import/export company, who had, some eight months earlier, reported a burglary at the company's premises. There was no commercial espionage involved. An investigation had led to the arrest of a petty thief who had stolen a laptop computer and a modest amount of cash.

Marcia had a hang-up about telephones since the call at her office of someone pretending to be Mattia. Even though it was her mobile ringing now, and only a few people close to her knew the number, the fact that it was past ten o'clock at night made her more than slightly nervous when she answered it.

'Don't panic, Marcia, it is me.'

'I recognized your voice right away, Gio. But the fact that it is late at night made me anxious.'

'I'm sorry. I wouldn't have phoned, but I need you.'

'At this time of night! Are you sure that you haven't got my number confused with one you've seen on one of those cards ladies of the night put up in telephone kiosks?'

'It is good to know that you have your sense of humour back, even though it is focused on twisted implications.'

'Don't try to sweet-talk me, Gio,' she warned with a giggle. Then in a serious tone, she asked. 'How can I help you?'

'Do you know anything about a guy named Dominic Wellman?'

'The name doesn't ring a bell. Is he well known?'

'Not to me but he's at the head of a large

import company named Wellman Imports.'

'Then I could well have something about him at the office. Are you in a hurry?'

'Yes.'

'Then I'll meet you at my office in around ten minutes.'

'No, don't. In the circumstances it is best that you play safe. Stay there and I'll drive over to pick you up.'

'This could result in a midnight tryst, Gio.'

'It won't, you can count on that. I'm at Crescent Street now and I'll drive straight over.'

Well wrapped up in a heavy coat, a woolly hat and a scarf on what was a bitterly cold night, she was waiting for him when he reached her apartment.

'It's good of you to turn out for me on a night like this,' he said gratefully as she got into his car.

'Don't get carried away. You haven't got my bill yet, and I warn you that I don't come cheap.'

'Remember that a DCI's salary doesn't amount to much.'

'That's OK. You can pay me in kind.'

'That's some sort of gender reversal,' he complained.

'You never struck me as being gay,' she laughed.

Their arrival at her office cut short a conversation which was heading in a direction that scared Mattia. But she became business-like once they had climbed the stairs and entered the office. Switching on a computer she sat in front of it pulling the keyboard forward ready for use. Then, a serious expression on her face, she reached for the mouse.

Standing close behind her, Mattia found that her fast, expert movements changed the vision on the screen so rapidly that he couldn't grasp what was happening. Sensing this she described what she was doing.

'Dominic Wellman. Ah, here we are, Dominic Lyall Wellman. This must be him. Born 26th January 1948. The only son of wealthy parents, he inherited the business from his father. I remember gathering information on him when he was prospective Tory candidate for this constituency at the 1997 General Election. He lost to the Liberal Democrat candidate, but it was a close thing. Two sisters. Veronica born 1953, Melody born 1956. Educated at Eton, he held an important position with a financial establish-ment in the City of London until ill health forced his father to retire and he took over the business. Married in 1973 to Linda Howard.'

'Hold it there, Marcia,' Mattia exclaimed,

in what for him was an excited tone. 'Can you see if she is anything to do with Rowland Howard?'

'The lawyer?'

'Yes.'

'Hold on.' Concentrating hard, Marcia's teeth had left an impression on her bottom lip as she reported, 'She is the daughter of a judge, Justice Howard. Does that mean anything to you, Gio?'

'It sure is on the right track. Are there any siblings?'

'Hold your horses. OK, here we are. Sister Lena Cheryl, brothers Richard William, and Rowland Henry.'

Hesitating only very briefly, Mattia said, 'Just one more thing, Marcia.'

'I thought there might be,' she murmured with a resigned sigh.

'Can you see if Dominic Wellman has any other business interests?'

'If he has, then I'll have it on file,' she promised. 'Ah, hold on to your hat, Gio. He owns the Mississippi Club.'

'Sole owner?'

'Sole owner.'

'You are a genius, Marcia. Switch off your PC and I'll take you home.'

When she was ready he held her coat for her at a distance that caused her to complain.

'Are you frightened of catching something if you come close to me, Gio?'

'I'm unable to trust myself,' he truthfully explained.

'Don't let that bother you,' she audaciously advised him. 'A woman will always forgive a man for making a pass, but never for missing out on an unclaimed opportunity.'

When leaving the office and on the journey back, they spoke little. Yet the atmosphere was electric.

'You are a work fiend, Gio,' she remarked when he stopped the car outside her apartment block. 'Have you taken time out to get yourself something to eat this evening?'

'No.'

'Then come in and I'll get you supper. You are welcome to stay here tonight.'

'Too many distractions.'

'There's only one of me,' she protested.

'Maybe, but there are many ways in which you distract me.'

'If I didn't know you so well, I might have construed that as a compliment,' she smiled.

He locked the car and followed her into the building. When they were in the lift familiar alarm bells were ringing inside his head. She was casting a spell that was weakening his resistance. He wanted whether or not he stayed the night to be his decision. The resolve to make that decision was rapidly deserting him. He'd had a lucky escape when Lewis Milford had kept schtum about seeing him with Marcia, and he had made a promise to himself not to take any more risks.

Desperate to stay faithful to Candace, he had an urge to rush back down to the car. However, it would be exciting, relieving, to stay there with Marcia. But because of Candace it would amount to no more than a practised technique as well developed as a set of symmetrical muscles. There would be kiss for kiss, caress for caress, a precise and calculated bargaining between two people. Motions but no emotion. An absolute sacrifice of the soul. He had made far too many sacrifices of that kind.

His feelings for Candace were of a much higher order than those for all the other women he had known. Materialism shouldn't be permitted to impinge on things spiritual but it couldn't be avoided since Candace had a demanding business to run, and his work meant meeting new challenges virtually every day, many of them involving attractive women. Maybe that unavoidable separation from the mystical was all that prevented him from finally closing the gap in his liaison with Candace.

But now it was Marcia and he who stood

facing each other. Though little more than acquaintances they were both all too aware that there was something stronger than the pulling between lovers tugging at them. The old hunger, the restlessness was stirring in him, the need to sip a dry Martini and a wet mouth. He had known that she would invite him in when they got back to her place, and that to drive away from her would require self-discipline of a kind he had never possessed.

'In my job it pays to keep an overnight bag in my car,' he said, hoping that by distancing himself from her he might be able to think up a feasible excuse to escape. 'I'll fetch it.'

He stepped out into the night and looked up to find a sky dotted with twinkling diamonds. He was momentarily in the grip of something instinctive, a need to be free of relationships. To have been orphaned at birth and go through life without serious involvements would be ideal. But that wasn't how it had been for him. Yet emotions, like gases under pressure, seek a vent, and Marcia presented the chance for relief.

The solution to any problem should not require a lot of thought. His firearm training in the NYPD had taught him that to dwell in the aim was unwise. It was necessary to make a snap decision. He did so. Taking his bag from the back seat, he locked the car and walked through a sickening mixture of garbage smells back into the block of flats.

In the lift, he stood motionless for some time before pressing the button. When he reached the top floor and the lift doors switched open, at least a full minute passed before he stepped out on to the landing. The door of her flat being ajar struck him as an ominous invitation to a disaster. Yet rationality stands no chance in a battle with a rampant libido. The prudent decision he knew he should make surrendered without a fight.

Walking into Marcia's flat, he closed the door behind him and put his bag on a nearby chair.

★   ★   ★

The evening had been a busy one in the restaurant. Earlier Candace had listened with pleasure when a Salvation Army band had played Christmas carols in the street outside. This introduction to the festive season had delighted her. Candace's only regret was that Mattia had not been there to share the moment with her.

A moment that had been marred a few moments earlier when Lewis had changed the subject during what had been a pleasant conversation. As always when the restaurant was closed and the washing up crew were at their mammoth task in the kitchen, her manager had waved his hand graciously for her to be seated before placing two steaming mugs of hot chocolate on the table for them.

'Christmas has always been my favourite time of year,' Lewis had said in a way that prepared her for one of prolonged reminiscences. 'It's really great here with you. I get so excited when we put up the decorations. Then there's the Christmas spirit that the diners bring in with them. Honestly, Candace, this is the best job I have ever had.'

'I don't want to ruin your happy hour, Lewis, but I'm curious. What was the worst job you have had in your career?'

'Oh, that's easy to answer, dear. Don't worry. I can laugh about it now,' he had said with a short, friendly laugh. 'That was when I was a reporter in Fleet Street for a Sunday newspaper. I spent most of my week inventing quotes to cover what the celebrities I had interviewed might have said if he or she hadn't been as dim as a Toc-H Lamp. Believe me, lovey, scriptless, the majority had the communication skills of goldfish with a chronic sore throat.'

Laughing, Candace had admonished him.

'That's a cruel thing to say, Lewis.'

'Maybe so, but it's the gospel truth,' he had countered, before becoming thoughtful, and asking wonderingly. 'Is it possible to be politically incorrect where a goldfish is concerned?'

'There is sure to be something fishy about it, Lewis.'

That had made him laugh before he had unexpectedly remarked. 'I could tell you were sad when the band was playing carols. It was plain that you were wishing that Giovanni was here with you.'

'I was,' she confessed.

'Though I would like it to be otherwise, monogamy just doesn't seem to work. Geoffrey and I are an exception, of course.'

'I see lots of happy couples every day,' Candace disagreed.

'Apparently happy, dear. Since my time as a journalist I have been a keen observer of *Homo sapiens* . . . you understand my use of the term *Homo* isn't in the sense so common today.'

'I understand that, Lewis.'

'Of course you do, sorry lovey. What I was about to say is that I study groups of men and women who come in the restaurant celebrating something or other. It is easy to spot who is the partner of whom, and I find it just as simple to fathom who is having affairs with their friends' partners. No matter how discreet they believe they've been something always gives the lover and the beloved away. I agree with writer Erica Jong's description of monogamy.'

'What does she say about it?'

'A string of profanities that I couldn't bring myself to utter in your presence, Candace.'

He was studying her through eyes that were feminine, dark lashed and terribly innocent. Candace could sense that he was trying to bring himself to tell her something, out of kindness not malice. Lewis was a good friend who was worried about her.

Did he know something about Gio that she didn't know? That wasn't possible, she reproached herself. Then she wondered if Mattia's explanation that he would be out of touch for a couple of days and nights was just an excuse.

She enquired tremulously, 'Are you trying to tell me something, Lewis?'

'Whatever made you reach that conclusion, Candace?' he asked, turning his face from her as he stood to collect their empty mugs.

★ ★ ★

Though he had intended to be up early the next morning, the brilliance of a fully risen December sun was illuminating Marcia's kitchen when Mattia walked in. Through the window he could see a street that twisted down a steep hill. Children were playing on the steps of the houses, while women stood gossiping in groups of twos and threes. It was a peaceful scene that for him held an ominous calm before a storm message. With the dawning of a new day had come realization that last night had been an error, a particularly foolish one on his part.

Marcia stood at a worktop preparing food with her back to him. She drew in a long, deep breath, and then spoke without turning. 'This is where we agree that last night was a mistake that must not happen again.'

The absence of a traditional 'Good morning' greeting alerted him. Turning to face him, wearing a woollen sweater and jeans, she struck a gunfighter pose with her thumbs in the thin leather belt at her waist.

Deciding that a casual response would be the wisest move, he asked. 'Is it?'

Saying nothing more, she remained silent as she put a cooked breakfast on the table and gestured for him to sit down. With her face void of make-up she looked young and very defenceless. Placing her own breakfast on the table, she sat opposite to him and poured coffee for them both. Still not speaking, she began eating. Mattia picked up his knife and fork. Finding the silence between them painful, he was the first to break it.

'Are you going to your office today?'

A shake of her head set the blonde hair swinging. 'No.'

'Perhaps it would be best for you to wait until I have checked out this Wellman guy. Then I will get back to you.'

'You will be in touch?' she checked without raising her eyes from her plate.

'I thought you knew that you could trust me.'

'I'd like to check with your other women before I could completely do so.'

'You don't know anything about my women, Marcia.'

'By saying that you have confirmed, as I suspected, that there are a lot of them,' she said sullenly, pushing her plate to one side, her breakfast only half-eaten.

Not having anticipated someone like Marcia would become possessively jealous, Mattia was dismayed. He watched her for a minute or two as she concentrated on tracing the outline of a red rose on the tablecloth with the tip of a forefinger. Staying quiet, she then gave one of those short and silly laughs that women often give before collapsing in floods of tears.

Then he witnessed another of her instant personality switches. She didn't cry, but offered a quickly spoken apology. 'I'm sorry, Gio. I'm being a right miserable bitch yet again. I have mood swings that would captivate a psychologist and cost me a fortune in appointments. One day I'm strutting around believing that I'm Cagney and Lacey rolled into one. The next day I'll be hiding away under a heavy black cloud of depression.'

'I can empathize, Marcia,' he assured her compassionately. 'More and more of late I have become disillusioned with my work. Probably I should have said disillusioned with my *life*.'

'I said we are two of a kind,' she said spontaneously, and then covered her embarrassment by saying quickly, 'Forget I said that. The self-assured mask that I wear to face the world conceals a very insecure person. I fully accept that the fact that I invited you to stay for one night doesn't make you my property. You are free to walk out of that door at any time you wish and not come back, Gio.'

'I would have to be callous to do that.'

'You did it last night. Not me but a

different door, a different woman.'

'That hurt, Marcia.'

'It was an unnecessary remark. Please forgive me.'

'It was true, so there is nothing to forgive,' he humbly told her.

'It won't stop you from keeping me updated?' she questioned him anxiously, going on to explain herself. 'I didn't say that in a selfishly demanding way. It's just that I've been so unnerved by all this that I want to know when I will be safe.'

'I understand, but there may be a slight delay. One of my team is off work.'

'The girl from the office. She worships the ground that you walk on, Gio.'

'That's just a kid's thing. Mandy is in love with the job that I am just a part of. I won't let you down.'

'I know that,' she said softly.

When he had fetched his jacket and put it on, she hesitantly moved close to him, fussing with the lapels of his jacket and straightening his tie before abruptly drawing back with a small sound of self-reproach.

She said diffidently. 'Just one question, with no strings attached. Do you regret last night?'

'Not in the slightest,' was the answer he felt obliged to give.

Their parting that followed was no more than a brief touching of hands.

* * *

The first hour or so after leaving Marcia had been an ethereal time for Mattia. His mind, blitzed by memories of an enchanted night spent with the lovely blonde, and crucified by guilt over his betrayal of Candace, seemed to have somehow split him from himself so that he had become an observer of his own actions. Though he could tell that Petters had noticed he was preoccupied, the sergeant made no comment as Mattia brought him up to speed on how Dominic Wellman had become involved in the Spencer murder investigation.

'Are we going to make a direct approach to Wellman, sir?' he enquired.

'I have spent the last hour trying to decide that, Melvin,' Mattia replied. 'If he is seriously involved, as seems likely, he is being used through the network by Stafford-Smythe to get Roland Howard, his brother-in-law, to represent Martin Spencer.'

'Represent Spencer, an innocent man, by having him plead guilty to manslaughter, thereby taking the heat off Stafford-Smythe.'

'Ever the quick thinker, Melvin,' Mattia

congratulated his sergeant. 'But Stafford-Smythe knows that he cannot relax until he takes possession of Tina Spencer's file on him.'

'My quick thinking has just stalled. How do we solve that problem, sir?'

'If we give either Rowland Howard, Wellman, or Stafford-Smythe even a hint that we are investigating them, there will be another murder.'

'Marcia Ridgely.'

'Exactly. That brilliant mind of yours wasn't hindered for long, Melvin. By charging Spencer with murder, Superintendent Bardon has prevented us from questioning him further. The best way to proceed is for us to pay Stuart Spencer a visit and persuade him to have his brother drop Howard as his defence solicitor. Do you agree, Melvin?'

'Totally, sir. But if he is successful in persuading Martin to get rid of Howard he, Stuart Spencer, will need to replace him with another solicitor at his expense.'

'Stuart Spencer's meanness is the largest hurdle we will need to get over,' Mattia agreed. 'So get your coat on. We'll go to see him and try our luck.'

Not having been close to Stuart Spencer's house when they had visited his car sales property, Mattia and Petters were impressed when they arrived. It was an old manor house that expert restoration, guided by the best architectural advice, had made ageless. It was a symbol of luxury, but utterly devoid of any of the garishness that spoils modern building ventures. The choice stone of the walls had been neutrally restored with great skill. The building could have stood there two hundred years or five without any change to its dignity.

'Seems like he would be financially capable of engaging counsel for his brother, sir,' Petters commented in a half whisper.

'Appearances can be deceptive, Melvin,' Mattia said advisedly, pressing the doorbell, mentally preparing himself as always to adapt to the people he was about to meet and the environment he would be stepping into.

An elderly maid-cum-cleaner answered the door and ushered them into the spacious hall that was done in plush, gilt and leather. In front of them were imposing Doric columns flanking the broad staircase which made it easy for Mattia to imagine a butler of yesteryear standing in subservient greeting.

They followed the maid into a luxuriously furnished room. The light from four wall lamps gave the atmosphere a warm cosiness. From somewhere in the house came the sound of a canary trilling mindlessly up and down the scale.

Estelle Spencer, as timid as ever, stood in the centre of the room, welcoming them with an uncertain smile. She squeakily voiced a humble apology. 'I am so sorry. Mr Spencer was at a meeting until very late last night. He is in the shower at the moment, but I am sure he won't keep you waiting for long. Please sit down.'

'Thank you,' Mattia just managed to say as a smartly dressed Stuart Spencer wafted into the room on a scented aura of body lotion and after-shave.

12

'Good morning, gentlemen. How can I help you?'

'We won't take up many minutes of your time, Mr Spencer,' Mattia began. 'There are just a few matters — '

'Pardon me for cutting in,' Spencer excused himself before addressing his wife. 'Hospitality, dear, hospitality. I am sure that Mr Mattia and the sergeant would both welcome a cup of coffee.'

Having just sat down, a chastened Estelle Spencer dutifully struggled to get her heavy body up out of an armchair. Her husband's inferior in many ways, intellectually in particular, there was a slavish look in her eyes that went with the tense way she held her shoulders. She had got herself out of her seat, pausing in a crouch when Mattia spoke.

'Thank you for the kind offer, but we don't have much time.'

The woman lowered herself steadily back into her chair, and her husband took a seat and apologized to Mattia. 'I am sorry that I interrupted you, Chief Inspector. You were saying?'

'I was about to ask you a question. Are you content to have Rowland Howard representing Martin?'

'Of course. I consider my brother to be fortunate to have this area's best lawyer in his corner. Why do you ask?'

Mattia thought carefully before answering. 'There are several relevant matters that prompt me to enquire, but they are part of our investigation so I am unable to divulge them at this time. What we do find strange is that Howard indicated at the magistrates' court that a plea of manslaughter would later be entered. That was a premature move, which is putting it mildly.'

'Ah, I'm with you.' Spencer nodded his head several times in understanding. 'That also perturbed me, so I had a word with Rowland Howard, who put my mind at rest.'

'That suggests to me that you believe that your brother killed his wife.'

'Well, the circumstances of Tina's death have me all but convinced. Martin doted on his wife, so he would be shattered to learn that she was not what he believed her to be. I take it that you don't share that opinion.'

'It is not my brief to form opinions, but to evaluate the evidence we collect.'

'Of course, of course. My closeness to Martin naturally has greatly influenced me, rightly or wrongly. As you will have noticed, my brother is now in a very bemused state. Rowland Howard set it out for me that the evidence is such that it would, although understated, be regarded as a crime of passion. For Martin to enter a plea of manslaughter would mean a short sentence considerably reduced by good behaviour.'

'If that is the way you see it, it is your business,' Mattia said, standing ready to leave. 'I'm obliged to you for your time, Mr Spencer.'

'You are welcome,' Spencer assured him. 'It has made me uneasy to sense that you regard Martin as innocent. In my desire to do right by my brother, is it possible that I am doing wrong by him?'

'That is a decision for you to make, Mr Spencer,' Mattia said. 'Thank for your help. We will keep in touch. Goodbye, Mrs Spencer.'

The timid woman gave a little jump, startled by someone having noticed she was there.

'Goodbye, Mr er . . . '

Petters added his farewells. Looking preoccupied he spoke despondently when they reached the car. 'We drew a blank there, sir.'

'On the face of it, yes. But we have planted a seed of doubt in his mind, Melvin.'

'I can appreciate his dilemma,' Petters said. 'If I had a brother who was in that situation I would be nervous of losing a free brief of Howard's standing.'

'If you had a brother in that situation, and you had Stuart Spencer's money, you would give Howard the push and engage a lawyer you could control. Howard seems intent on getting Martin Spencer sent down.'

'What would be the motive, sir?'

'As we discussed earlier, to keep Stafford-Smythe out of the investigation.'

Glancing out at the surroundings through which they were passing, Petters presumed, 'I take it that we are heading back to Crescent Street, sir.'

'We are. I want you to spend the rest of the day finding out if Mark Willis is still in town. If you do find him don't approach him. Just tail him for a while to discover what he's up to and who he's mixing with. I'll probably be away for the rest of the day, if I can get through to Danny Wood, the guy in the Met who found Willis for me. If he knows anything, or can find me anything, about the situation that Tina Spencer was mixed up in with Stafford-Smythe, I'll drive up to see him.'

★ ★ ★

Mattia had telephoned Danny Wood, who explained he had been a uniformed constable at the time of the Harmon incident, but arranged an interview for him that afternoon with an Assistant Commissioner Meech. Partly hidden behind a bulky wooden desk from the era of gaslight, and wearing a Neville Chamberlain stand-up shirt collar, Meech was on the telephone. Absently waving Mattia into a seat, he put down the phone and stood to shake Mattia's hand.

Indicating a file of documents on his desk, he said, 'I have had a keen interest in this matter which I understand is connected with a murder case in which you are SIO, Chief Inspector.'

'Yes, sir. Tina Spencer, the murder victim, who was the Carol James in the file that you have, had been blackmailing a government minister who, I presume, is also in your file.'

Using a nod as silent confirmation Meech replied, 'The investigation was weighted down with political difficulties. I would guess that you were in the States at the time?'

'I was, yes.'

'Though the Profumo episode was long gone, we had to tread carefully.'

'I assume that Kath Harmon hadn't drowned. Was the cause of death established?'

'Not conclusively, although the body was

270

surprisingly well preserved.'

'The time of death being when the girls had attended a certain party?'

'An *alleged* party, yes. The sole mention of which, and the host's name, was in Carol James's statement. There was nothing in that statement to establish a prima facie case.'

This was a blow to Mattia. Carol James's statement being considered inadequate meant that the dossier she had, as Tina Spencer, left with Marcia would be as unreliable.

Meech commented, 'It is always difficult to reopen a case after so long a period of time.'

'I am not looking to reopen the case, sir,' Mattia clarified.

'All that I can offer at this stage, DCI Mattia,' Meech proposed, 'is that if you can come back to me with evidence of a substantial link between the murder case that you are investigating, and this incident that occurred back in 1994, you will have my full support.'

'I very much appreciate your kind help, sir,' Mattia said as he stood to shake hands.

'I have just realized something,' Meech said in the manner of someone hit by a stray thought. 'The dead girl had two close friends. Yet you have mentioned only Carol James.'

'I didn't know there were three girls.'

'Give me a moment,' Meech said, as he began leafed through the file. 'Ah, here we

271

are, Carmel Summers. She was a singer with Carol James in some short-lived West End show. That was when they met Kath Harmon and became toms.'

'If the Summers girl is still alive, and can be traced, this could be really useful, sir.'

Still thoughtful, Meech suggested, 'It may well pay you to revisit your friend DI Wood before you leave London. Detective Superintendent Norman, at Wood's station, was on the Harmon case.'

'Your kind help is very much appreciated, sir.'

'My pleasure. I wish you luck, Chief Inspector.'

★　★　★

For close to two hours Petters had been sitting in an unmarked police car watching the Mississipi Club. He came alert at the sight of Mark Willis leaving the club with a burly companion, and walking to a grey-coloured Audi A4.

Petters moved out on to the main road to follow the Audi at a discreet distance. Willis pulled up outside a large warehouse the upper part of which was an office block, and the lower section a warehouse. There was a WELL-MAN IMPORTS sign on the smaller building.

Half an hour had passed without Willis and his companion re-emerging, when Petters' mobile phone buzzed.

'Are you able to talk?'

It was Mattia. Petters replied, 'Yes, sir, but I may have to break off. I'm outside Wellman Imports. Mark Willis went in there with another guy half an hour ago. Where are you now, sir?'

'Still in London. When I get back I will want you to drive out of town to collect the Tina Spencer dossier she left with Marcia Ridgley. I'll give you directions later.'

Petters delayed answering as a door opened in the Wellman building. Then he spoke tersely. 'There's something happening, sir.'

'Stay with it, Melvin,' Mattia said urgently, before continuing, talking fast. 'I won't ring you direct again. Who is the duty desk sergeant?'

'Sergeant Davis, sir.'

'Good. I will phone Cal Davis with the directions, when I get them from Marcia.'

The two men were walking towards Willis's car. 'I've got that, sir. I must go.'

★   ★   ★

Snow was falling in huge, lethargic flakes when Mattia arrived back in Sandsport.

Marcia pouted as she let Mattia into her apartment. 'Oh, you haven't brought your overnight bag.'

'I won't be staying, Marcia,' he said, gently easing her away when she tried to cling to him. Detective Superintendent Norman's recollection of Carmel Summers had exactly described a young Cammy Studland, and he was keen to return to the investigation. 'I could do with your help.'

'Fine, I'll do what I can for you, Gio,' Marcia responded. 'I'll make us coffee.'

When she returned with two cups, they sat together on a settee. She smiled at him. 'This is cosy, but you want to talk business.'

'Work is pressing. I need the briefcase that Tina Spencer left with you.'

'That's no problem, Gio. When do you want it?'

'This evening. I'll send my sergeant to collect it if you give me the address.'

'It's Briar Cottage out at Elm Tree Farm on the Winchester road. I had better telephone Cheryl to warn her.'

'I was going to suggest that. Tell her it will be a Detective Sergeant Petters who calls.' Mattia checked his watch. 'He should be there at around nine o'clock.'

Marcia made the call. Replacing the receiver, she immediately picked it up again, holding it out to Mattia. 'I assume you will want to ring your sergeant.'

'I'll pay for the call,' Mattia promised. He got through to Sergeant Davis. 'Hello, Cal. I want to leave a message for DS Petters. He is expecting it.'

'Fire away, sir.'

'He is to collect the package at nine o'clock this evening from Cheryl Mannering at Briar Cottage on Elm Tree Farm — that is some twelve miles out on the Winchester road.'

'I've got that, sir. I'm expecting Melvin to be here within fifteen minutes.'

'Now it is goodbye-Marcia-time,' Marcia guessed as Mattia put the phone down. 'On an evening such as this we should be sitting on the floor in front of a blazing log fire sipping mulled wine as we look for faces forming in the leaping flames.'

Tempted, he used humour as a defence. 'You don't have a fireplace.'

'That was a crass thing to say, Gio. I was being poetic but you made a fool of me.'

Ashamed at having hurt her deeply, he said, 'It's me that's the fool. Duty leaves me no alternative but to go now.'

'Then go, Gio, before one of us weakens and ruins everything for you.'

★ ★ ★

After a day spent following Mark Willis and his companion, Petters had gone home for tea and to spend a few precious moments playing with his baby daughter. He reached Crescent Street at half past seven, where the duty sergeant passed him Mattia's message.

'You are lucky to have a reason to get away from the station this evening, Melvin,' an envious Sergeant Davis remarked.

'Why so, Calvin?'

'Because Assistant Chief Constable Wilkes got here about half an hour ago. He is on the warpath. Frank Wyman called me away on something to do with a custody matter, and when I came back Wilkes was behind my desk, rummaging through all the papers.'

'What was he after, do you know?'

'I have no idea. He asked if D/Supt Bardon had been at the station this evening. I told him he had called in, only staying for a short while. But it was Mattia he was frantically interested in. When he asked when Mattia would be back and I couldn't tell him, he stomped off in a real hissy fit. I'll do my best to warn Mattia before the old man gets to him.'

Worried over what Mattia's latest transgression was, Petters surmised, 'It must be pretty bad to have the assistant chief constable around at this time of day, Calvin.'

'That's what I was thinking.'

'Oh well, I had better be on my way,' Petters said, his former enthusiasm for the task ahead diminished by his concern for Mattia.

★　★　★

'Good evening, sir.'

Mattia greeted Assistant Chief Constable Wilkes, surprised to find him at Crescent Street at that time of night, especially outside the entrance. Preparing himself for a verbal attack, he was astonished when Wilkes welcomed him as a colleague.

'Thank God you are here, Mattia,' the fraught Wilkes exclaimed.

'What's the trouble, sir?'

Wilkes put an arm round Mattia's shoulders, saying urgently, 'Let's go to my office.'

Following him up the stairs, which he took two at a time, Mattia found Wilkes holding open the door of his office. Both remained standing when they were inside.

'You have sent DS Petters to collect a file that is of importance.'

Mattia made a concise reply. 'In connection with the Spencer murder, sir.'

'We have an emergency. DS Petters is in

danger,' an agitated Wilkes informed him.

'I don't understand, sir. Only Sergeant Petters and I knew about his brief this evening.'

'You telephoned Sgt Davis with the final details this evening.'

'That is true but — '

Wilkes stopped him. 'Sergeant Davis's integrity is not open to question.'

'I am aware of that, and I had no intention of implying otherwise, sir.'

'I know that, Chief Inspector, I was wrong to interrupt you in mid-sentence. The thing is, Sgt Davis made a note when you telephoned.'

'So someone had access to the note.'

'It was behind his desk, as is usual. This adds to the worrying matters I have been investigating in recent weeks. But I digress, and time is of the essence. I will bring you up to date tomorrow. I understand that DS Petters will be collecting this file at nine o'clock this evening from Elm Tree Farm.'

'That's right.'

Wilkes checked his watch. 'An hour's drive, would you say?'

'Perhaps more due to the snow. The roads are being gritted here in town but the country roads will not have been treated.'

'Then you must get out there at once.

Someone is intent on getting that file, and I am certain that DS Petters is in danger. Take back-up with you, by all means.'

'That won't be necessary, sir. I can get going now, and move faster on my own.'

'But what if you encounter a mob, as is very likely?'

'I will deal with whatever it is, sir.'

Permitting himself the ghost of a smile, Wilkes agreed. 'I am sure that you can.'

'I'll be on my way, sir.'

'I'll be here until I hear from you that everything is satisfactory.'

'I will keep you fully informed, sir,' Mattia promised.

It was snowing heavily when he stepped outside. He liked snow. It obscured visibility and put a soothing hush on a noisy world, making it easy to think. Snow gave you a strange sense of isolation even in the crowded centre of a town. You felt alone even though you weren't alone. In the dry hot days of summer he was always nostalgic for winter and snow.

It allowed him now to consider what difficulty Petters might be facing. Wheels spinning a little in the car-park, he drove out carefully on to the gritted main road then put his foot down hard on the accelerator. A glance at the dashboard clock daunted him. It was twenty minutes past eight. There was a real possibility that the forest roads might by this time be impassable.

Mattia made good progress until he came up behind a line of cars slowed to a crawling pace by the car in the lead being nervously driven. Lowering the window beside him, Mattia reached up to place his blue police light on the roof of the car. He switched it on, then chose his moment and swung out and overtook the line of vehicles, breathing a sigh of relief as he reached the front car without incident.

All went well then until he came to the untreated roads on the outskirts of town and had to reduce speed. It became worse when he left the built-up area behind and had difficulty keeping the car moving in a straight line. Successfully climbing a short hill though losing traction several times, he found himself facing a long downward slope. To apply the brakes would be disastrous, so he changed down a gear but the wheels spinning and sliding prevented the car from slowing.

Close to the bottom of the hill his whispered prayer of thanks was premature as the car zigzagged crazily, straightened out, and then slid sideways into a shallow ditch. With the car refusing to go forwards or to reverse, Mattia got out. He was pleased to discover that only a few random flakes of snow were falling. The snow on the ground made it easy to see what his problem was. Both nearside wheels had sunk a few inches into a snow-filled gully at the side of the road. The solution was to dig away at the front of each of the wheels, but that required a shovel that he didn't have.

With no alternative, he caught hold of the front wing of the car while he used his right foot to move the snow and slush away from the front of the wheel. It was an uncomfortable and time-consuming task. Eventually satisfied, although hopeful would be a better term, he moved to cling on to the back wing and perform the same operation. When he had finished the snow had gone over the tops of his shoes to soak his socks.

Until he got back into the car he hadn't realized that his feet were painfully cold. Trying to ignore this, he started the engine. Before putting the vehicle into gear he tried to remember what he had learned long ago in a snowbound America. The highest gear possible in the situation was necessary. He moved the gear lever into second, keeping the revs low as he eased the clutch in. The car moved an inch or two and then came to a stop again, the wheels spinning.

If it was possible for his despair to sink any

lower, it managed to plummet when the clock warned him that it was five minutes to nine. Petters would be at Briar Cottage now, or more likely had already left the place. Ramming the gear into reverse, he kept his foot off the gas pedal and controlled the clutch and felt the vehicle slowly regain the couple of inches backwards that he had lost.

Another glance at the clock showed that nine o'clock had passed. He put the lever into third gear. Intent on revving the engine enough to move the car, he gently let in the clutch and was rewarded as the vehicle moved forward gradually but positively and the car moved out on to the snow-covered road.

Gradually building up the speed until satisfied that the car could safely handle the straight road ahead, Mattia moved along fast. There was no hope of making up for lost time, but worry over Petters determined him to avoid any further delay.

★ ★ ★

Elm Tree Farm was a huge confusing place as all the tracks that could be followed were hidden by snow. The lighted windows of a cottage up ahead caused Petters to hope that, by luck rather than judgement, he had reached his destination. Rather than risk driving into the deep snow banked up in front of the cottage, he parked the car some distance away. Trudging through deep snow, he walked the final fifteen yards to the cottage and knocked on the door. He then stood with his back to the cottage, getting pleasure from looking out over the Christmas-card scenery.

The door opened behind him, and he turned to see a black-haired woman wearing a red satin dress that broke the chiaroscuro contrast of her hair and complexion to stunning effect. Petters decided that she was of Romany stock. She wore an uncertain smile on her face.

'Ms Mannering?' he asked. 'I am sorry that I'm late. I got lost a little way back.'

Her smile gained strength to become special. 'Sergeant Petters. Please, do come in. Getting lost on your way here is nothing to be ashamed of.'

He followed her into a room heated by a traditional log fire and with the décor of a bygone age. It was a strange experience for Petters. She moved a wooden clothes-horse on which were draped a child's garments back from the fire, the woman invited him to take a seat.

'Thank you, but my superior officer is waiting for me back in town,' Petters explained why he was refusing.

'Of course, you are on duty.' She accepted his explanation graciously, walking across the room to pick up a leather briefcase. 'This is Marcia's case, the reason for your visit. I haven't seen Marcia for a little while, how is she?'

'I am sorry, Ms Mannering, I — '

'Call me Cheryl.'

'Thank you, I'm Melvin. I have to confess to never having met your friend. It is my boss who has been in contact with her.'

'Ah, give me a moment.' She held up a hand to stop him speaking again while she searched her memory. 'It's Italian, I am sure of that. Let me see . . . yes, it is Giovanni. Is that right?'

'You have it.'

'I should have remembered it easily. Marcia never stops talking about him.'

'He does have that effect on women,' Petters told her, thinking how different the present situation was likely to have been had it been the DCI and not him who was here with this unusual woman.

She passed him the briefcase, then walked to the small lobby inside of the door, kicking her slippers off and stopping to put on a pair of Wellington boots.

'I'll walk you to your car.'

'There is no need,' Petters protested.

'I would like to. This is an ideal area to enjoy the night, but the wrong one for a woman to risk going out alone.'

'I appreciate what you mean,' Petters said. 'By all means walk with me and I will stay outside the car until I see you go safely inside cottage.'

'Thank you, that is most thoughtful,' she told him, as they went out.

When they reached the first trees she slowed, seemingly waiting for something. It appeared to the bemused Petters that everything seemed to be waiting, somewhere.

Coming to a halt, she said softly, 'Let's give them a moment.'

'Who?' Petters enquired, mystified.

'The creatures of the woods,' was her hushed reply. 'Didn't you hear them whispering of our approach? Can't you feel the tension?' She raised a hand for silence. Then she gave a satisfied sigh. 'There now, it's over. They know there's no danger, but they've marked our trail as a warning to others.'

Petters' ears caught the scampering of small animals, the flapping of wings as birds flew off. He was relieved that the woman had been speaking of real things, even though they were beyond his understanding.

There was something magic but sublimi-
nally savage in these surroundings, that
affected the minds of the sensitive. Looking
around him, he remarked, 'As a town man I
envy you living in this environment, Cheryl.'

'Living crowded together among the
chimney pots is what has ruined the world for
most people,' she explained. 'Being close to
nature is essential, but not to conform in this
world means having crazy people dancing
around the image they make of you. Many
around here regard me as some kind of
modern witch.'

'That's ridiculous. However, it is a real
pleasure to meet someone like you with the
courage to be yourself rather than be shaped
by those around you.'

'That's why I am a single mum, never
married. Living through a husband or anyone
else is the easy option — a kind of
semi-suicide.'

'Giovanni Mattia is someone who shares
your philosophy.'

'Don't tell Marcia that,' she warned.

'I won't, and although I will tell my wife
about you I'll omit some of the conversation
we have had. If I don't she'll keep on at me to
bring her out here for a card reading.'

This caused her to smile. 'Fortune telling is
a risky business. Intuitions and hunches are

286

either misunderstood or unappreciated. Guess wrong and it will be forgotten. Get it right and you're under suspicion.'

Aware that Mattia would be waiting, he opened the rear door of the car and placed the briefcase on the seat. Shutting the door, he straightened up to discover she was looking at him intently.

'Can I say something, Sergeant?' He nodded and she continued, 'I just want to say that you must take care, take great care.'

This alarmed him. Had she seen something in his aura? Had he been wrong in connecting the omens he had received of late to Mandy? Were they related to him? There was nothing selfish in him dreading that was so. Leaving Zeeta and Sunil alone in the world was his concern. He decided to question her, but saw that she was hurrying off through the snow.

At her door she turned to wave just once. Then she was gone. Slowly getting into his car he was taken aback to notice that the beautiful seasonal scenery had taken on the appearance of a bleak winter's night.

★ ★ ★

A pair of headlights coming towards him over the brow of a hill some distance up ahead was the first movement Mattia had seen since

287

rescuing his car from the ditch. He knew that it had to be Petters. It was unlikely that anyone else would have cause to travel a dangerous road like this on such a night. The lights disappeared as he drove along a straight road, and then appeared once more, to illuminate a left bend some way up ahead. Then he clutched the steering wheel hard as a second set of headlights appeared behind the first car, gaining on it fast.

Throwing caution to the winds, Mattia stepped on the gas. But a terrible scene evolved as the first car came round the distant bend, the second pair of headlights swinging out to overtake it.

Then the headlights were four abreast across the road before the outside car cut in on the vehicle on its left. Watching sparks shower in the darkness as metal grated against metal, Mattia didn't realize that he had forgotten to breathe until the breath was forced out of him explosively. Apprehensively he watched as the inside car hit the bank and climbed fast before catapulting into a somersault as it reach the top. Then it disappeared.

The second car came on at speed, the driver and passenger both covering their faces with a hand as they passed him. Fearing for Petters' safety, he sped on towards where he had seen the car leave the road.

Near the corner, he could see where the snow and earth had been churned up by the car. There was a pull-in on his side on the road outside a small building surrounded by an iron fence. He pulled in, switched off the engine, and jumped out of the car to run across the road and climb the bank.

Aided by the fallen snow reflecting the starlight, Mattia saw Petters' car on its roof at the bottom of a slope. Slipping and sliding down to the car, he was thankful to see that the roof wasn't badly crushed. Using both hands, and with a foot against the car's body, he tugged at the driver's door. It resisted at first then opened with a grinding of metal. Reaching in, he pulled Petters out and laid him in the snow.

13

Dropping to his knees to reach for Petters' pulse he was startled when the sergeant spoke. 'Thanks for getting me out, sir.'

'Jesus, Mary and Joseph, Melvin, why didn't you groan first as a warning.'

'Would you like me to groan now, sir?'

'Leave it until I can give you a kick up the ass.'

'Could you first help me up, sir?'

He helped Petters to his feet, and put the sergeant's right arm over his shoulders to support him, asking. 'Do you think you can make it to the top of the hill, Melvin?'

'I'll be able to make it. Hang on a minute, sir.'

Petters stretched an arm into the rear of the car to grasp the briefcase and bring it out.

'Mission accomplished,' Mattia said gratefully, taking the briefcase as they started off up the hill together.

Weakened by the effort, Petters needed to rest before they reached the top. Mattia could see headlights swinging round some distance away and rapidly becoming brighter.

'They have turned to come back,' he informed Petters.

'How many are there, sir?

'I saw only two.'

'We can handle them, sir.'

'We aren't going to handle anyone, Melvin. You need to rest. Come on.'

Mattia assisted Petters down the bank and across the road, putting him in the front seat of the car. He said firmly, 'I'm going to lock you in. You stay put. Do you hear me?'

'I hear you, sir,' Petters answered in a manner that warned he would disobey.

Crouching beside the front passenger door, Mattia saw the other car stop. To his surprise, three men got out to climb the bank, their voices carrying clearly on the still night air.

'One track down to the car, two tracks back up. What does that tell us?'

'The guy who was driving that car over there went down and got the other cop out.'

'So, if they are back up here the briefcase will be with them.'

Going to the driver's side of Mattia's car, one of them called, 'Someone is in here.'

'The driver?' one of the other two enquired.

'No. He's in the passenger seat.'

Mattia tensed as a shadowy figure came round the back of the car. Then a large man was in front of him, grinning as he spread both arms wide in an arrogant what-have-we-here gesture. His grin slowly faded as he moved closer to Mattia.

Mattia moved fast. Aiming a punch at the man's stomach, he snapped his hand into a fist just before his knuckles made contact. This added terrific power to the punch, and he twisted his hand to screw his fist into the man's body. The man staggered backwards, his ugly mouth dropping open squarely like that of a ventriloquist's doll. But he wasn't finished. Bending low, he lunged forwards to drive a shoulder into Mattia's midriff.

Mattia was sent flying through the air. Winded, realizing that he would be finished if he hit the ground face down, he tucked his head in so that he struck the ground with his shoulders and rolled to come up on his feet to deliver a hard rabbit punch to the roll of fat at the nape of his attacker's neck. The big man crashed to the ground like a felled oak and lay still.

Still gasping for breath from the impact of the shoulder to his stomach, Mattia dropped to his knees. Hearing movement, he raised his head to see another man had moved in and was aiming a kick to his head. With no time to avoid it, the sole of the newcomer's boot caught Mattia on the side of the head to send him crashing flat on his back.

Then a kick was aimed at his stomach. The sound of the third member of the gang smashing one of the car's windows warned Mattia that Petters was in danger. Intercepting the kick by catching the booted foot, one hand gripping the heel and the other the toe, Mattia twisted the foot to slam his attacker face down on the ground. Still holding the foot, Mattia got up on to his knees. Folding one of his own legs behind the man's knee he bent the leg double and fell on it with all his weight. The sound of ligaments tearing could be heard over the victim's scream of pain.

Now standing upright, Mattia was intent on helping Petters. As he turned, so did the first man he had downed, spring to his feet to grab him from behind. With his forearm crushing Mattia's throat, the man backed against the car, applying more pressure as the third man came around from the other side of the car.

Facing Mattia, the man was moving nearer when Mattia recognized him as Mark Willis. His staring eyes were wildly insane. His top lip was pulled back from his teeth in a wolf-like snarl as he struck out with his right hand at Mattia's chest. The scrape of steel against his ribs made Mattia realize that the scarfaced man held a knife. As Willis withdrew the knife and took a step back, Mattia, who was close to blacking out, managed to deliver a vicious kick to Willis's groin that doubled him over. This brought Willis's head into Mattia's range. Kicking out once again, he caught the knifeman full in the face with the flat of the shoe on his right foot. There was such force behind the kick that Willis did a complete backward somersault.

Taking him by surprise, Mattia was able to drag the man holding him a step forward. Estimating the location of the car's wing mirror, Mattia dug his heels in to thrust one step backwards. He was rewarded by a grunt of pain, the smashing of glass and breaking of metal as the mirror dug into the small of the man's back.

Grabbing the wrist of the arm that had been throttling him with both hands, Mattia twisted it so that the hand was palm upwards. Moving his right shoulder forward a little, he laid the man's elbow on it and jerked down hard on the wrist. Mattia heard the sinews of the elbow joint make odd stretching, snapping sounds as they were torn asunder.

Pivoting on his heel, Mattia saw the man bent double nursing his shattered right arm. His mouth was moving in a soundless plea for mercy. Compassion was not uppermost in Mattia's mind. With a chopping blow with the side of his hand to the throat, he felled him instantly. He lay at Mattia's feet, trying to breathe through his smashed airways.

Moving fast, Mattia found the window of the front passenger's door had been smashed. Sitting inside, head resting on his chest, clutching the briefcase on his lap, Petters was covered by a layer of small pieces of glass. Alarmed by his white-faced appearance Mattia unlocked the door and pulled it open. Then his worst fears were confirmed. Melvin Petters was deeply unconscious.

★　★　★

'It's DCI Mattia, sir,' Sgt Davis called, holding the telephone receiver out at arm's length to Assistant Chief Constable Wilkes.

Almost snatching the phone, Wilkes asked abruptly, 'What is happening?'

'DS Petters' car has been forced off the road, sir.'

'Is the sergeant injured?'

'Yes, sir. I locked him in my car before I was attacked by three men from the other car. He's unconscious now.'

'Give me your location and I'll send an ambulance at once.'

'It would be too late. I am going to drive him to the hospital now, sir.'

'Where are the men that attacked you?'

'I've handcuffed them to some iron railings, sir,' Mattia explained, continuing to give Wilkes directions to what he had discovered was an electricity substation inside the railings.

'Are they injured?'

Mattia looked down to where the breathing of the man with the mashed throat was an irregular snorting sound in an otherwise soundless night. The other two glared at him silently.

'They could use an ambulance, sir.'

'That had already occurred to me. Are you hurt, Chief Inspector?'

Trying to stem blood from the knife wound, Mattia reported, 'Just a scratch, sir.'

* * *

Ending the phone call, Mattia drove off with the unconscious Petters at his side along a road made more treacherous by snow that had frozen. His clothing was now blood-soaked, and he was acutely aware that in his fast deteriorating condition he would have difficulty in reaching the hospital. Glancing through the side window he was astonished to recognize how close he was to the town. But it wasn't an encouraging realization. He knew that he must have blacked out some time ago and had been driving instinctively before regaining consciousness.

He kept going, and then knew nothing more until he came to just in time to brake to avoid crashing into the doors of a garage at the end of a private drive up which he had driven. A light in a bedroom of the house was switched on. He reversed out fast into the street. Driving off, fading in and out of consciousness, he knew to continue could result in disaster.

He slowed the car to take a look around and he couldn't believe his luck. The hospital was situated at the end of the road he was in. He drove on into the hospital grounds slumped over the wheel. Dimly aware of people running and shouting, he knew no more.

★　★　★

'What is the latest, Reg?' a fraught Freya Miller asked Wilkes as soon as he entered the room.

'Both Mattia and Petters were in a bad way when they got to the hospital. The staff there regard it as some kind of miracle that Mattia reached there in his condition.'

'How is he now?' the chief constable

enquired, noticing Wilkes's quizzical glance.

He replied in the order she didn't want. 'The sergeant's spine has been injured. He was conscious for a while. Now he is in a medically-induced coma. The knife missed Mattia's heart by a tiny fraction of an inch. It's all right, Freya. The wound has been sutured and the doctors say that a man with his constitution can return to duty if he takes care.'

'Which is something he won't do, Reg.'

'He's being discharged and should be here within the hour,' Wilkes advised, the twinkle in his eye pleasing her rather than annoying her.

★　★　★

With much to explain to Candace, Mattia stopped off at the restaurant. The sight of his bloodstained clothing alarmed her but he made light of being stabbed and told her that Petters was in a bad way.

'Oh no! Poor Melvin. Will he be all right?'

'We must hope so. He has a spinal injury. His wife has been with him all night.'

'Incidents like this terrify me.'

'Melvin obtained evidence last night that should permit us to close the case.'

'That will be a relief,' Candace sighed. 'It

298

has been keeping us apart, Gio.'

'That has been on my mind. I have to get to Crescent Street but I will be back with you soon. Then we will be able to make up for lost time.'

★   ★   ★

The reception given Mattia by Freya Miller and Reginald Wilkes centred on concern over Petters' and his injuries. Then Wilkes explained that he had already contacted the Metropolitan Police about the Tina Spencer file. The Met believed there was sufficient evidence in it to enable the Kath Harmon case to be reopened.

He said, 'The file shows that there was a third young girl with Tina Spencer and Kath Harmon in London. That girl is of the utmost importance to the Met, who hope to find her.'

'I knew about the girl, and believe that I have found her,' Mattia said. 'She is here in Sandsport. She will need our protection as Crescent Street is not safe now.'

The chief constable reluctantly concurred. 'Sadly, I have to agree.'

'We also agree that this Mark Willis fellow was sent here to stop the deceased's blackmail. Whether he killed her remains to be established,' an anxious Wilkes remarked.

'I appreciate that. But we have Willis in custody, sir.'

'When he is fit to be interviewed we will need to establish how he gained entry to the bungalow, there being only two sets of keys, both accounted for on the night of the murder.'

The chief constable said. 'By the way, Chief Inspector, DC Snelling returned to duty this morning. But you will need a replacement for DS Petters until he is well.'

'That won't be necessary, ma'am,' Mattia said, as he stood to leave. 'Do we know how it was that someone knew about the briefcase and from where it was to be collected?'

'That is still being investigated,' Wilkes replied guardedly.

★　★　★

Exhausted by her long vigil at the cot-sides-up bedside of her husband, Zeeta Petters was dozing when she was snapped fully awake by an eruption of action around her. She heard a nurse shout 'He's tachy-cardic,' and another nurse's panicky call. 'Fetch Dr Carter.'

Getting swiftly to her feet, hysterically needing to take a closer look at Melvin, a nurse gripped her firmly by the arm as the doctor came hurrying into the single room.

'You must leave this to us, Mrs Petters,' the nurse advised as she moved her away.

'Will he be all right, Nurse?'

Leading her backwards towards the door, the nurse replied without committing herself. 'Doctor Carter is here now.'

'Start compression,' Zeeta heard the doctor order, and she saw a sister with both hands resting flatly on Melvin's chest rhythmically applying forceful pressure.

Left alone out in the corridor she watched through slatted window blinds as the doctor with an instrument in each hand, called a 'Stand clear' warning to his staff as he applied the instruments to Melvin's chest.

Seeing her husband convulsing, coming up off the bed, his legs jerking violently, was too much for Zeeta. As she slid down the wall, she heard a cry of alarm and the sound of running footsteps echo hollowly and far distant as everything went black and she slumped to the floor.

★　★　★

On route to Cammy Studland's home with Mandy in the seat beside him, Mattia was aware of a difference in her that he couldn't define. She was still the same friendly girl, a colleague it was a pleasure to be with, but some vital part of her was missing.

He mentioned this. 'But there is something not quite as it should be about you.'

'I have been intending to talk to you, to ask your advice, sir,' she admitted humbly. 'I was enthusiastic when joining CID. But that is no longer the case, maybe because I was attacked. What has happened to Melvin hasn't helped. Now I am uncertain that I want to continue in the police.'

'I am sorry to hear how you feel, Mandy, as you were destined for great things in the force. It would be wrong of me to advise you, as it is your life. Anyway, it would be difficult for me to do so because I have been disillusioned for some time. I have delayed making a decision until this case has been brought to a successful conclusion.'

Instantly more cheerful at hearing this, Mandy said, 'That idea appeals to me. Do you mind if I join you in that, sir?'

'Glad to have you on board, Mandy,' he responded.

★ ★ ★

'That's her.'

Cheryl Mannering took a sideways look as she ate her meal. She questioned. 'That's

302

Mattia's intended?'

'That is Candace Dvorak, the owner of this place,' Marcia Ridgely confirmed.

'She sure is stiff competition, a real looker like you, Marci.'

'I have a huge advantage,' Marcia confidently advised. 'Gio has been in love with the ghost of Veronica Lake for ages. I just replaced the phantom with flesh, and that was it.'

'I get labelled a witch while people like you put a hex on unsuspecting guys,' Cheryl complained humorously. Her mood changed and she asked, 'That sergeant, Melvin?'

'Petters. He made an impression on you. You have gone white as a sheet.'

'It was nothing like that,' Cheryl protested. 'He was . . . I tried to warn him but I didn't want to make a fool of myself. I don't know how to explain this. It was as if he was shrouded in a strange kind of shadow. I've known this sort of thing before, and it's not good.'

'An omen. You thought he was doomed,' Marcia presumed. 'Why do you always get these gloomy feelings, Cheryl? Do something cheerful for a change; cast a spell on Candace Dvorak right now. Make her step right out of Giovanni Mattia's life.'

Marcia found her own request to be

hilarious. But Cheryl Mannering was not laughing.

★ ★ ★

It was a delicate subject that he had handled with tact, yet Mattia was still extremely uncomfortable after revealing his knowledge of her teen years to Cammy Studland. She covered her disquiet by reaching for a teacloth and wiping some crockery that was in a rack on the draining board beside her; it appeared that she was about to cry.

Recovering sufficiently to speak, she asked, 'Does this mean it is all going to be dragged out into the open? I am thinking of my daughter, who is old enough to understand.'

'There is nothing that will involve the Sandsport police. The Metropolitan police will want to speak to you. But that will only be as a witness for the prosecution, and I would assume, but I can't say for sure, that you will be granted anonymity.'

'Thank you,' she gratefully responded. 'What about reprisals? They were powerful people we mixed with then, and they would be even more powerful now.'

'The London police will give you witness protection,' Mattia informed her. 'But I have to tell you that Tina Spencer brought the distant pasts of her and yourself to the attention of some local people.'

'I don't understand.'

'Tina was blackmailing Stafford-Smythe, and getting a monthly payment in cash here. So the London people have contacts in this town.'

'Does that mean I could be in danger here?'

'That isn't likely. We found you only from a file of evidence that Tina had compiled. That file is now held by the police here at the Crescent Street station.'

'Good. I appreciate both of you coming here to forewarn me, but it occurred to me that you may have another reason for doing so.'

'An ulterior motive?' Mattia surmised. 'No, but I am now wondering if you ever saw any indication that Tina was regularly receiving large amounts of cash?'

'None whatsoever. She was a good friend but a very private person. Though I liked her a lot, I don't suppose that I ever really knew her.'

'That observation fits in with what we have gathered, Cammy,' Mandy confirmed.

'We will keep you up to date with all developments,' Mattia promised as they left.

★　★　★

'Do I need to make an appointment?'

The well-dressed man stood in the doorway of Marcia Ridgley's office, awaiting a response to his question. He was expensively attired and well-mannered.

'I have a quarter of an hour now if that is any use to you?'

'That will do me fine.'

'Then please take a seat and tell me how I can help you.'

'Thank you.' He gave her a nice smile as he sat. 'I'll begin by saying that you have been recommended to me as a streetwise operator who knows most of the important people in this town better than they know themselves.'

'I'm not sure that I can live up to that,' Marcia modestly replied.

'Now that I have met you I am convinced that you can. I have a difficult assignment for you but I am prepared to pay well above the normal rate.'

He had Marcia's full attention. She enquired, 'Is this a business or a marital matter?'

'Neither. It is an unusual mission that you may well wish not to accept.'

'Try me.'

'I want you to arrange a meeting for me with a dangerous man.'

'A convicted criminal?' Marcia asked.

'No, but dangerous nevertheless. What I seek is a meeting with this gentleman in a public place, but not too public. What I am trying to suggest without appearing to be class conscious, is an establishment frequented by hoi polloi rather than the middle-class.'

'I get the picture.'

'There is just one other thing. I want you to attend the meeting with me.'

Holding up both hands, palms facing him in a hold-it-right-there signal, she made her position clear. 'I am a private investigator, not a minder.'

'You misunderstand me,' he said with a flicker of a smile. 'I want you there simply as a reliable witness should violence be threatened or result.'

'Fine.' Marcia reached for her pad and pen, 'Give me the details.'

          ★   ★   ★

After dropping Mandy off at her flat, Mattia pulled up in a quiet street and reached for his cell phone. It was now seven o'clock and bitterly cold. A whole evening for which he had made no plans stretched ahead of him. Candace would be at her restaurant until around 10.30, and he would be welcome to have a meal there and stay until she was ready to go home. However, he should be doing something constructive in the murder investigation.

Tapping in a telephone number to enquire whether pathologist Mike Probert had returned to his office, he was pleased when the man himself answered.

'This is Gio Mattia, Mike. How are you doing?'

'Hello, Gio. I'm not exactly glad to be back, but I am sorry to have missed out on this murder you are investigating. How can I help?'

'Do Marcus Bellingham's notes include the love bite on the deceased woman's neck?'

'I have only taken a glance at them, but I can take a look in the morning, Gio.'

'I would be grateful if you would. Bellingham was going to investigate the possibility of obtaining DNA from the bite, Mike.'

'Do you want me to follow it up?'

'If DNA is present I expect it is that of a prisoner in hospital named Mark Willis.'

'Leave it to me, Gio. I will get in touch.'

'Thanks, Mike.'

He was putting his phone in the glove pocket when it beeped. There was a 'You have one new message' announcement. It was Marcia Ridgely.

'Gio, I have arranged a meeting for tonight with someone for whom it is important for you to speak. He doesn't want to give you his name at this stage, but says that it will be in your interest to meet him. Please be at the Rose and Crown at eight this evening.'

★ ★ ★

Though the instructions she had been given were cloak and dagger stuff, Marcia followed them to the letter. Driving through a shopping area sparkling with bright Christmas decorations, she reached her destination of a central car-park. She slowly circled the car-park as instructed. Partway round she braked as a figure stepped out from the shadows between parked cars.

'Right on time,' the man congratulated her as he quickly opened the car door and got in. 'I can rest assured that you have made the arrangements?'

'I have. His line was continuously busy, but I left a message,' she lied. Lacking the nerve to spring so unusual an invitation on Mattia, she had avoided speaking to him.

'Will he keep the appointment?' he asked worriedly.

'I know Gio Mattia well, and I can guarantee that he will,' she answered with a confidence that surprised her.

* * *

Having telephoned Candace to say that he would pick her up from the restaurant at 10.30, Mattia arrived at the *Rose and Crown* at just before eight o'clock. He stood to one side just inside the door. Scanning the bar he spotted the unmistakable style of Marcia's blonde hair in a dimly lit corner. A man sharing a table with her was in deep shadow and unrecognizable.

Mattia was just feet from the table when he recognized the man. He halted, undecided as to his next move as Ace Durell stared at him apprehensively.

Marcia stood up and came to give him a quick kiss. 'You seem to know him, Gio.'

'I do. He is Ace Durell, the asshole who manages the Mississippi Club.'

'He didn't tell me who he is. What he did say was that he must speak to you.'

'Now that I am here I might as well hear what he has to say.' Mattia shrugged.

There were no handshakes before Mattia sat at the table. Durell seemed embarrassed as he started to speak. 'I fully realize that in the light of our previous association you will find this situation to be difficult. Let me first explain that I have left the Mississippi Club and tonight I will be leaving here to return to my native London for good. There are things that I want to tell you, information that will be very useful to you.'

'I would feel easier about this conversation if I knew why you want to help me,' Mattia queried. 'I doubt that altruism is a factor.'

Though disconcerted by this, Durell remained calm. 'My parting from my associates was acrimonious. The action you take on the information I give you means less chance of the threat to me becoming a reality. Perhaps it would be best if you ask me what you want to know.'

'We can give it a try,' Mattia agreed. 'Did Stafford-Smythe have Wellman recruit the guy you know as Rory Wilton to eliminate Tina Spencer?'

'That's right. But the way she died causes me doubt. The man in London made it clear to Wellman that it must look like an accident. If Wilton did do it he slipped up badly.'

'It is unlikely that someone skilled in assassination would go that wrong.'

Durell shook his head. 'Not in this case. Wilton is a psycho.'

One feeble hickey didn't strike Mattia as the work of a psychopath, but he let that pass, and said, 'I appreciate you telling me this. Have you anything else to say?'

'There is just one important thing. Do not trust your colleagues at Crescent Street. The London people already know some of the contents of that file you recently acquired.'

Alarmed, Mattia asked, 'Do you have a name or names of the police informants?'

'No, I was never really accepted, and was not privy to that sort of information.'

'That's a pity,' Mattia said. He stood to leave. 'I am grateful to you for this, Durell, and hope everything works out for you in London.'

'Thank you,' a surprised Durell responded, before turning to Marcia with an enquiry. 'Will you run me back to my car, Miss Ridgley?'

With a nod to confirm that she would, Marcia asked Mattia, 'Will you be waiting at my place when I get there, Gio?'

'No,' was his abrupt answer as he walked away, his mind occupied by what he had just heard.

★ ★ ★

He reached Candace's restaurant at twenty minutes past ten and filled in waiting time by using her landline to telephone Assistant Chief Constable Wilkes at his home.

'This must be important, Chief Inspector,' Wilkes commented with great interest.

'It is vitally important, sir,' Mattia declared. 'Can I see you in your office as soon as you get there at nine o'clock tomorrow morning?'

'No. I'll make sure that I am there at eight o'clock to discuss whatever it is.'

★ ★ ★

Regenerated by a pleasant night spent with Candace, Mattia was in Wilkes's office before eight o'clock the following morning. He reported the details of his meeting with Ace Durell, and ended by expressing his deep concern. 'The leak we have here is a serious one, sir.'

'It is indeed perturbing,' Wilkes agreed. 'I am greatly concerned for the safety of this Carmel Summers girl, or I should say *woman* now.'

'There is no worry on that score. I discovered who she is, the name she now goes under by absolute chance when I was in London, sir.'

'I am relieved to hear that. You have told no

one here at the station, Giovanni?'

'Only DC Snelling knows, and she is aware that it is top secret. How many have seen the Tina Spencer file, sir?'

'Just a few senior ranks.'

'Including Superintendent Bardon, sir?'

Not giving a direct answer, Wilkes warned, 'As you know, it is evidence not suspicion that counts in these matters, and I am working on that.'

'That's fine. I am ashamed that I have neglected to ask how DS Petters is, sir.'

'It isn't good news, I'm afraid. He is out of danger now, but there is a real possibility that he will never walk again. Maybe you could spare time to visit him this morning.

'I will make time, sir,' Mattia vowed, shaken by the dire news about his sergeant.

Further conversation was prevented by a knock on the door followed by Sergeant Calvin Davies entering to announce. 'I am sorry to interrupt, sir. A call has just come in of a burnt-out car with a body inside on Barnes Common.'

'That is the Met's problem, Sergeant.'

'That's so, sir. But the car is registered to A.C.E. Durell at the Mississippi Club. The body has yet to be identified.'

'Thank you, Sergeant,' Wilkes said, and

when Davies had left, he remarked to Mattia, 'I don't think we need to wait for the identification. In the circumstances your presence may well be required in London. Confine yourself to just visiting DS Petters, then come straight back here.'

'Very good, sir.'

14

The day had been a hectic one for Mattia. Visiting Petters at the hospital had been a distressing experience. Mattia had spoken of the guilt that had been plaguing him. 'I feel that this is my fault. I must have exacerbated the injury to your spine by dragging you from the overturned car.'

Petters had denied this. 'Had you left me in the car they would have killed us both.'

Not once during the time Mattia had spent with him had Petters complained personally. His regret had been concentrated on the effect his disablement would mean to his wife and child. Mattia had still been affected by the visit when he returned to Crescent Street.

Wilkes was waiting for him with the news that the Metropolitan Police needed him in London. Durell had no relatives in London, and there was no one else in the capital city who could identify him. Mattia drove to Barnes Common, to where the burnt-out car had been cordoned off, and identified himself to the uniformed inspector who had met him.

'I am Inspector Rawlings, sir,' the young officer introduced himself. 'You have an unpleasant task ahead of you. All that is left of the deceased is a badly burnt body, which may just be identifiable. Forensics have refused to remove the body from the car until you have seen it. Obviously because any attempt to move it would cause it to crumble into ashes.'

Mattia ducked under the tape the inspector raised for him to go to the fire-blackened car. It had taken him some five grim minutes study of the charred corpse to identify Ace Durell. Though he hadn't liked the man, he had felt sorry that the new life Durell had been heading for the previous night had not even had a chance to begin.

Following the identification, Mattia was asked to go to Scotland Yard for a meeting with Assistant Commissioner Meech, who already had a copy of the Tina Spencer file on his desk beside the 1994 cold case file containing her statement. Mattia spent three hours at the Yard telling Meech all that he knew of Stafford-Smythe's connection with Wellman in Sandsport, and the activities of Mark Willis there. Meech was certain that the 1994 case could now be reopened, and that he would require Mattia's co-operation.

It was late in the evening when Mattia returned to Crescent Street to find the station to be a hive of activity. He had been puzzled as to what was going on, but all was revealed when he had been told that Assistant Chief Constable Wilkes urgently needed to see him. He found Wilkes in his officer together with Chief Constable Freya Miller. The atmosphere was fraught with tension, and the exchange of greetings was perfunctory.

Then an uncomfortable Wilkes made a terse announcement. 'Willis escaped from the hospital earlier this evening. Some kind of distraction was arranged with two apparently drunken patients becoming violent. When they had been subdued it was discovered that Willis had escaped during the now obviously staged fracas.'

'What sort of a threat does this present, Chief Inspector?' the chief constable enquired.

'I don't — ' Mattia began before being interrupted by a call on his mobile phone. He excused himself to his two superiors. It was Marcia.

'Don't get cross, this is serious,' she pleaded. 'I have been trying to get you all day.'

'I have been in London on business with my cell phone switched off,' he explained, prior to giving her the benefit of the doubt by asking neutrally, 'What is it?'

'When I took Durell back to his car last night he passed me an envelope containing my fee in cash. I didn't open the envelope until I got to my office this morning. There was a pencilled message in with the banknotes that was obviously meant for you. It says that those in London are aware that Cammy Studland is Carmel Summers.'

Coming straight after learning that Mark Willis had escaped, this was dispiriting news for Mattia. Durell obviously had good reason for not sharing this knowledge while still in Sandsport. It was ironic that his death was on the cards, regardless.

Letting it sink in for a moment, he then told Marcia, 'You are right; this is serious. It is good of you to inform me, and I apologize for it being difficult to get through to me.'

'You sound very formal, Gio. I guess you are in the company of top brass.'

'That's right. Goodbye, and thank you again.'

'Goodbye, Gio,' she said then made a kissing sound that he prayed hadn't reached the ears of Freya and Wilkes, who were waiting patiently.

'We have a problem,' he told them. 'I have just been informed that Stafford-Smythe and his people know who Kath Harmon is and where she is.'

'Which is why they have got Willis out,' Wilkes decided with a sigh. 'We have to protect her immediately. You know her address, Giovanni?'

'Yes, but she will be working at this time of night.'

'Willis will be armed, so we must send an armed response vehicle to the club.'

'With respect, sir,' Mattia interjected. 'The arrival of an ARV will either mean that the attack on the woman will be postponed, or the situation will be made worse. I suggest that I go out to the Mississippi and call in if an armed response is necessary.'

'I think that is the best way forward,' said the Chief Constable, giving Mattia her support, with the proviso, 'That is providing that you have recovered sufficiently from having been stabbed.'

'That will cause me no problem, ma'am. It will be best if I go it alone.'

Nodding his agreement, her assistant said, 'Very well. But I will have an ARV on stand-by.'

★ ★ ★

Having driven into the Mississippi Club car-park, Mattia parked away from the club's door, checking his watch as he got out of the car. It was 10.30. He hoped he wasn't too late. He found a dark place from where he could watch the club's door without being seen. It was bitterly cold but he wasn't uncomfortably aware of it. Two men came out through the double doors. Idly watching them go, he came instantly alert as the doors opened again and Cammy Studland stepped out into the night with a man close behind her. When the lighting favoured his view, Mattia saw that the man holding her arm tightly was Mark Willis. They came at an angle to where Mattia stood, heading for a car parked to his right. Still gripping Cammy's arm, Willis unlocked the front passenger door.

Preparing to run to his car to follow them, Mattia had to change his plan as he saw Willis take a handgun from the glove compartment. Willis put the weapon in his pocket and closed and relocked the door before dragging Cammy off across the carpark. They were heading for a semi-derelict single-storey building in a dark corner of the car-park. Aware that the club was a converted ancient manor house, Mattia guessed that the building was a long disused laundry. The kind of place in which girls in Catherine Cookson novels worked for a shilling a week and their keep.

Using a shoulder to open the heavy wooden door, Willis pulled Cammy inside and pushed the door closed behind them. Through a glazed window in the side of the building Mattia saw a brief flash of torchlight as Willis must be looking around inside. Mattia was unable to formulate a plan. The only entry was a slow one through the weighty door, which would probably result in Willis shooting both Cammy and him.

He made his way to the far side of the building where he found a sparse hedge was all that separated the laundry building from the road. He waited for the headlights of the next passing car to come along, and spotted a low window in the wall, unglazed with a tattered piece of tarpaulin loosely nailed to the wooden frame.

Quietly, moving away from the window, Mattia telephoned Wilkes. Relating what had happened so far, and describing the location of the laundry building in the car-park, he requested an ARV, although aware that he had to ensure the safety of Cammy Studland before the arrival of armed officers.

He heard the droning sound of a slowly approaching heavy lorry and put together a plan of action. It was a plan with no more than a dauntingly slender chance of success, but it was all he had. Picking up a short length of timber, carefully judging the sound of the lorry, he chose what he hoped was the right moment to sprint round to the other side of the building. He raised the timber and smashed in the window's glass. He heard the crack of a reactionary but pointless shot from Willis's gun as he raced back to the other side of the building.

The window was bathed in light from the lorry's headlights. Ripping the tarpaulin down, he jumped in through the window. Luckily he landed in an empty space, but toppled sideways and hit the concrete floor. This proved to be fortunate as he actually felt the breeze of a bullet pass close to his head as he fell. In the now dimming light from the lorry's he saw a heavy table on its side, and dived behind it as he heard Willis fire again and the thud of a bullet burying itself in the thick wood of the table.

'Is it you, Mattia?' Willis questioned.

★   ★   ★

Mattia's eyes had adjusted enough to make out Willis's outline. He called, 'It's me, Willis.'

'Then come out of hiding, or the next bullet will be in the girl's head.'

Sure that a figure huddled on the floor to Willis's right was Cammy, Mattia groped around on the floor beside him. His fingers connected with what had to be a brick.

Grasping it, he said. 'Fire at the girl, Willis, and the flash will show me where you are and I'll have you.'

'What purpose will that serve?' Willis questioned contemptuously. 'The girl will be dead, which is what I was hired to do, and I'll pump a bullet into you before you can get to me.'

Still gripping the brick, Mattia was undecided. What Willis had said was totally logical. He was at such a disadvantage right then that any attempt Mattia made at saving Cammy Studland would more likely result in her death. Yet there was no alternative.

Standing up from behind the table, he threw the brick at Willis with all his strength. Seeing the missile thud against the gunman's chest, knocking him backwards, he was unprepared for his rapid recovery. Before he could duck back down behind the table, he heard the crack of the handgun, saw the small flare from the barrel, and realized that he had been hit in the left shoulder. There was no pain, but Mattia knew from his time in New York that the hurting would soon begin.

Then he watched in helpless horror as he saw Willis take aim at Cammy Studland.

★ ★ ★

After briefing Sergeant Turpin who was in charge of the ARV, Wilkes then went on a hurried search for a senior officer to oversee an exercise that was certain to be beset by problems and likely to fall prone to an Independent Police Complaints Commission inquiry.

His hoped for choice, Detective Inspector Rideout, was heading a drugs raid on the far side of town. The only senior officer available was D/Supt Bardon, and Wilkes reluctantly had to accept that he must use him. Even so, Wilkes still had misgivings as he stood in the vehicle section and watched Bardon drive out behind the ARV.

★   ★   ★

Aware that it would be a useless move, Mattia was about to launch himself at Willis when the pain arrived in his shoulder. It was a profound agony that temporarily robbed him of movement. Held in its grip, he could only wait for Willis to pull the trigger.

Unable to credit what was at least a minor miracle, Mattia heard a click as Willis pulled the trigger on an empty chamber. He heard the unmistakable sound of an arriving ARV as his paralysis suddenly switched off, and he leapt up from behind the table to rush at

Willis. Swinging his uninjured right arm, he landed a terrific blow to the side of Willis's head, felling him.

As Mattia hunkered at the side of a sobbing Cammy, Willis scrambled to pick up his empty weapon and struggle to his feet as a megaphone voice crackled outside.

'Come out, Willis, with both hands held high.'

Willis wrenched open the door and, pausing for a moment, stepped out, waving the gun in his right hand. Starkly aware what was about to happen, Mattia ran to stand at one side of the open doorway.

He shouted, 'This is DCI Mattia. He has no ammunition. The handgun is empty. Do not fire!'

'What do I do, sir?' the Armed Response Unit sergeant asked anxiously.

A short period of silence followed. Then Mattia heard the shouted command. 'Fire!'

There was a fusillade of shots. Willis seemed to take a few convulsive steps backwards before his body crumpled and he flopped to the ground.

★ ★ ★

The next morning an informal inquiry was being held in Wilkes's office. Present were

Freya Miller, Wilkes, and Mattia. His shoulder had been treated at the hospital and had given him no problems since.

'We are probably wasting our time discussing this in the light of the IPCC having already instituted an inquiry.' Wilkes expressed his opinion in a worried tone.

'Detective Superintendent Bardon had Willis shot in the full knowledge that his gun was empty.'

'We can't be sure of that, Chief Inspector, until we know the outcome of the inquiry.'

'I was there. I know that it's true, and I'll swear so on oath, as I am sure Sgt Turpin will if no pressure is brought to bear.'

'This incident has cast a dark shadow over the force,' the chief constable censured Mattia. 'Your suggestion that Sgt Turpin may be persuaded, as it were, not to give false evidence is uncalled for.'

'From experience I consider it to be a probability rather than supposition, ma'am.'

'I don't think this kind of talk will help.' Wilkes voiced a reprimand.

'It could well help Martin Spencer,' Mattia argued. 'Mark Willis's death will commit Spencer to a life sentence if the truth is concealed.'

'Are you suggesting that that was behind Superintendent Bardon's decision to order the armed officers to fire?'

'Can you suggest another motive, sir?'

The chief constable and the assistant chief constable fell silent until the latter said, 'I think this meeting has ended, Chief Inspector.'

Ready to leave, Mattia said, 'Mike Probert called me earlier. DNA taken from a love bite on Tina Spencer's neck does not match that of either Mark Willis or Martin Spencer.'

A doleful Wilkes groaned. 'Where does that leave us?'

'In one hell of a mess and without a murder suspect,' Mattia replied.

★ ★ ★

'Can I have a word, sir?' Mandy Snelling asked, hesitantly, looking at the grim expression on Mattia's face as he entered the CID office.

'You have no need to ask, Mandy.'

Gratified by his faith in her, she told him, 'Several residents in Orchard Avenue have reported seeing lights late at night inside the Spencers' bungalow.'

'Seems like we have exchanged a prime suspect for a ghost,' Mattia complained. 'Check it out, Mandy. Talk to whoever has seen the lights, and if you think there is anything in it find out the times that it happens, and for how long the lights are visible.'

'I will do my very best, sir.'

'I know you will. I can see that you have your special spark back,' Mattia delighted her by saying. 'Report to me later. For the next hour or two I'm being grilled by the IPCC.'

* * *

Armed with a list of names of householders who had reported strange lights in the unoccupied bungalow, Mandy started with the first woman to have contacted the police. Expecting to encounter some crone with an over-active imagination, she was surprised when a very attractive woman in her early thirties answered the door when she rang the bell.

'Mrs Andrews?' she asked, her warrant card ready to be produced.

'Yes.'

'I am DC Snelling. You reported an incident to the police.'

'That's right. Please come in. It was two incidents, really,' the woman said as Mandy followed her into the house. 'It was last night and the night before.'

'What sort of lights did you see, Mrs Andrews?'

'Make it Karon. It wasn't the main lighting system. I would say torchlight.'

'What time was this?'

'Just after ten o'clock the first night, and roughly half an hour later last night. It was really creepy.'

'How long did it go on, Karon?'

'No more that twenty minutes either night.'

'Was there a car outside the bungalow, and did you see anyone enter or leave?'

'There was no car, and the scary thing is that I didn't see anyone go in or out, even though the streetlighting is more than sufficient. Would you like a cup of coffee?'

After having coffee with this pleasant, intelligent woman, Mandy got a similar account from three of Karon's neighbours, a middle-aged woman, a teenage girl, and an elderly man. All three were frightened by what they had witnessed in a bungalow where a woman had been very recently murdered.

★ ★ ★

A bespectacled man with a long face and wearing a dated suit asked Mattia a final question without looking at him. 'After you

330

had shouted that the now deceased man was unarmed, the ARV opened fire. Being in the doorway of the building, it could be that you weren't heard.'

'No chance. Sergeant Turpin heard me, and asked Detective Superintendent Bardon for instructions. He gave a one-word answer — Fire!'

'I will be speaking to Sergeant Turpin later.'

'I am certain that he will tell you the same,' Mattia said confidently.

★   ★   ★

'What do you intend doing, sir?' Mandy enquired, after she had read out from her notebook the interviews with the four residents in Orchard Avenue.

'I'll be in the bungalow before ten o'clock tonight, waiting.'

'On your own, sir?'

'I take it that you won't be volunteering, Mandy?'

'I wouldn't even be keen on obeying orders. Won't you find it spooky, sir?'

'Nowhere near as frightening as where I am heading first this evening,' Mattia said with a grin.

'Where's that, sir?'

'For dinner at Marcia Ridgley's place.'

'All that is required is your confirmation that we accept his resignation, Freya,' Wilkes clarified the situation persuasively.

'It seems to me that would be letting him off lightly, too lightly, Reginald.'

'The IPCC found him to be blameworthy, but there was insufficient evidence to charge him with even a summary offence.'

'Very well, I will accept Bardon's resignation. I will leave it up to you to explain this decision to Mattia.'

'I doubt that it would be wise to do so, Freya. It would probably result in him beating the living daylights out of Bardon.'

★ ★ ★

When she opened the door to him, Marcia's blonde hair was in Lake's peek-a-boo style. The sheer silk of her royal-blue gown clung to the slender shape of her body, making his desire a threat to the evening. When he handed her a Christmas present in gratitude for the help she had given him, she became emotional. She explained that she had invited him to dinner to have a memory of one evening to ease the loneliness she endured every Christmas.

He put off telling her that he had to leave early, even though he knew that delaying would make it more difficult for him. He was relieved when the conversation at the start of a superbly prepared dinner centred on the Tina Spencer murder.

'How is your investigation proceeding, Gio?'

'It isn't. The DNA of the main suspect, who was linked with the London people in the file Tina Spencer left with you, is not a match with the DNA found on her body.

'What about Dominic Wellman and the other guys here in Sandsport?'

'They will eventually be brought into the investigation, Marcia.'

'Is Baileys Irish cream OK with you, Gio?' she enquired after dinner, as with a bottle in one hand and two glasses in the other, she came towards the settee on which he was sitting.

Raising her glass, she proposed a toast. 'Here's to us.'

'To us,' Mattia warily responded. Then he took a big mouthful like a long kiss. It settled smoothly against his tongue and went down like a nun's blessing.

The sexual tension in the atmosphere had them both empty their glasses swiftly. She took his empty glass from him and placed it on a small table.

'I could use another of those,' he complained, certain that she was planning something he would be desperate to avoid.

'All in good time,' she said, moving close. 'A Christmas kiss is in order right now.'

Distancing himself from her as far as the settee would permit, he cancelled out her suggestion. 'It would restart something that we both know can't end happily.'

'Correction. One of us *thinks* that it can't end happily,' she argued, moving nearer.

Pushing her away, he stood up. 'I am sorry, Marcia, but the evening has to end here.'

'It shouldn't,' she said, looking sorrowfully up at him. 'When a man and a woman have shared what we have shared, they can never be completely separated from each other.'

'Spiritually perhaps,' Mattia agreed, 'and I will have something of you with me for ever. Something very precious to me. But we met too late and in the wrong circumstances.'

No longer needing to excuse himself for leaving early, he reached for his coat. He unsuccessfully tried not to notice the unshed tears glistening in her eyes. It was an image that he couldn't free himself from as he walked to his car.

He arrived at the top end of Orchard Avenue shortly after 9.30, parked his car and walked the rest of the way. Entering the bungalow, he closed and locked the door behind him. He shone his torch down the passageway. At the far end the door of the room in which Tina Spencer's body had lain was wide open. He opened the door to the lounge and saw the curtains were closed, filtering the exterior street lighting into a dim illumination. He shut the door, waiting for his eyes to adjust, then sat down in an armchair to wait.

Half an hour passed quickly, his mind being busy with regrets about Marcia and his plans where Candace was concerned. The latter did not help him feel less guilt over the former, but it gave him a target to concentrate on. He was so absorbed with this that something similar to an electric shock violently slammed all the joints in his body together as he heard footsteps passing down the passageway outside the room. He was easing himself up out of the chair when a door was slammed loudly.

Stepping out of the room, Mattia shone his torch to reveal an empty passageway. But the door at the end of the passageway was now closed. He made his way down the passageway and thrust the door open, but using his torch to search the room, he discovered it was empty. Mystified, he made his way back to the lounge and the armchair to resume his vigil.

Doors don't slam shut on their own and visible people make the sound of footsteps. Trying but failing to find a rational explanation, he tensed at the slight scraping sound of a key sliding into one of the front door locks. He remained still, unmoving, listening to the other lock being turned, then the front door opening and closing. Footsteps came along the passageway to halt outside the closed door of the lounge.

Mattia's body was ready to spring into action as the door was opened, very slowly. The silhouette of a woman stood in the doorway. She had started to enter the room when he shone his torch and she shrieked piercingly. He switched off the torch and she suddenly went quiet. Mattia ran across the room and grabbed her. She started screaming again as he held her with one arm and switched on his torch to find that he was holding Estelle Spencer.

Raising the torch beam to illuminate his face, he spoke soothingly, 'It's all right, Mrs Spencer, it is me, DCI Mattia.'

Her screaming gradually abated, and he helped her across to a settee, explaining, 'We can't put the light on, it would panic the neighbours. What you are doing here?'

'Give me a moment to get over my fright,'

she pleaded tremulously.

'Start at the beginning. Where did you get the keys?'

'When my husband had the security door fitted for Martin, he had three sets of keys cut.'

'Why did he want the extra keys?' Mattia questioned.

'I have been anxious to share this with someone. This is my third night coming here searching for a bundle of love letters that Tina kept hidden from her husband.'

'You want to find them to save Martin from further grief,' a sympathetic Mattia assumed.

She shook her head violently and burst into tears, sobbing as she continued, 'No. It's because I learned that Stuart was having an affair with Tina. I wanted to save my marriage.'

'Is your husband aware that you know?' Mattia asked, mentally constructing a completely new and unexpected murder scenario. One that had not occurred to Estelle.

'He doesn't suspect that I know, and that's the way I intend to keep it. I regret what happened to poor Tina, but Stuart and I have become very close once again since the murder.'

'Just one question, Mrs Spencer. Then I

suggest that you get yourself home.'

She checked her wristwatch. 'Yes I must, Stuart will soon be home from his meeting. What is it you wanted to know, Mr Mattia?'

'Some of the residents here have reported seeing lights in the bungalow but not seeing anyone coming in or going out. How do you do that?'

With an ironic little smile, she replied, 'I learned from following my husband. I park in the next street and come through a gap in the hedge into the back garden, then come down the side of the bungalow.'

'I see. Now, we had better be on our way.'

'What about the love letters? I desperately need to find them.'

'We have to go now, but I'll try to get them for you very soon,' Mattia lied.

★ ★ ★

Eyes closed, Reginald Wilkes lay back in his chair the next morning when Mattia had finished his oral report. He spoke at last without opening his eyes. 'This is stunning, Giovanni. Everything pointed to Willis before the DNA thing pulled the rug from under us. Now this! How would you suggest we proceed?'

Mattia had told Wilkes everything apart

338

from the mysterious footsteps and the slamming of the door in the bungalow. That was something that he would never speak of to anyone. He answered, 'Stuart Spencer has to be arrested, but we must act in a way that as much as possible, protects both Martin and Estelle Spencer from further distress.'

'I agree wholeheartedly.' Wilkes opened his eyes and sat up straight. 'No offence, Giovanni, but you usually advocate a 'kick 'em in the thingies' policy.'

'I do have a sensitive side, sir,' Mattia blithely protested. 'If you agree, I will go to Stuart Spencer's place right now and, providing his wife is not nearby, bring him in.'

'Both the wife and the brother will have to know sooner or later.'

'I'd prefer it to be later,' Mattia admitted.

'So would I. Go ahead with your plan, Gio.' Wilkes readily sanctioned the idea.

At the car sales premises a salesman pointed to where Spencer was standing some distance away, by the open driver's door of a sleek new sports car. Spencer peered questioningly at Mattia, and remarked, 'I wouldn't say this is a friendly visit, Chief Inspector.'

'It's a difficult one that I hope we can both keep as low-key as possible, Mr Spencer.'

Surprising Mattia with a smile, Spencer said, 'Just my luck to have a clever cop on my case. As a prospective condemned man might I make one request?'

'It's a bit premature, but what is it?'

'Cars have been my life,' Spencer replied, gesturing towards the sports car. 'This is a new model with many innovations. I have not yet had chance to try it out, and I never will if I go with you now. If you would kindly permit me to have a short test run, with you accompanying me, of course, I will come quietly, as the old saying goes, when we get back here.'

'If I have your word on that I don't see why not.' Mattia shrugged.

As they got into the car Stuart Spencer showed remarkable insight by promising. 'You have my word. I have no more wish to involve my wife than you do.'

He drove at speed out of town, climbing a steep hill to a grassy plateau that gave a panoramic view of Sandsport. It was a place popular with visitors to the area. Spencer stopped the car with the engine still running some twenty yards from the edge.

'What do you think of her?' he asked Mattia.

'It sure is a fast car, but not the type that interests me.'

'Let's find out what she can do!'

15

Before Mattia realized what was happening, Spencer had put his foot down hard on the accelerator. Within seconds they were heading for the edge of the plateau at a speed that braking couldn't stop on the grassy surface. Mattia broke out into a cold sweat. They were so close to the edge that he could no longer see it through the windscreen. Surprising him, Mattia's panic switched suddenly into calm acceptance of his imminent death. He closed his eyes, but then opened them in renewed panic as Spencer suddenly pulled the steering wheel hard to the right. As the car turned in a tight half-circle Mattia felt the rear wheel on his side of the car drop off the edge. The car tilted alarmingly. Through the side window he looked down on the buildings below, now miniaturized by distance. But the momentum of the car and its front-wheel drive pulled the rear wheel back up on to firm ground. Spencer chuckled as he drove the car away from the edge. 'That had you worried, Detective Chief Inspector.'

Mattia was convinced that Spencer's intention had been to kill them both. Why he had changed his mind at the last moment was a mystery that Mattia was thankful for. Yet his mute celebration at being alive collapsed as Spencer turned the car and stopped it facing the edge in a similar position from which the whole terrifying episode had begun.

Preparing himself to reach across and snatch the ignition key, his voice was hoarse when he said, 'You have had your fun, Spencer, but this is where it ends.'

'I know that,' Spencer, obviously having regained his sanity. 'I can only apologize for scaring you. The only excuse I can offer is that I wanted to take a last tilt at authority before spending the remainder of my miserable life obeying it.'

'We are facing the edge again, Spencer, which more than suggests to me that you haven't finished.'

'I'm finished, believe me,' Spencer assured him fervently, opening the car's door. 'You are in charge now, Mr Mattia. Here's where we change places and you drive us back.'

Spencer got out of the car. Mattia opened his door and swung his legs out, keen to get into the driver's seat to ensure there would be no more crazy antics from Spencer. But he had only just placed his feet on the ground and stood up when Spencer leapt back into the car and started the engine. There was a roar from the car's twin exhaust as it raced forwards. The passenger's door swung hard against Mattia, knocking him to one side as it slammed shut. He stood watching helplessly as the new car sped towards the edge. Fighting a strong urge to turn away, he forced himself to observe the car leaving solid ground. It seemed to be suspended in the air for a split second before it dropped out of sight.

He ran to the edge and looked down. Far below on a disused railway line the sleek new car was a mangled wreck shrouded by a thin mist of smoke and dust.

★   ★   ★

'I am in agreement with the chief constable, Mr Cartwright,' Wilkes told the chairman of the County Police Committee. 'Having explained that shortly before her death the murder victim had ended a long-running affair with her husband's brother, who had a set of keys to her home, I concurred with DCI Mattia that everything pointed to Stuart Spencer as the murderer.'

'We are presently awaiting confirmation that the DNA sample taken from the deceased woman is that of Stuart Spencer,' Freya Miller added supportively.

'It is very unlikely that it won't be,' Cartwright assented. 'Our problem is that Mattia went to arrest Spencer and took a car ride with him to a place where the suspect committed suicide in the presence of the arresting police officer.'

The chief constable didn't argue with this summary of the situation but said in mitigation, 'DCI Mattia knew that Martin Spencer was completely unaware that his wife had been having an affair with his brother, although Estelle Spencer did know about the affair, and that Tina Spencer had ended the clandestine relationship. However, Estelle refuses to believe that her husband murdered Tina.'

'Both Estelle and Martin Spencer have become very fragile mentally since the murder of Tina Spencer. DCI Mattia's actions in the failed arrest of Stuart Spencer were prompted by his desire to cause neither of those two innocent people further distress,' Wilkes stated.

'Can we substantiate that for the inquiry into Stuart Spencer's death?' Cartwright asked.

'I am convinced that we can,' the chief constable assured him.

'Then you have my support.'

★ ★ ★

The county constabulary's Christmas Dinner was as usual held in the prestigious Melbury Hotel. Entering the foyer with Candace on his arm, Mattia knew that the evening ahead would be an ordeal. He had been devastated on his last visit to Melvin Petters to see how his condition had deteriorated. Ever since he had fought against accepting the obvious, that Petters had only weeks rather than months to live. Melvin's beloved child's first birthday was the only one he would ever witness. The trials and tribulations of the Spencer family also weighed heavily on his mind. But for Candace's sake he would keep his depression concealed throughout the long hours that lay ahead.

One bit of good news was that Mandy Snelling had decided to continue her career in the police. Earlier that day she had enquired what his plans for the future were, broadly hinting that her question included his *romantic* liaisons. She had laughed when he had admitted, 'In the unlikely event of both Eva Longoria and Halle Berry chasing me at tonight's ball, I would be wondering if Sandra Bullock wouldn't be the best option.'

Now, as he saw the chief constable and her press officer approaching, he was determined that the humorous answer he had given Mandy was the old him. The new Giovanni Mattia had been matured by the traumatic events of the past few days.

He introduced Candace to Freya Miller and Sinéad Mayo. 'This is my partner, Candace Dvorak.'

Proud to be with Candace, and pleased with the immediate rapport between her and the other two women, he felt reassured that he was a reformed character where women were concerned. Nevertheless, unwillingly acknowledging that the presence of Freya Miller had unsettled him, he tested himself by considering what his reaction would be if Marcia Ridgely should unexpectedly walk in.

There was still no result from this self-examination when he and Candace were seated at the top table, and he had introduced her to Wilkes.

'I couldn't believe how beautiful the chief constable is, and she is really nice,' Candace confided, when Wilkes had seated himself further along the table from them. 'But the assistant chief constable strikes me as being a bit weird.'

'He's all right when you get to know him, Candace.'

'I'll take your word for it.'

'Don't do that, I haven't got to know him yet,' Mattia wryly advised.

Already immensely enjoying the evening, Candace had a good laugh at that. She was in good form later when, after Wilkes had stopped to inform him that he was to be seconded to the Metropolitan Police on the Kath Harmon cold case after Christmas, he returned to find Candace conversing on first-name terms with Freya Miller. Welcoming him back with a smile, she informed him, 'I have been drumming up business, Gio. Freya has booked Christmas Dinner at the restaurant for her and her friends.'

'That's nice,' Mattia said, dreading what difficulties it might cause him.

'I take it that you will be present, Gio.'

Put off balance by the chief constable's use of his first name, Mattia joked, 'I will probably be doing the washing-up, ma'am.'

The conversation was brought to an end by Wilkes's rapid arrival.

'Excuse me, folks,' he apologized, before making an old-fashioned bow and a sweeping gesture towards the dance floor. 'The band is playing my favourite melody. Would you do an old man the honour of joining me in this dance, Ms Dvorak?'

With an amused glance at Mattia, Candace went off with Wilkes. Freya Miller joined him in watching her go, commenting, 'You are a lucky man, Gio.'

'I am a stupid man for not recognizing that fact long ago, ma'am.'

'There you go with that *ma'am* again. Are you unable to put that few minutes we spent together on that balcony out of your mind?'

'Have you, Freya?'

'*Magic Moments*, as the Perry Como hit of yesteryear described such times. No, and I never will. We have to control our emotions. We must accept that some things can never be.'

'I have always found that difficult to do, Freya.'

'I have had no trouble doing so until just a few evenings ago,' she confessed very quietly as the dance ended and Wilkes returned with Candace.

It both surprised and gladdened Mattia to realize that this admission by Freya Miller did not have anything like the extreme affect on him that it once would have had. Enjoying a waltz with Candace, he welcomed rather than diverted an uncharacteristic advance from her.

Even under the subdued lighting of the dance floor he could detect her blushing as she said, 'You introduced me as your partner earlier. What nuance should I place on that?'

'It means that perhaps we two could rescue something from recent tragedies. Please believe that I am a changed man where permanent relationships are concerned.'

'What changed you?'

He couldn't answer her. Having been appalled at the tangled life Tina Spencer had lived, it had come to him a short while ago that, in a different way, his life was equally reprehensible. He hadn't been the same since his paranormal experience in the Spencer bungalow. In his more meditative times it seemed that it had been a message from Tina.

'I will tell you at some time, Candace,' he promised. 'I was going to ask if you would come to Midnight Mass with me on Christmas Eve.'

With a gasp of astonishment, she said, 'But you know that I'm not a Catholic, Gio.'

'Nevertheless, Candace, I am joining the Met for a short while straight after Christmas, and consider it would be a firm foundation for a church wedding when I return.'

'I . . . ' she began before temporarily losing her voice. 'Can I put my trust in what you have just proposed?'

'You have every reason to be suspicious, but I swear to you that I meant every word.'

The dance ended and in the ensuing silence between them he offered up a mental prayer that a long overdue return to his boyhood religion would give him the resolve to keep his promise to her. Putting an arm around her he pulled her close, and she clung to him, weeping tears of happiness.

At that moment, he knew that whether or not his prayers were answered he had stepped over the border into a new and very different life. Detective Chief Inspector Giovanni Mattia had grown up.

THE END

We do hope that you have enjoyed reading this large print book.

Did you know that all of our titles are available for purchase?

We publish a wide range of high quality large print books including:
Romances, Mysteries, Classics
General Fiction
Non Fiction and Westerns

Special interest titles available in large print are:
The Little Oxford Dictionary
Music Book
Song Book
Hymn Book
Service Book

Also available from us courtesy of Oxford University Press:
Young Readers' Dictionary
(large print edition)
Young Readers' Thesaurus
(large print edition)

For further information or a free brochure, please contact us at:
Ulverscroft Large Print Books Ltd.,
The Green, Bradgate Road, Anstey,
Leicester, LE7 7FU, England.
Tel: (00 44) **0116 236 4325**
Fax: (00 44) **0116 234 0205**

LET ME DIE YESTERDAY

Theresa Murphy

When hired to trace a village girl who went missing in the 1960s, private investigator Gerry McCabe anticipates an early end to his assignment with the discovery of female remains. Instead, it plunges McCabe into the dark and hostile labyrinths of rural life. Intent on mending his broken marriage, he is distracted by the vivacious Beth Merrill — the missing girl's sister — and the alluring widow Sharee Bucholtz. Unwittingly causing a local tragedy, a distraught McCabe struggles to continue his investigation and resolve his own relationship difficulties. But can he succeed on either case?

THE SECRETS MAN

John Dean

When DCI John Blizzard visits a friend in hospital, he is intrigued when an elderly villain in the next bed reveals much about Hafton's criminal gangs. These revelations attract a series of sinister characters to the ward. Blizzard wonders if they are seeking to silence the old man, but fellow detectives believe that the pensioner is suffering from dementia. It's only when people start dying that his colleagues take the DCI seriously. Blizard faces a race against time to save lives, and must face a part of his past he's tried to forget — and with the one man he fears.

DEAD SHOT

June Drummond

Leading industrialist Trevor Cornwall was found dead at the gates of his daughter's estate. It was remarkable not only that he had been mysteriously shot but also that the murderer had already delivered an obituary notice to a newspaper. Then there was another murder. Were the murdered men victims of a crazed killer or someone who had felt wronged by these prominent personalities? This was to prove a baffling case for DCI Dysart and Dr John Thorneycroft and there would be many surprises before the killer was finally unmasked.